A Sacrifice of Honor

Erik Lewis

PRESS

DEDICATION

To DeAnna. Thank you for all the love and support
you have shown me and our children. I couldn't
have done it without you.

CHAPTER ONE

Vietnam 1972

The cool morning breeze swept through Lt. John Miller's hair as he walked across the flight deck of the aircraft carrier U.S.S. America. The smell of the ocean filled his nostrils and he suppressed an early morning yawn. John hadn't gotten much sleep the last few nights, but then neither had anyone else. Knowing that Christmas was three days away, his son's third birthday two weeks after that, and that he was going to miss both of them had put him in a mild state of depression. Most of his fellow officers would drown their sorrows in a bottle of beer, but John was a teetotaler. Despite all the glamour and glory life in the Navy had once seemed, it was in reality a lonely life, and as he was learning, hard on a family. He now understood why the divorce rate with Navy officers was so high. In the last week, John had done some soul searching to decide if a career in the Navy was what he really wanted. Did he really want to spend twenty more years being shipped around the world for months at a time leaving his family behind and wondering if his children would even remember who he was? But this was the life he had wanted. He had chosen this career. It had been his dream and he had to take the bad with the good.

John Robert Miller was born on June 28, 1946, to a family with a strong military heritage. His great-great grandfather had survived the famous Pickett's charge at Gettysburg. His grandfather had fought in World War I and his father was a decorated Marine who fought at Iwo Jima. For as long as he could remember, John had wanted to be a soldier. He played soldier as a boy, read books about soldiers, and loved to hear his father and grandfather's war stories. It came as no surprise to anyone when John was admitted to the Naval Academy.

John, a star athlete in high school, had been quarterback of his high school football team and forever won the hearts of the town of Wilson when during his senior year, he threw four touchdown passes and won the state championship. He made all American in football and basketball. John Miller was what they called a home-town legend. He was not only the best athlete in Wilson High School, he was also the smartest. He was captain of the debate team, editor of the yearbook, and valedictorian of his class. With all of his abilities, though, he was never arrogant. After winning the state championship in 1964 and being carried off the field by his teammates, he was quoted in the newspapers as saying, "It was a team effort. I threw the passes, but somebody had to catch them." John had an air of dignity about him. He looked people in the eye and gave a firm handshake. He was confident and likeable. At 6'1" with brown hair and hazel eyes, some people said he reminded them of a young John Wayne. In fact, his first day at the Naval Academy someone commented on his Wayne like appearance, and from that moment on, he was nicknamed "Duke" Miller. One of his fondest memories from the Academy was when the real John Wayne came to visit, and he had his picture taken with him. That picture was proudly displayed on John's mantel back home in Wilson, North Carolina.

John was just the kind of man the navy wanted. Reared in a strict Baptist home, John had been taught that a man's loyalty was God, family, and country. The happiest day of his life came in May 1968, the day he graduated with honors from the Naval Academy. That day he fulfilled two lifelong dreams. One to become an officer in the United States Navy, and the other to marry his high school sweetheart, Rebecca Evans.

John and Becky had been going together since the ninth grade. They had known each other since the fifth grade. John was the school's star athlete. Becky was the studious type. A pretty blond with blue eyes, Becky had other boys after her, but she, like many others, was attracted to John's quiet, confident demeanor. It embarrassed him when people (especially his parents) would brag about him, because he knew that the next time he might drop the ball or miss the shot and they would be disappointed in him.

John was also incredibly calm in stressful situations. Once during English class his sophomore year of high school, Mr. Jenkins, the teacher, had a heart attack right in the classroom. John calmly sent two students to the office to call the ambulance while he administered CPR. He was credited with saving Mr. Jenkins life. His coolness under fire was a quality that would serve him well in the military.

John joined the Navy with one goal and one goal only in mind. He wanted to be a fighter pilot. He lived, breathed, and dreamed airplanes. It was during flight school training that on January 9, 1970, Shawn Allan Miller was born. John could not have been more proud. For weeks Shawn was all he talked about. It got to the point that people would hide when they saw him coming. Unfortunately, the life of a Navy officer left John little time for anything else, but he spent as much time as he could with his wife and son. He was a family man, when the Navy permitted.

All of that seemed worlds away as he stood looking out over the Gulf of Tonkin. As a child, John used to imagine himself as one of the brave RAF pilots fighting the Luftwaffe in the Battle of Britain battling it out in a death struggle to save his country from the evil Adolf Hitler. That was a war. It had a purpose, a mission, and an enemy. Vietnam was not a war. It was insanity. He hated it. He hated the politicians who thought they knew more than the generals. He hated having an enemy he couldn't see and fighting for people who didn't appreciate the sacrifice. He hated the protesters in the United States who had cursed him and spit on him, and most of all he hated being away from his family at Christmas. Whatever he felt about the war, though, he was a man of honor. He had sworn an oath to the people of the United States, and he would serve here and do his job to the best of his ability whether they appreciated it or not. Whatever his feelings about Vietnam, he would keep them to himself. John loved his country, even if his country didn't always love him.

John met up with his partner Lt. David Connors, the only bright spot in John's life at the moment. The two men had developed a close friendship in the four months they had flown together.

Dave was a black officer two months John's junior. They had much in common. From an early age, both had wanted to be pilots. Both had gone to the Naval Academy where they knew of each other. However, Dave's family history was very different from John's. John was born and raised in North Carolina with a long history of southern tradition. Dave's parents, Joe and Anna, had immigrated to the United States from Jamaica in the late 1930's. His father had started a laundromat in New York and had done his best to instill in his children a sense of pride and self worth. They were poor, but they were a loving family who worked together through the hard times. From his earliest years, Dave's father had drilled into him that he would succeed in life through hard work and determination. One of Joe Connor's favorite motto's was "never give up." Joe was a quiet man, yet he held an unquestionable air of authority in the home.

The closest Dave ever saw his father come to losing his temper was when Dave was thirteen years old and quit his school's football team. His father asked why he was home early and Dave told him that he quit the team because he thought the coach was going to cut him anyway. Through piercing eyes and some carefully chosen words his father reprimanded him. "I did not come to this country and work twenty years to have one of my children quit anything. You WILL go back to your coach, tell him you changed your mind, and you would like another chance to make the team and do not come back into this house until you do!" "Yes, sir," was Dave's response. Dave turned to leave. "I'm NOT done!" Dave stopped dead in his tracks. "Son, you go out there and give it your best. If you've done your best and you're cut from the team, then hold your head up with pride, but don't ever tell me you quit anything. Is that understood?" "Yes, sir." Dave did understand. That lesson went with him through his life. He did make the football team. By his senior year he was the star running back. Sometimes he won, sometimes he lost, but always he gave it his best. His fierce determination, along with his intelligence and sense of patriotism won him the attention of many, including his congressman who saw to it that Dave won an appointment to the Naval Academy. The day Dave left for the Academy was the proudest day of Joe Connor's life. It was one of the few times Dave had ever seen his father cry. They were tears of joy. Twenty-five years of hard work and determination in his adopted country had paid off in the life of his child.

Dave was a source of pride for his whole neighborhood. Parents would often remind their children of what they could achieve if they worked hard like David Connors. One week after Dave left, Joe was sitting in the local barber shop and he overheard two men talking. One was new to the area and said that he had heard that a young man in the neighborhood had been appointed to the Naval Academy. "Why yes," the other one replied, "that's Joe Connor's boy."

Dave had done very well at the Naval Academy. He earned high marks and was often used in their promotional materials. Dave's appointment came at an opportune time. The civil rights movement was in full swing, and the Academy wanted to display their diversity. Dave had always been a good-looking kid, but in his uniform he cut a dashing figure.

In fact, he was wearing that dashing uniform the first time he met Mary Turner. He was home for a few days leave and Mary was babysitting Dave's nephew David, named after him. Dave went to see his sister Carolyn and her husband Bill and little Dave whom he had never seen. Dave thought he would surprise them. He knocked on the door of their apartment, and that's how he met Mary Turner. It's anybody's guess as to which one of them was more surprised. When she opened that door, Dave saw the prettiest girl he had ever seen in his life. Mary was a high school senior at the time. Mary was not expecting a handsome, young soldier at the door. They stared at each other for a few seconds before Dave finally spoke. "I must have the wrong apartment." (Knowing he didn't) "I'm looking for my sister Carolyn."

"Oh, she's out. I'm babysitting her son."

"That would be my new nephew David."

"You must be her brother in who's in West Point. Nice to meet you."

"Nice to meet you. Actually, I attend the Naval Academy. I was wondering if I could take a peek at my nephew. I've never seen him." At that moment, Dave could have cared less about seeing his nephew. He wanted an excuse to meet this beautiful young lady. "Sure. I think that would be fine."

It was nearly two hours before Dave saw his nephew. In his defense, little Dave was sleeping, so he sat on the couch and talked with Mary. He didn't want to leave but he had a date with someone else that night. He told Mary he had to go to the library.

Mary was not only beautiful, but she, too, was very intelligent. She later graduated from college with a degree in Elementary Education and taught for a year while Dave finished flight school. They married on Valentines Day 1972. Six months later, Dave was on his way to Vietnam.

Another way Dave and John were alike was that their religion was very important to them. Dave and his family faithfully attended mass on Sunday and prayed together every night. He and John would often pray together in the cockpit before taking off.

The two men became close friends during their tour of Vietnam. They not only flew together, they spent much of their off duty time together. They ate most meals together, played pool, and spent many long hours talking. Over the course of the year, that to these men seemed a lifetime, they formed an unbreakable bond. Simply put, they trusted each other.

John had exactly 365 days from the time he arrived in Vietnam until the time he was supposed to leave. On any given day he could tell exactly how many days he had left.

December 22, 1972, the last thing John or Dave wanted to do was fly over North Vietnam, but they had their orders. After eating breakfast together the two men boarded their plane. Only an hour into their flight, it happened. They were flying at 30,000 feet when suddenly from out of nowhere a surface to air missile hit the plane. An explosion shook the plane. Looking out the window, both men could see flames shooting from the back. Before either man could say a word, the plane shook violently and the nose dipped down toward the ground. It was no use. Both engines were gone. The plane was going down. The only thing they could do was bail out.

It was a strange sensation. One minute they were sailing through the sky going hundreds of miles per hour, the next they were being hurled in the air like cannonballs. John was thankful that both he and Dave had made it out alive. His parachute snapped open and he began to float to the ground. He saw Dave off in the distance. He was alive and his parachute was open. John had a gash in his shoulder and a deep cut on his face, but things could have been worse, much worse.

Things did get worse. First of all, John smashed into a branch on the way down and was knocked nearly unconscious. He didn't actually land. His parachute got caught in the tree, and John was hanging six feet off the ground. He used his knife to cut his straps, but when he landed, he sprained his ankle. He estimated that Dave was a hundred yards away. He knew better than to call out his name. They were behind enemy lines. He started limping in the direction he had seen Dave's parachute land. He found him a half hour later. Dave was lying on the ground as if he hadn't moved at all since he landed. It was obvious his friend was wounded. John had been afraid of this. He could tell something wasn't right when he had seen Dave floating toward's the ground. "I wasn't sure I'd find you." Dave tried to move but instead he groaned.

"Where are you hurt?" Dave's face grimaced in pain.

"All over. I hurt all over." His teeth were clinched. "I know my leg is broken. I think I broke some ribs." Once again he tried to move. This time the pain was so bad he yelled when he moved. John got out the first aid kit and began to bandage up the cuts as well as wrap the broken leg. He ignored his own wounds. He would get to them later.

"Where are we, Duke?" John hesitated to tell him.

"I don't know." He said as he continued to work. Dave was getting frustrated.

"Well, where do you THINK we are?" John let out a sigh. There was no fooling Dave.

"I have some good news and some bad news."

"Let's hear it."

"We're only ten miles from the border."

"That's the bad news?"

"No, that's the good news. The bad news is we're on the wrong side of it."

"Duke, you know they're already looking for us." John continued to work. "They will find us!"

"Do you have any more words of comfort and cheer?"

"You better get going. Leave me some rations and come back for me."

"We'll go as soon as I'm done patching you up."

"Duke, I can't walk. Heck, I can't even stand up. Go get help and come back for me. Leave me a few rations." John continued to tape the bandages on.

"John, I appreciate what you're trying to do, but really I'll never make it out of here . . . "

"If you say one more word that's not positive and comforting, I'm going to use this tape for something other than bandages, and I promise you I won't be gentle. Think positive."

Dave laughed. "All right, Norman Vincent Peale. Before you go, though, you'd better patch yourself up. You lose any more blood from your wounds and we'll both be in trouble."

A few minutes later they started out. John had to practically carry Dave. John had one arm around Dave's waist and Dave had his arm around John's good shoulder. Fortunately John was a bigger man and fairly muscular, but he had lost quite a bit of blood and was feeling weak. Using his compass, they headed south. The jungle was so thick they could only see a few yards in front of them. They talked just above a whisper as they went.

"We're lucky we landed in the jungle." Said John

"Why's that?"

"We're less likely to be spotted."

Three hours passed, and they finally stopped to rest. John had no idea how far they had come. He guessed about two miles. Dave was pale and in great pain. John gave him some food and water from their MRE's. They both sat quietly.

"My leg, I . . . It's going numb. Duke, you gotta leave me . . . "

"I still have that tape," a look of concern came across John's face. "Hang in there, buddy." Just then, both men heard a rustling sound in the bushes. Through the thickness of the jungle they saw someone coming. They were wearing what looked like black pajamas and yellow straw hats. There were at least a dozen of them and they all carried rifles.

"Dave," he said in a whisper.

"I know. We have company. You do have a gun, don't you?"

"Yeah, but there's a bunch of them." John looked around. A few feet away was a ditch with some thick grass.

"Our best bet is to hide." Quietly, they scrambled into the ditch. John had to carry Dave, but it wasn't far. Through the leaves they could see someone coming. There was no mistaking the black pajamas and yellow straw hats. John could hear men talking in Vietnamese. He knew enough Vietnamese to know they were looking for them.

"Here they come," John whispered. They were coming right toward them. John held his breath in case the Viet Cong might hear him. They stopped in front of the ditch and it sounded to John like they were deciding which way to go. At one point they were so close John could have reached out and grabbed one of them by the leg, but miraculously he and Dave were never spotted. After talking a few minutes, the Viet Cong continued on their way. He and Dave waited half and hour before they moved.

"That was close," said John

"No kidding. We're not out of the woods yet," said Dave with a slight chuckle. John just looked at him.

"It's either laugh or cry."

They continued on their way, walking a little slower and not talking. By nightfall John figured they'd gone five miles. Both men were thoroughly exhausted. They got in the middle of some shrubbery and laid down.

It was actually more comfortable than John would have expected. The grass was soft, and he took off his shirt to make a pillow. They didn't get much sleep that night, though. The mosquitoes kept biting them all night.

The next morning they finished the last of their provisions. John estimated that they had five miles to go before they would be across the border; however, it would be more difficult than the first five. John's shoulder was in great pain and Dave could no longer walk at all. John had to put him on his back and carry him. He had no idea, really, where they were. He had been heading south, but that was all he knew. He hoped that eventually they would run into someone friendly.

As soon as John heard the rustling of the bushes, he knew they were in trouble. This time there was no chance to hide. He heard voices before he saw them. Two men came toward them shouting and gesturing for him to get his hands in the air. He carefully laid Dave down and raised his hands to the air. The two men had their rifles pointed at him. They were dressed in the same black clothes and straw hats as the other men. John couldn't understand everything, but from what he could tell, it sounded like one of them wanted to shoot them and the other wanted to take them prisoner.

Neither John nor Dave ever figured out what caused the noise. Later John said he thought it was a twig snapping, but he was not sure. Whatever it was, it saved their lives. For one split second, both of the Viet Cong soldiers turned their attention to the direction of the sound. It was only for a second, but that was all John needed. The soldier closest to John never saw what hit him. With lightening speed, John reached down, grabbed the .45 in the back of his pants and shot the first one right between the eyes. The second soldier managed to fire off one shot but he had not taken the time to aim carefully so the bullet only grazed John's leg. John shot him right in the chest. For one solid minute neither Dave nor John said anything.

Dave finally broke the silence, "I thought they called you Duke because you look like John Wayne, not because you shoot like him."

Both men were getting weaker by the minute. John knew he had to get help soon or Dave might die. There was more wrong with him than a few broken bones. John feared he might have been bleeding internally. They still had several miles to go before they were anywhere near safety. Hours went by and John was beyond the point of physical exhaustion. A hundred times he wanted to collapse on the warm earth, but he couldn't. Something kept driving him on. He imagined his family being over the next hill and if he could just make it he would see them again. Dave was going in and out of consciousness, but he knew that John was on the verge of collapsing.

"Duke."

"What, Dave?" John said irritated. "I'm kind of busy at the moment."

"Duke, you have to . . . " John had all he could take. He threw Dave to the ground careful to make sure he fell on his unbroken leg.

"I've had it with you! Shut up! I can handle the jungle, the mosquitoes, no food or water, the Commies shooting at me, being wounded, and even carrying you, but if I hear you say one more time to leave you, I'm going to knock you out with my bare fists, throw you over my shoulder and then at least I'll have some peace and quiet!"

"You're beautiful when you're angry." Dave said wryly.

A very faint smile crossed John's face.

"I'm sorry, Duke. You won't hear from me again until we cross the border."

John softened a little. "It's all right. We're in this together."

That afternoon they finally reached the road. It wasn't Interstate 95, but John decided to keep close to it. He figured they had traveled between nine and ten miles.

"We're getting close, Dave." Dave made no response. John heard the roar of engines and quickly jumped into the woods. Looking through the bushes, he would be able to see the jeeps without being noticed.

"More visitors?" Dave said barely above a whisper.

"I'm afraid so."

Dave managed to get himself in a position where he could see the road also. In a minute the vehicles appeared. As soon as he saw them, John started laughing and shouting and hugging Dave. The jeeps were American.

After a week in the hospital John felt like a new man. The doctors finally released him. Apart from a very ugly six-inch scar on his left shoulder, he was none the worse for wear. Dave's recovery was much slower. He had nearly died. The doctor said that if he had not gotten help within two more hours, he probably would not have made it. Dave would make a full recovery, but he would not be dancing the tango with Mary for a while. After John was released, the nurse told him Dave wanted to see him. John was glad for the opportunity to talk to Dave. He walked into the ward where Dave was and sat down next to his bed. Dave looked much better, but he still had a ways to go.

"How you feeling?" John said, putting on his best smile.

"Wanna dance?" said Dave smiling.

"I'll let Mary have that honor."

"Because of you, she will." John looked down at the floor.

"You'd have done the same for me?"

"I'd certainly like to think so." Dave got a little choked up. " I want to thank you for saving my life. My family and I will always be grateful."

"And I want to thank you for being a true friend in a lonely and miserable place. You made my experience in Vietnam bearable. Without your friendship, I'd have gone crazy. I'm not sure who saved who." John got up to leave. He reached over and shook Dave's hand.

"Good bye, friend," said Dave.

"Good bye, friend," said John. As John reached the door, Dave said,

"One more thing. Would you really have knocked me out?" John smiled.

"Of course not. I was just trying to scare you."

"Well, it worked."

CHAPTER TWO

Norfolk, Virginia 1980

It had been nearly eight years since John and Dave had been shot down. Both men were awarded the Purple Heart and John was awarded the Navy Cross which had been pinned on by the Secretary of Defense.

Though the two men didn't see each other much anymore, they still kept in contact. They called each other a couple times a year, sent Christmas cards, and occasionally visited each other when their jobs crossed paths. Both men were promoted to Lt. Commander. Dave worked at the Pentagon, and John was stationed at Norfolk. Dave and Mary had a baby, and the last John heard they were expecting one more. John and Becky had twin daughters Sara and Shannon in March of 1974. Both men had done very well in their careers. Dave worked with the Chief of Naval Operations. John worked with the computer operations system aboard ships and submarines which set up the system that navigated the ships as well as launched nuclear weapons. Almost everything about John's job was classified.

John was fortunate because he worked under a man that he greatly admired and respected. His commanding officer was Captain Russell Anderson. A tall, quiet man, he was not like many commanding officers in the military. In the year they had worked together, John had never seen Captain Anderson raise his voice even once. He was polite to everyone who worked under him.

When someone did not do his job properly, Captain Anderson would not berate him in front of others. The matter would be dealt with privately. He was respected by those under him as well as over him. He was not, however, a pushover. He demanded a great deal from those who worked under him as well as himself and when people did not perform, they were dealt with sternly.

John's pride and joy was his son Shawn. Shawn was ten years old and the best friend John had. John loved all of his family, but Shawn was his buddy. They would go fishing together, and he would even take him hunting sometimes, though he never let Shawn have a gun. Occasionally he would take Shawn golfing with him. When he had time, John would sometimes help coach Shawn's little league baseball team. He was not able to go to all the games, but he did make it to most of them. Shawn loved the time he spent with his father. John was careful not to show favoritism with Shawn. He loved his girls too. Sometimes he would take them somewhere and leave Shawn at home with his mother, but most of the time they did things as a family. John tried to set aside some time every week that he could spend with his family. They were very important to him. Unfortunately, his job sometimes sent him away for a week or two at a time and he could not tell them where he was.

Perhaps one reason Captain Anderson and John got along so well were that they had a number of things in common. Both of them had graduated from the Naval Academy. Both had served in Vietnam. Both had a wife and three children and both worked hard at their jobs and expected everyone else to. They had a good working relationship. They weren't to the point where they would classify each other as 'friends,' but they did see each other outside the workplace. Captain Anderson had two sons, the youngest of whom was two months older than Shawn. He played on Shawn's Little League team, and on one occasion Captain Anderson had taken his two sons fishing with John and Shawn.

Everything changed in July of 1980. It was discovered that someone in the chain of command was selling top secret information to the Russians. Captain Anderson had always considered himself patriotic. The idea that someone under his watch was betraying his country made him angry. He determined he would find out who the mole was, and until he did he didn't trust anyone including Lt. Commander John Miller. Anderson worked with Naval Investigation to find out who it was. After two months they found their man. It was the second in command. Commander Matthew Walton. Next to himself and Captain Anderson, Commander Walton was the last man John would have ever expected. He also was a Naval Academy graduate. He had served two tours of duty in Vietnam where he received the bronze star and the purple heart. He had commendation after commendation. He was happily married with a lovely wife and two beautiful daughters. His wife was president of the officer's wives club. Becky knew her well. He went to church every Sunday, was seen praying before his meals, and even kept a Bible on his desk. He even had the American flag hanging behind his desk. John had heard him talk about the anger he felt when protesters would burn the American flag during the Vietnam War. Yes, he seemed to be a genuine, red-blooded American.

The whole thing was devastating to the department, but especially to John. Commander Walton's office was right next to John's and they talked often. John was a man of strong religious faith and Commander Walton seemed to be also. They had openly talked of God, and Commander Walton, like John, would not touch alcohol. He was a likeable man and easy to work with. He did not fit the profile of a traitor.

The damage was massive. The information he had sold to the Russians about submarine operations put the United States back at least ten years. He gave them information about submarine design, computer operations, and worst of all, how to track them. Before this, the Russians had a difficult time tracking American submarines, and now they could track them much easier because of the information Commander Walton had sold them.

It made John sick to his stomach to think what that man had done to his country. What was even more amazing was how he did it. He walked into the Russian embassy and told them he had some secrets to sell. He would place the information at a prearranged drop sight. The Russians would leave cash in small bills to be untraceable. This went on for two years. He had sold his country out for money. Not because he had a bone to pick or because he was secretly a Communist sympathizer, it was money. Plain, old-fashioned greed. He had betrayed two hundred million Americans for what amounted to $100,000 dollars. The thought of it made John so angry he couldn't stand it.

The only bright spot was that the whole ordeal was over. The spy had been caught, the flow of information stopped, and if this man was found guilty he would surely receive the death penalty, which according to John was the very least he deserved.

But it wasn't over. That's what John found out on the morning of September 16th. He noticed that Captain Anderson was not at work. John didn't think it too unusual. He just figured Anderson was sick. After what he had been through, what they all had been through, it certainly wouldn't surprise him. It did strike John as odd though that it was the first time in nearly two years that Captain Anderson had missed a day of work. Around 10:00 John reached into his lunch bag to get an apple. He noticed a note inside his bag. It was a man's handwriting written in a hurry. How did it get in his bag?

'John, meet me at 1630 at the place we went the day after Thanksgiving. IMPORTANT. Tell no one, not even Becky. Make sure you're not followed. RA'

John felt a big knot in his stomach. Something was wrong. He had noticed Captain Anderson had changed, but he figured it was because of the investigation. There was something else, and he would do as he was asked.

CHAPTER THREE

John called Becky and told her that he would be late. He was not sure when he would be home, but told Becky to eat dinner without him and he would pick something up. He would come home late at least once every week or two, so this was nothing unusual. She learned not to ask why. He couldn't tell her most of the time anyway.

John left the office at 3:30. It would take him at least an hour to get to the lake he and Captain Anderson had taken their sons fishing the day after Thanksgiving. It was a beautiful place out in the country that Captain Anderson often took his children. Shawn had a really good time when he went. John had just bought him a new fishing pole for his birthday and he had been anxious to use it.

At precisely 4:30, John pulled up to the lake. There was Captain Anderson sitting in his truck. John got out and walked over to the truck. Russell got out and shook John's hand. John could tell by the look on his face that there was something terribly wrong. Anderson was white as a sheet and John saw fear in his eyes. The Captain looked all around just to make sure no one was watching.

"You weren't followed were you?"

"No, Russell, what's wrong?" John had never called him by his first name before.

"John, I'm sorry I have to drag you in on this; God knows I didn't want to, but I need someone I can trust and right now you're the only one." John had never heard Captain Anderson say he trusted him before.

"Trust me with what? What's going on?"

"It's time I told you the truth."

"I'm listening."

"For the last two years I've been working with Naval Investigations to uncover a spy ring."

"You mean Commander Walton."

"He was part of it."

"You mean there's more."

"Yes, a lot more, but it's probably best if you don't know."

"What do you want of me?"

"I need you to hold on to something for me." Anderson handed him a thick envelope full of papers.

"What's this all about?"

"It really is better if you don't know."

"Captain, I have all the respect for you in the world but I'm not taking anything unless I know what it is and who it's for. Especially in light of what's been going on lately."

Russell rubbed his chin and thought for a moment.

"You may not want to hear what I have to say."

"I'll take that chance."

"All right." Russell sat down next to a tree and John followed suit. Russ was quiet for a moment.

"This has to do with Matthew, doesn't it?" Russell reached into the envelope and pulled out a manila folder.

"Take a look at this." Russell handed him a photocopy of something. John looked at it for a minute.

"This is Matthew's birth certificate."

"That's right. Matthew Henry Walton, born in Oklahoma City, Oklahoma on January 16, 1936, to Peter and Helen Walton."

"So I have one too somewhere in my basement. It doesn't make me a spy."

"Now look at this." He handed John another photocopy.

"This can't be. This is impossible."

"Oh it's real all right. Matthew Henry Walton died on June 12, 1942 at the age of six. He died after falling from a tree." He handed John a cut out of an old newspaper article. The headline read "Boy Dies of Fall."

"Well, if the real Matthew Walton died of a fall nearly forty years ago, who was that guy that worked next to me for a year and a half?"

"He was part of a Russian spy ring." He cleared his throat and continued. "His real name was Ivan Mihiel Sevinsky. He was born in Kiev in 1934." John's face registered complete incomprehension. "In 1937, our friend and ally Joseph Stalin started a project to infiltrate the American military. It was actually the KGB's idea but Stalin backed it up. They took young children from all over Russia ages three to seven and placed them in a special training camp in the Ukraine. The KGB built a small town to look just like an American Midwest town. It had a grocery store, post office, church, school, and houses. There were several hundred children who were tested to be genius or near genius in intelligence. They were raised in this town in a school patterned after American schools. The kids spoke only American English. They learned American history. In school every morning they said the pledge of allegiance, read a Bible verse, and sang the Star-Spangled Banner. They even listened to American radio programs. They wore American style clothes. They were also highly trained agents. For years they were educated in American culture and also how to spy on America's best kept secrets."

"You definitely have my attention." Said John.

"After ten years of training, the KGB narrowed the field from several hundred, down to twelve. Twelve highly trained, teenaged agents. They then sneaked them into the United States through Canada and Mexico and into homes of Soviet agents working in deep cover in the United States. Birth certificates, passports, school records, medical records, were all forged for these kids. They were moved into homes with their newly adopted parents. The plan was brilliant. They spent years researching identities they could steal. In each case they took the identity of a child and parents who were all dead. They specifically looked for families that had few close relatives alive. With a legitimate record of their birth and no relatives to contact, it was very difficult to trace their true identity."

"So you mean, Matthew Walton's parents weren't his real parents."

"No, the real Peter and Helen Walton died in a car crash in

1946. Both were an only child and both of their parents were deceased."

"And I'll bet Matthew had no brothers or sisters."

"Correct."

"So who were the parents really?"

"They were actually Americans who betrayed their country. They were George and Elizabeth Morris, both born and raised in California. Active members of the American Communist Party."

The families were placed in twelve different states from Washington to Florida. To all outside appearances they were new families moving into a neighborhood. They even had school ribbons from previous schools they supposedly attended. The parents were all professional people who were well respected in their communities. They looked as American as apple pie and baseball. No one ever suspected that the nice family with the smart kid next door were actually spies. These kids were all trained to pursue careers in the military, the FBI, or the CIA. Four of them made it to the CIA, three to the FBI, and five in the military. They seemed to be the ideal candidates, smart, hard working, loyal Americans just wanting to serve their countries. All the while they were trained to spy or assassinate, whatever their informant told them to do. One even made it into the Naval Academy, graduated with honors, and earned medals in Vietnam.

"Commander Walton?"

"That's right."

"You said something about assassinate. They didn't actually kill anybody did they?" Russell reached into the envelope and looked for a minute. He pulled out a file that was about five typed pages.

"I shouldn't be showing you this, but I'm going to because I don't want to leave any doubt in your mind how dangerous these guys are. Read this." John spent several minutes reading. After the second page he looked up, his face white as a ghost.

"I'd ask you if you're kidding, but I know you're not. Did they really kill President Kennedy?"

"I won't take the time, but the evidence is all in there. There's no doubt. The four that made it into the CIA were the ones that killed him. Lee Harvey Oswald was just the fall guy. He never killed anybody."

"But why kill Kennedy?"

"Because of Vietnam. Kennedy wouldn't commit combat troops to Vietnam. He only sent in advisers."

"You mean the Russians wanted us in Vietnam?"

"Absolutely. They could have cared less about taking Vietnam. Vietnam was nothing to them. The Russians knew from the Korean War that when America goes to war it goes all the way. They wanted us in Vietnam because . . . "

"Because if we sent a bunch of soldiers over there it would drain our sources in other parts of the world."

"Exactly. We'd spend so much time and money in Vietnam that it would take pressure off the Russians in other parts of the world, most notably Eastern Europe. Remember the Hungarian Revolt?" John stared at the ground, completely dumbfounded.

"Keep reading. It gets worse." John finished reading the second and third pages. Once again he looked at Russell with a look of complete incomprehension.

"Martin Luther King Jr., I'm sorry, this makes no sense. I might understand the Russians wanting to kill the President of the United States but why would they care about a civil rights leader preaching equality for all Americans? What could they possibly gain from killing him?"

"John, think of the time period. By 1968 there were many who wanted to take a more radical approach to the Civil Rights Movement. King had always preached non violent protests."

"I know. I was in my last month at the Naval Academy when he was assassinated. But why kill him?"

"They were hoping for revolution. They were hoping that by killing King the leader of the non violent movement, his followers would think non violence doesn't work so let's use violence. They were hoping to overthrow the United States government. Then the Russians would have won the Cold War. They darn near succeeded." John kept reading. When he finally finished, he handed it back to Russell.

"So they killed Bobby Kennedy too. Why?"

"They didn't really kill him. They just found someone willing,

Sirhan Sirhan and helped him along."

"Why Bobby?"

"He would have ended Vietnam early." Russell continued, "John, as bad as that is that's not all of it. We have learned of one, possibly two more assassination plots in the making."

"Who?"

"Have you been keeping up with the Presidential race?"

"Of course, who hasn't."

"If you had to guess, who would you say will win the election in November?"

"Unless things change, I'm guessing Governor Reagan."

"That's what the Russians think."

"You mean they're going to take out Reagan? But why?"

"Only if he gets elected. He scares them. He wants to build up the military, and he has pledged to fight Communism whenever he can." John said nothing, his eyes wide.

"Do you know when?"

"We don't know any details. We only know they plan to take him out within two months of taking office."

"I'm afraid to ask who the other one is?"

"Well, we're not sure, but we have reason to believe they may try to assassinate a Middle East leader."

"Who?"

"We're not sure. Possibly Prime Minister Begin of Israel, or King Hussein of Jordan, but our most likely guess is Anwar Sadat of Egypt."

"Dare I ask why?"

"They want to show what happens to Arab leaders who befriend Israel."

"John, I haven't even told you about all the military secrets they have been feeding to the Kremlin. It's put the Russians way ahead of us."

"Dear God, how could this have happened?"

"These men will not stop until they have completely destroyed our country. We can't let that happen."

"How did you find out about this?"

"About six months ago we had a Russian pilot defect to us. The man risked his life to make it to this country. Anyway, during his debriefing, he mentioned that his brother-in-law is a high-level KGB agent. One day while talking to his brother-in-law, he hinted that there was a spy ring in the American military. That's what got the ball rolling. Naval Investigation assigned two men to investigate. One was my roommate at the Naval Academy. He called me two days ago and told me the story. He told me that his partner had died in a plane crash that he believed was murder. He was worried he was next, and he needed to trust me with some vital information."

"So what happened?"

"They found his body yesterday. He had committed suicide with a shotgun and a typed suicide note. If they get to me, the information dies with me. I can't let that happen." Anderson let it sink in before he continued.

"Now the bad news."

"The bad news? If what you told me was the good news . . ."

"The fact we caught them, at least most of them, is the good news."

"Oh no. You mean you don't have all of them?"

"We have ten of them. Two of them are unaccounted for."

"So you're telling me there are two Russian spies floating around this country, and we don't know who they are?"

"That's right. This is why I have to give you this information. I am the only one left, and if they got to me, the information would die with me. Tomorrow I have a meeting in Washington. I'm pretty sure they know nothing about me, but I want to be safe. If you hear of my untimely death, see to it that this gets to the proper authorities."

"John," he said very seriously, "if they find you with this information, they will kill you. Be careful, my friend."

"I will."

"Good, I've made copies of everything. It's all here. Photographs, maps, locations, what information was sold, everything. I want you to hide it somewhere where no one will find it and whatever you do, don't tell anyone you have it, and don't read it. The less you know the better. If all goes well, I'll pick it up from you in two days and we can both go on with our lives knowing we did something to help our country in its greatest hour of need."

"You have my word, Captain."

"Just make sure it gets to the right people."

"What do I do now?"

"Go home, pretend nothing's wrong or else they'll get suspicious."

"You mean they're watching me?"

"It's possible."

"I'll be careful then." John turned and walked away. As he did Russell put his hand on his shoulder.

"You're a good man John. I wish we had gotten to be better friends."

"Me too." That was the last time he saw Captain Anderson alive.

CHAPTER FOUR

After John left the lake, he did not go home. As he drove, he glanced down at the large yellow envelope and couldn't help but wonder what information was in it. He would keep his promise to Russell and not look through it. He decided he would not hide the information in his house. If anyone thought he had it, that would be the first place they'd look and besides, he didn't want to put his family in danger.

John had a friend in the church he attended by the name of Allen Stewart. Allen owned a cabin in the mountains about forty-five miles from Norfolk. He allowed John to use it whenever he wanted and even gave him a key. John would sometimes go hunting and spend the night in the cabin. It was in the middle of nowhere. John decided he would hide the information there. His friend was in Florida until the middle of October, so there was no chance that he would accidentally find it. Less than a dozen people even knew of its existence, and trying to find it would be difficult for someone who had never been there.

As John drove up to the cabin the sun was setting on the horizon. He walked into the cabin and looked around. It was cozy, but not luxurious. It had a living room with a fireplace, two bedrooms, a bathroom, and a kitchen. John decided to hide the envelopes behind the deer head mounted on the wall above the fireplace. Allen had shot the deer many years before but was still very proud of it. Hopefully, John would be back in a couple of days to pick the information up, and Allen would never know anything about it.

John didn't get home until almost 11:00. The light was on when he drove up the driveway. Becky was sitting on the couch waiting for him.

"Hi, honey. Everything all right?"

"Yeah, just some trouble at work. I think it's all going to work out though."

"I suppose you can't talk about it can you?"

"No, I wish I could. Sorry. Are the kids asleep?"

"Yes."

"I'm going to check on them."

"Are you sure everything is all right?"

"Yes, why do you ask?"

"Well, it's just that you sounded like something was wrong on the phone."

"I'm fine. I'm going to check on the kids, be back in a minute."

"Did you eat any supper?"

"No."

"I saved you some. I'll get it ready."

It was midnight before John finally got to bed. The phone rang at 5:30. John answered it and immediately recognized the voice. It was Mike Parker, the chief homicide investigator for the Norfolk Police Department. His wife and Becky were very close friends.

"Hello, John, I'm sorry to bother you. This is Mike Parker."

"Yeah Mike, what can I do for you?"

"I need to talk to you as soon as possible." A cold chill went down John's spine as he suddenly remembered what Mike did for a living.

"Mike, what's wrong?"

"I'd rather wait until I can talk to you face to face."

"Mike, I have to know now, what's wrong?"

"I really don't think I should tell you over the phone." There was a pause for a moment, then Mike said,

"It's your commanding officer, Russell Anderson. He's been murdered." The phone fell out of John's hand. He quickly grabbed it.

"Where are you?"

"Actually, I'm calling from his house. We just got here. A

neighbor called an hour ago and said she heard something going on and . . . "

"I'll be there in ten minutes."

"John, don't come here. You won't like what . . . " John hung the phone up before Mike finished his sentence.

Exactly ten minutes later John pulled up to the Anderson home. The place was crawling with cops. He noticed several military uniforms as well as policemen. Mike walked up to him as he got out of the car. John didn't even stop to speak to him. He just started walking toward the house.

"John, where are you going?" John kept walking. "John, JOHN!"

"You can't go in there."

"You'll have to arrest me to stop me." For one brief moment Mike considered doing just that.

"John, I know you liked Anderson. I knew of him, he was a good man, but please don't go in that house. I've been in homicide fifteen years and I've never seen anything that horrific. I've already had to send three of my men home, and they deal with this all the time. I'm asking you not to go in there."

"And I'm telling you, get out of my way."

"I won't stop you, John, but you will regret this." John walked up the steps, opened the screen and walked into the living room. Several policemen as well as military personnel were working, taking pictures and dusting for prints.

"Hey, you can't be in here!" said one policeman.

"It's all right. He's with me." Mike said.

What John saw was the most horrible thing he had ever seen in his life. No horror movie producer could have imagined what met John's eyes. Even the most battle-hardened soldier would shutter to see this. Nothing could have ever prepared him for what he saw. There lay the bodies of Captain Anderson, his wife, and three children. Blood was everywhere. There were severed body parts strewn around the room. Next to John's foot was the severed hand of the daughter, rings still on the fingers. Captain Anderson had been stabbed so many times in the throat that his head had been severed from his body. His wife, who had been a beautiful woman, was slashed in the face beyond recognition. His daughter had her clothes torn completely off. Her entire body slashed and John did not even want to dwell on what that sweet girl went through before she died. Anderson's older son had been stabbed in the eyeballs and the knife was still in him. But by far the worst thing he saw that day was what they did to the youngest son, the one only two months older than Shawn.

Russell Junior was known as Rusty to distinguish him from his father. In fact Shawn had been in this very house nearly a year ago for Rusty's tenth birthday. John had watched this boy play baseball with Shawn only a week ago. He had blond hair and blue eyes like Shawn. When John saw the severed body parts of that boy lying around the room, he could take it no more. He felt the bile coming up his throat and he immediately ran to the door. He just made it outside in time. As he stood in the yard heaving, Mike walked up to him.

"John, I'm so sorry. Even I got weak when I saw that, and I investigate murders for a living." John continued heaving. "Now you know why I didn't want you in there." John wiped his mouth and looked up at him.

"How could anybody be so cruel?"

"That's not the worst of it."

"What do you mean?" Mike shuffled his feet and then said quietly,

"Sit down for a minute. We need to talk." John took a seat on the steps next to Mike.

"John, can I be frank with you?" John nodded.

"Besides the brutality of it, the likes of which I've never seen, there's something else that bothers me." Mike turned away and looked off into the distance. "I can't figure out a motive. Whoever did this broke into this house in a well-lit neighborhood that is regularly patrolled by both police and a neighborhood watch. They took all five family members, tied them up then ransacked the house literally from one end to the other and did not take a single thing. This definitely was not a robbery. They left jewelry, money, electronic equipment. I don't think they took a single thing." John just listened, too upset to even respond. Mike continued,

"They were looking for something. I'd bet my entire pension on it. They were looking for something and couldn't find it, and here's the part that'll really make you sick. Anderson was the last to die. From what we can tell, they slowly tortured his wife to death, then his son, his daughter, and by the time they got to the last child they were desperate so they made that one especially brutal. They taped Anderson's eyes open and forced him to watch, and then they literally hacked him to death." John threw up again.

"I'm sorry, John. I shouldn't be so honest but I said all that to say this. They wanted something he had or wanted some kind of information, and he wouldn't tell them. My first thought was Mafia but even the Mafia isn't this ruthless.

"When I called you this morning, your reaction was most unusual. I sensed that you already knew something bad might have happened to someone you knew. You seemed almost in panic coming down here and wanting to go inside. My guess is that whatever these men were looking for had something to do with Russell's work, and since you work with him you may have some clue as to who did this and why. " Mike put his arm around John's shoulder, "We need your help. Is there anything at all you can tell us, no matter how small that will help us catch them?"

John was caught in a difficult situation. He could not tell Mike what he really knew; that would endanger his life and yet he had to tell him something or Mike would get suspicious.

"Anderson didn't come to work yesterday. He never misses work, ever. I don't know where he was all day. He'd been acting differently. Like something was bothering him." Then came the question John had been praying Mike would not ask.

"Did he contact you at all in the last twenty-four hours?" John hesitated in his answer.

"He did call me yesterday."

"What was the call about?"

"There was a lake where he and I took our sons fishing. He wanted to meet me there sometime. Look Mike, I've helped you all I can. I really should get home. After seeing this, I would like to check on my family." John hid it well, but Mike knew fear when he saw it. He looked John straight in the eye.

"I know Anderson had an important job in the Navy and I know there was some kind of trouble. You know more than you're letting on, John."

"You know I can't discuss my job, Mike."

"I know that, but we have reason to believe this murder was connected to his job. You worked with him. I don't want the next screams in the night to be at your home."

"I have to go."

"All right, but I think the military is going to have some questions for you too."

CHAPTER FIVE

John got home at 8:00. The kids were already at school. Becky was waiting for him when he came in. John called his secretary and told her he would not be in today; he was sick. He didn't elaborate, but he was telling her the truth. He felt so physically ill, he would not have been able to work. As soon as he hung up the phone, he sat down on the couch next to Becky. They were home alone.

John was a strong man both physically and emotionally, but this time he just broke down and cried. For ten minutes he couldn't compose himself enough to tell her what was wrong. Becky had seen her husband shed tears, but never cry like this. He told her that Captain Anderson and his family had been murdered and they were trying to find out who did it. He did not tell here how or why he was murdered.

"John, I'm so sorry," was all she could say. John spent an hour talking with Becky about Anderson. What a fine gentleman he had been. He was a fair and honest man who treated everyone with respect. He had not deserved this. He talked about when they had gone fishing and how he had shown Shawn how to hold his pole. His son Rusty was first baseman on Shawn's baseball team. Becky couldn't quite remember what Rusty looked like so John got out Shawn's team picture. He played for the Pirates. They had yellow jerseys and black pants. He pointed out Rusty Anderson in the picture. Tears filled his eyes again as he looked at the smiling, freckle faced little boy in the photograph. Becky finally remembered who he was.

"He was a cute little boy."

"And he was a good kid too. Shawn always liked him."

"When should we tell him?" asked Becky.

"I haven't thought that far in advance." John thought a minute. "I'll tell Shawn tonight. We'll go out for dinner, and when we come home, I'll have a talk with the whole family. The girls need to know, too. It'll be all over the news tomorrow." John felt like he was going to throw up again. The room was spinning. He grabbed hold of the counter to balance himself.

"John, go lie down for a while. You need some rest." This was not a request.

"Would you like something to eat?"

"After what I saw I may never eat again."

"John, go lie down. I'll get you a glass of tea and put on some quiet music."

"All right." John walked down the hall and went into the bedroom. The bed was made but John just lay down on top. He heard Becky moving around in the kitchen. John closed his eyes. He lay there for a full five seconds when like an asteroid crashing to the earth, it hit him. The envelope behind the deer head. In all the commotion and shock he had nearly forgotten about his promise to Russell. John sat up in bed, just as Becky came in with a glass of iced tea. What should he tell her? He couldn't tell her. Not after what he saw. But how would he get it? The cabin was an hour and a half away. Were they watching him? Would they follow him to the cabin? Would they murder his family while he was out? Did they even know he had the information?

"John, is everything all right?"

"Yeah" he said as he reached for the glass of iced tea. "I just need to be alone and rest for a little while. Thanks for the tea." Becky left and John put the iced tea on the night stand. He had to think things through. He decided against going and getting the information right then. Russell had warned him not to change his routine too much. Right now he would stay with his family. Their safety was his number one priority. He opened his night stand and got his .38 revolver. It was unloaded. He got up, went to his closet, reached to the back of the top shelf and retrieved the box of bullets.

He took out five and loaded his gun, leaving one chamber empty. Somehow, holding a loaded gun made him feel safer.

John decided that there was no way they could know he had the information. At worst they might suspect he had it but the only other person in the world who knew he had the information was now dead. He was safe for the moment. He contemplated destroying the envelope and forgetting the whole thing. However, he knew that was out of the question. He loved his family, but he loved his country also. He had to get this information to the proper authorities. Should he call? They might be tracking his calls. Could he use a payphone? But what if he were followed? Who would he call? The FBI, the CIA, Naval Investigation? How far did the spy ring run? If he talked to the wrong person they might kill him before he had a chance to turn it over. He could take his family and run. No, that wouldn't work; the Russians would know he had it and they would track him down.

Slowly, a plan formed in his mind. He would leave for work tomorrow morning the same as he always did. Instead of going to work, though, he would drive to the cabin, pick up the envelope and drive to Washington. He would walk right into the Pentagon and ask to speak to the Secretary of Defense or some other high ranking officer. He would personally hand it to a high-ranking officer and ask for protection for his family. If he timed it right, he could be back home before the kids were home from school and Becky was back from shopping. He would not tell Becky where he was going. She would think he was going to work as usual. He could be home the same time as usual and everyone would think he had just been to work. It was a good plan, but even this had a problem. If whoever was watching him saw him leave and then called his office, they might find out he did not come to work and get suspicious. It was a chance he would have to take.

Usually the kids rode the bus home from school. This afternoon Becky picked the kids up at school. This didn't happen often, but it did happen enough that most would not suspect anything including the kids themselves. Becky told them that they were going out for an early dinner. Sara asked, "Are we going to McDonald's"

"No, I'm afraid not."

"Ah, Mom" the kids said in unison. They decided on the S & K Cafeteria. It was a buffet style place that had great food at a reasonable price and good service. For one price it was an all you could eat. The kids liked it because there was ice cream on the dessert bar. All three kids loved chocolate ice cream.

They were just finishing dessert when the waiter came over to John.

"Excuse me sir, but are you John Miller?"

"Yes, is something wrong?"

"You have a telephone call." John got up and followed the waiter.

"How did you know who I was?"

"The caller said you were a tall man with brown hair with a wife and three young children with blond hair. You're the only one here who fits that description." John picked up the phone.

"Hello. This is John Miller."

"John," It was Sam Patterson, his next door neighbor. "I'm sorry to bother you. Becky told Ruth you were going out tonight. You need to come home right away." A sickening feeling crept into John's stomach.

"What's wrong?"

"You just need to come home. Don't worry, nobody's hurt, but you do need to come home as soon as possible."

"Sam, just tell me what it is."

"I'm sorry to tell you this. Your house is on fire."

"I'll be there as soon as possible." John went back to the table.

"We have to go." There was a coldness in his voice.

"Dare I ask what it is?" said Becky.

"I'll tell you in the car." The kids by this time knew something was up. As soon as they got in the car Shannon asked, "What is it, Daddy?" They all looked at John.

"I'm afraid our house caught on fire. I don't know how bad it is, but we can all be thankful we were not in it." John could see the smoke and hear the sirens' two blocks away. As he pulled up, he saw his entire house engulfed in flames. Three fire trucks were there and the men were working to put the fire out. It was a losing battle. It was obvious that nothing would be saved. A man who was apparently the fire chief came up to him.

"Are you the family that lives here?"

"Yes," John couldn't say much at this point. His wife and children were behind him crying.

"I'm genuinely sorry about your house."

"Actually we were renting this home. I'm stationed at Norfolk."

"Do you have insurance?"

"Yes, we do."

"Good. You should be able to recover your losses."

"What happened?"

"You have a gas stove, don't you?"

"Yes, we do."

"From what we can tell, someone left the gas stove on wide open. Apparently you forgot to put out the furnace also. The house was filled with gas and was lighted by the furnace. A lot of fires are started that way. I'm truly sorry." John's mind went back a few hours too just before they walked out of the house to eat dinner. Becky had turned the stove on to boil some tea bags. Becky had never left the stove on before. John began to feel afraid. Something was not right. The more he thought about it the more afraid he became. They hadn't used their furnace since March. Becky called him aside. She spoke softly so no one else could hear.

"John, I don't want to call that man a liar, but I distinctly remember turning the stove off. Maybe one of the children did it." John spoke to each of the children privately. All said the same thing; none of them had touched the furnace or the stove. John could tell when his kids were lying. They weren't.

As John looked into Shawn's big blue eyes, he thought of the horror he had seen at the Anderson's home a few hours before. This was no accident. Whoever did this was sending him a message. They weren't sure if he had the information or not, but this was their way of saying they would take out his entire family if he turned over what he had to the proper authorities. John had been shot down over the jungles of Vietnam and he was not as scared then as he was now. This time it was personal. This time it was his family. He called Becky aside once more.

"Honey, I need you to do something, and please don't ask me to explain."

"Okay."

"I want you to take the kids and check into a hotel for the night. In the morning, I want you to drive to your brother Henry's house and stay there for a few days."

"I suppose I can't ask where you are going?"

"I'll be all right. Here's some money. If you need any more use the checkbook or credit card." Becky started crying again. John's heart went out to her and his family, but he reminded himself that this was for their safety. He got into his Ford truck and drove up to the mountains to the little cabin. He took down the deer head and took the envelope from the back of it. He stared at it for a while as he thought about what he was going to do.

An entire lifetime's worth of emotion fell on him at once. His family was in danger and so was his country. Should he sacrifice one to save the other? He had to talk to somebody. Somebody he could trust not only his own life but the lives of the four most important people in the world to him. There was only one man John trusted that much. He picked up the phone and dialed the number from memory. The phone rang three times before it was answered.

"Hello. This is Dave."

"Dave, this is John."

"Duke, good to hear your voice. I just told Mary yesterday I was overdue to call you. Listen since I got you on the line, I was wondering if . . . "

"Dave, we gotta talk."

The Saturday, September 21st edition of the Wilson paper had this story in the top corner of the second page.

VIETNAM HERO DIES IN CAR CRASH

"Lt. Commander John Robert Miller, the former all star high school quarterback, Naval Academy graduate, and war hero was driving back to Norfolk Friday night from Washington, D.C. when his car went over a railing, down a cliff, and exploded killing the driver. He is survived by his wife Becky and his three children, Shawn, Sara, and Shannon. Police have determined that he was driving under the influence of alcohol. His death is considered a tragic accident."

The case was officially closed.

CHAPTER SIX

April 2004

It was a cold, rainy morning as Shawn Miller drove to work. When his alarm clock went off this morning, Shawn would have loved to just turn it off, roll over, and go back to sleep. In fact, he had briefly toyed with the idea of calling in sick, but he had already used up all his sick days. From the back seat six-year-old Heather asked, "Daddy, can we go to the park after school today?"

"We'll see, Sweetie, I doubt it though. It's supposed to rain all day."

"Then can we go to the mall?" Shawn laughed quietly. His daughter was the determined type.

"I'll tell you what, if I can't take you today, I'll take you tomorrow. Okay?"

"Okay." Shawn and his daughter were alike in many ways. Both had blond hair and blue eyes, both were highly motivated people, both were smart, and both had lost a parent at a young age.

Shawn's wife Amanda had died of a brain tumor in August of 2003 after six months of radiation, chemotherapy, and some experimental treatment. It had been a crushing blow to Shawn and Heather, and yet it had brought them closer together. Shawn knew what it was like as a child to lose the most important person in his life.

Even though it was twenty-four years ago, Shawn could remember every detail of that awful night. He remembered where he had been, what he had been wearing, he even remembered the exact time it had happened. He and his mother and sisters had gone to his Uncle Henry's house. Henry was the oldest of the five Evans' children. Becky was the youngest. He was nine years older than Becky and since both of their parents were dead, he became the patriarch of the family. September 19th, 1980, was the day that Shawn's life changed forever. He was sleeping in the spare bedroom of his uncle's house. Shannon and Becky were sharing another room, and Sara was sleeping on the floor of Robin's room, Henry's only child. At 12:30, his Uncle Henry woke him up and said his mother needed to talk to him. Shawn knew something was wrong. Uncle Henry's voice cracked a little and he had a serious, sad look on his face. Shawn went down into the living room. His mom was there crying like Shawn had never seen her cry. She was hugging Sara and Shannon.

"Children," she began. "I'm afraid I have some terrible news." Tears streamed down her face as she spoke. "Your father was killed in a car crash tonight." All three children began to cry too. Their mother just hugged all three and they wept together. After a minute she continued, "Children, I want you to know something and don't ever forget it. Your daddy loved the three of you very much. There's nothing he wouldn't have done for you. You were his pride and joy."

"He loved you too, Mom." Shawn said trying to encourage his mother. She smiled through tears. "I know he did, Sweetheart. He was a wonderful husband as well as father. He loved all of us more than life itself. He's in heaven now, but he still loves us." She paused for a moment, "and we will always love him." More tears, more sobbing, "Love never fails. That's what the Bible says children. Love never fails."

That was the saddest night of Shawn's life until twenty-three years later. The loss of John Miller was a loss none of his family ever quite got over. Of the three children, Shawn took it the hardest. His dad had been his best friend. They had done many things together, hunting, fishing, golfing. Almost every happy memory of his early childhood involved his father; the only exception was when he was nine and he kissed Jennifer Morgan, the prettiest girl in the third grade, but even then his father was involved when the teacher called and told on him.

Shawn had wanted to be just like his dad when he grew up. He wanted to be in the military. In particular, he wanted to join the Marine Corps. His mother absolutely forbade it. She did not want to lose her son the way she had lost her husband. Shawn and his mother were close, but some of the harshest words they ever had were over this. He wanted to join the Marines, and she did not want him to. They never did agree, but they did reach a compromise. Shawn decided to go into education like his mother. After John's death, Becky finished some course work, got her certification, and became an outstanding public school teacher. Shawn followed in her footsteps and became an elementary school teacher. His mother did finally consent to allow him to join the Army National Guard.

Shawn's life changed in more ways than just losing his father. After the funeral, Uncle Henry suggested that the family stay in Wilson, North Carolina and live there. Becky had already had the same idea, so it was agreed. Shawn had moved five times before his tenth birthday. After his father's death, they settled in North Carolina, and that's where they had lived for the last twenty-four years. They lived with Uncle Henry, Aunt Bonnie, and Robin for three months. Uncle Henry became like a second father to Shawn. Shawn had always liked his uncle. In fact, Henry was his favorite uncle.

Henry Evans was very much a man's man, and in that way, he was like John Miller. He was different in that he was loud, opinionated, and occasionally obnoxious as opposed to John who had been quiet, even tempered, and low key. Some people said that Henry reminded them of Archie Bunker, from the popular TV series, 'All in The Family,' and indeed their similarities were startling. However, Henry was a lovable man. Everybody liked him. He irritated a few people sometimes with his opinions, but he was funny and warmhearted and he was kind, especially to his nephew who had lost his father. Henry became that father in all but name. It was a case of two people needing each other. After Robin was born, the doctor told Henry that he and Bonnie would not have any more children. Henry had wanted a son very badly, and he knew he would never have one. That was until Shawn came into his life. Even before John died, Henry had spent time with Shawn and loved him dearly. After John's death, that bond became even stronger. Uncle Henry loved to go hunting, and many times he took Shawn with him. Henry loved to travel, and twice he had taken Shawn, who also loved to travel, with him. Once, Henry went to Israel, Greece, and Egypt with a church group. He took Shawn with him and his family. Shannon and Sara never forgave him. Another time he took a two-week trip to Europe. Shawn went with him again. These trips were among the most exciting times of Shawn's life and it instilled in him a love of learning, particularly the history and culture of people. His family never could quite understand this, but Henry did because he shared that same spirit.

Becky and the family received $200,000 in life insurance money from the Navy after John's death. She had no idea she would get that much money. They also received $10,000 from the insurance company for their house and all its contents. With that money, Becky bought and paid for an adorable three bedrooms, two bath house on Pine Street for $40,000. The house was worth $45,000 but the bank had foreclosed on it. She spent another $4,000 fixing it up and buying furniture. She still lived in that house. She had taken the remainder of her money and invested it in treasury bonds. That, along with her teacher's salary provided her family with a comfortable, though not excessive income.

Shawn, Shannon, and Sara enrolled in Moore Elementary School in October of that year. Shawn was in the fourth grade and Shannon and Sara were in the first grade. The next year, Becky was teaching sixth grade in that same school district, except she was teaching in a different school. John Miller would have been proud of Becky. She was the most popular teacher in the school district. She loved kids and that radiated in her classroom. She pushed her students hard to do their best, and they did simply because someone who loved them was asking. Year after year her former students would come and visit her and tell her how much she meant to them, but as hard as she pushed her students, she pushed her own children harder. She found that rare combination of being a loving but demanding parent. Losing John had made her realize that life was short and that we should cherish the ones we love and tell them so every day.

Two things kept Becky going during those awful months after

losing John. One was her deep, abiding faith in Christ. Becky had accepted the Lord as a sixteen-year-old during a revival meeting. This had given new meaning to her life. She was not her own. She was "bought with a price." She had tried to share her faith with her then boyfriend John, but he was not interested. John had been raised in a Baptist home, but it was not until he was a senior in the Naval Academy that he became a believer. Every morning, Becky would spend at least twenty minutes reading her Bible and praying. Becky was never bitter toward God for the loss of her husband. In fact, in some ways losing John had drawn her closer to God. She had to rely on him even more. She didn't have a husband to talk to, but she often talked to God.

She never remarried. She came close once in 1986. In her Sunday school class at church she met a fellow Christian, Dr. Seth Green. He was a cardiologist. He was eight years older than Becky, divorced for many years, and a recent convert. Their friendship started out innocently enough. Both liked to bowl, read classical literature, and eat fine Italian food. And since they went to the same church, they saw each other every Sunday. Most of the time they did things with other older singles in their church but occasionally they would go to dinner or bowling alone. They spent a lot of time together and soon rumors were flying. There was no doubt that Dr. Green was very interested in Becky. He seemed the perfect catch. He was a Christian, he was handsome, financially secure, she genuinely liked him. Even her children got along well with him. It was June of 1986. Shawn was off at summer camp for two weeks and the girls were at a slumber party. Seth had asked her to dinner at the Italian Garden. He told her he had something important to talk to her about. Becky agreed. They spent half the meal talking about Shawn's experiences at summer camp and the new love of twelve-year-old Shannon's life, her young, handsome history teacher, Mr. Lewis.

"Becky, we've been friends for a several months now, and I want you to know you are very special to me."

"You're very special to me too, Seth."

"I'm not very good at this kind of talk, but I'll try." Becky just listened. " I've been alone for twelve years now. I don't like it. I don't like waking up in the morning to an empty bed and coming home to an empty house." Becky interrupted him,

"What about Missy and Ben?" they were Seth's kids. Seth looked down at his plate.

"I don't see them much. They're so busy studying and working. They rarely come home. Besides, they're still bitter about some of the things I did before I knew the Lord. Particularly toward their mom." Seth's face took on a sad look. "I guess I don't blame them. I was a lousy father."

"Don't be so hard on yourself. That's all behind you now. You've obviously changed. You're a dear sweet man, and the best friend I have. Seth, you can't change the past, but you can show your children they're important to you now and you love them. You'd be amazed how forgiving they can be."

"I know, but the point I was trying to make is that I'm tired of being alone. I have enjoyed getting to know you and you are a dear friend of mine too. I was wondering if you would ever consider remarrying." Becky had somewhat expected this.

"Is this a proposal?"

"It is. Will you marry me?" Becky was quiet for a moment. "You don't have to answer now. I know it's a big step. Why don't you think about it for a little before you answer?"

"When would you like an answer?"

"Dessert will be here in a few minutes." Becky smiled, she knew Seth was joking.

"I might need a little more time than that. Why don't you come over to my house tomorrow night for dinner?"

"Dinner with an attractive woman two nights in a row? How lucky can a guy be?"

The next night Becky sent the girls out and baked a delicious chicken Parmesan with Caesar salad, and strawberry shortcake for dessert. Seth was at the door precisely at 6:00. He looked nice. He was wearing a blue, long sleeved polo shirt and khaki pants. They had a wonderful meal. They talked about church, their children, what passages of scripture they had read that day, and sports. After dinner Becky put on a pot of coffee and they had coffee and dessert in the living room. They sat on the couch next to each other.

"Becky, I love you." This was not going to be easy, but she had to do it.

"I love you too, Seth, very much. Which is why what I'm about to say will be very difficult for me."

"I know, I know. Let me say it for you. Seth, you're a nice guy and you'll make some little lady a fine husband, but I'm as attracted to you as I am the fungus I scrape off the toilet." This is not going well, thought Becky.

"Seth, you're patronizing me and I don't like it."

"I'm sorry. You go right ahead."

"First of all, I really do love you. You're a dear sweet man and you're wrong about not being attracted to you. I'm more attracted to you than any other man I've ever met." Seth looked up in surprise. She continued. "Except one. He's the reason I can't marry you." Becky put her hand on his. "It's not you, Seth. If Tom Selleck asked me to marry him, I'd turn him down. I'm still in love with John Miller."

"Becky, I'm not asking you to forget about him. From everything I know about John Miller, he was a brave and honorable man and he'll always be your first love. I know that. But he's gone, and one day you're going to have to let him go."

"You may be right. But today is not that day."

"Becky, I do know what it's like to lose someone you love. My wife didn't die. She just walked out on me after twenty years of marriage and never looked back."

"I know and I'm sorry." Said Becky.

"No offense, but in some ways that was even more painful than if I had been widowed. You lost your husband through no fault of your own. My wife left me. God knows I wasn't a perfect husband, but I did love her."

"Seth, even if I wanted to forget him, I couldn't. The cruelest thing I could ever do is marry one man when I love another." She squeezed his hand. "If I ever were going to remarry, you would definitely be the type of man I would be looking for. You're a kind, loving, attractive man, but I'm sorry, I can't marry you." Seth smiled for the first time.

"Believe it or not, I understand. Will this kill our friendship?"

"It better not. Seth, I'm flattered, I really am. You've been nothing but a gentleman." They talked for another two hours before Seth left. Becky walked him to the door and gave him a hug. Seth kissed her on the cheek and left.

The two did remain friends. Seth did eventually get married, and Becky was at his wedding. He married another lady in the church who was also a friend of Becky's.

CHAPTER SEVEN

It had been nine months since Shawn's wife Amanda, affection-ately known as Mandy, had passed away. It seemed the Miller family had known more than their share of loss. To lose one's father at an early age and then to become a widower at the age of thirty-three seemed so unfair. Shawn had gone on with his life after the loss of his father. It was hard. On his eleventh birthday he cried the whole day. His dad wasn't there and no amount of consoling would change that. God, however, had brought other people into his life to help fill the void. The Bible says that God would be "father to the fatherless" and Shawn had learned that truth. He had accepted the Lord when he was eleven, and he, like his mother, had to rely on God for his needs.

As he drove to school, his mind went back nineteen years to when he was a fifteen-year-old sophomore in high school. That was the day he met Amanda Lynn Thomson. September 5, 1986. A faint smile came over his face as he thought of her. She was without a doubt the prettiest girl in Wilson High School. Amanda had long wavy brown hair and beautiful brown eyes. She was stunningly attractive, and when she smiled she had the most beautiful smile Shawn had ever seen. He used to joke that he could sell a million tubes of toothpaste if he had Amanda's smile on the box. He was forever grateful to his tenth grade history teacher Mr. Johnson for putting him next to Amanda during World History. It took him two weeks just to get up enough nerve to speak to her. When he finally did, she just ignored him. Mandy had guys flirting with her every day. Why did this guy, who was short and had a lot of pimples, think he was something special? It was love at first sight, though, for Shawn and he knew he would not rest until he got a date. He knew he could not just ask her out to her face. She would probably say no and he would just die. He asked her out the cowardly way. He slipped her a note during history class. It was short and to the point. "Mandy, will you meet me at the mall on Saturday and we can have a milkshake together? Thanks, Shawn." She slipped the note back with an answer, "Thank you for asking, You seem like a sweet guy, but I can't. Have a nice day." She had politely broken his heart.

Shawn was determined, though, and decided that he would wait a while and try again. If Shawn was anything, he was ambitious. A month later, he asked her out again. This time like a man, he asked her face to face. She may turn him down, but at least she would respect his boldness. He met her between classes at her locker. She was talking to Brad McKenzie, the handsomest guy in the school. Shawn didn't care. She looked at him. "Hi, Shawn."

"Hi, Mandy." Brad glared at him with a smart aleck look on his face.

"One of the kids you babysit, Mandy?" Mandy may not have been interested in Shawn but she didn't like people who belittled others.

"Brad, don't be mean."

"Well," said Brad, "I'll leave you two lovebirds alone." Brad left. Mandy just sighed.

"Jerk." She looked at Shawn. "Is there something you want?"

"Mandy, uh, I was wondering if you . . . well, I mean if you're not doing anything Friday, would you like to go out for pizza?" "Not again." Thought Amanda. She felt sorry for Shawn. She knew he didn't have a father, some of the other kids had been making fun of him because of his pimples, and he was a sweet kid. She didn't really want to go out with him, but it would crush him. She looked at him for a minute. He was kind of cute in his own way. Those blues eyes and that Opie Taylor type face. One date wouldn't kill her. It wasn't like she was going to marry him.

"Oh, all right, I'll go out with you." Shawn looked up.

"Really?"

"Yeah, really." Shawn smiled a huge smile. "But just this once. And if you tell anyone I went out with you, I'll deny it to the grave."

"Thanks!" said Shawn. He turned and walked away.

"Aren't you going to tell me what time you're going to pick me up?"

Shawn was so sure she would say no he hadn't even planned how he was going to pick her up.

"Uh, I'll pick you up at 6:00." Shawn turned again to walk away.

"Don't you want to know where I live?"

Shawn laughed. "Yeah, I guess I'd better."

Amanda wrote down her address. "See you Friday."

"See you, Shawn."

Somehow Shawn managed to talk his cousin Robin, who was in college, into driving him to Amanda's house, taking them to the Pizza Place, and taking them home. It was very generous on her part and she only agreed when Shawn promised to wash and vacuum her car, walk her dog, and give the dog a bath, an agreement Shawn happily made.

Robin picked up Shawn at 5:30. Shawn liked Robin. Tall, beautiful, funny, she was like an older sister to him. He particularly liked it on the few occasions she would pick him up at school. She was blond, beautiful, and drove a brand-new red mustang. He never mentioned to the boys that she was his cousin. He always tried to make sure some of them were around when she picked him up. He loved the attention.

"Wow. You look nice." She said as Shawn got in the car. He was wearing khaki pants and a green pull over shirt and brand new white tennis shoes. Robin was nearly knocked out by the cologne Shawn was wearing. She was sure her asthma would act up. She could hardly breathe.

"Shawn, may I make one friendly suggestion?"

"Sure."

"It's your cologne."

"You don't think I have enough?" Robin laughed.

"No, I think you might have over done it just a bit."

"You think it's too strong?"

"I'd just hate for your first date with Mandy to end up with her in the hospital, sick from the fumes." Shawn ran back inside and washed his face and some of the cologne off. He came back.

"Much better." Said Robin. She started the car and pulled out of the Miller's driveway.

"You really like this girl, don't you, Shawn."

"Yeah, I'd better enjoy tonight though. This will be my only date with her."

"You go with that attitude and it will be."

"Wait til you see her; she's way out of my league."

"Oh, I don't know about that. She's going with you isn't she?"

"Any suggestions?"

"Yeah, just be yourself. DON'T try to impress her. Most guys that do that make jerks of themselves."

"Sounds like the voice of experience."

"I've had many a first date that never became a second date because of that. In fact, the reason I'm dating Brian now is because the first time I met him he struck me as a nice, down to earth guy. He was friendly, but not overly so. Shawn, just be yourself. She'll either like you for who you are or she won't."

They arrived at Amanda's house right at 6:00. As Shawn got out of the car, Robin whispered,

"Don't forget to compliment her on how she looks."

"What if she dresses in a clown outfit?"

"You want this girl to like you or not?"

"What do you think?"

"Oh, and one more thing, don't eat spaghetti on a first date."

"Why?"

"It's messy. You want her to think you have class."

Amanda lived in a nice neighborhood. Her dad was an accountant like Uncle Henry and they knew of each other. Shawn went to the door and rang the doorbell. Amanda's mom answered the door. Shawn immediately saw where Amanda got her good looks from.

"Oh, you must be the young man who's taking our daughter to dinner."

"Yes, ma'am."

"Please, come in, Mandy will be down in just a minute." Shawn looked around the house. It was nice but not too luxurious. There were pictures of Amanda, her sisters, and brother on the mantle above the fireplace. They were a beautiful family. Amanda's sisters were as pretty as she was, and her brother looked like he could be a model. "Take a good look," Shawn thought, "This is the last time you'll see this place." Amanda came down the stairs. She was wearing blue jeans, white tennis shoes, and a pink striped sweater. Her hair was all curled and she looked wonderful. She took Shawn's breath away.

"I'm ready, is Shawn here yet . . . Oh, hi Shawn, this is my mom."

"Oh, I already met this nice young man." Amanda's father walked through the front door. He had just finished a round of golf. Her dad was a big man, at least 6' 2" and he had huge biceps. He must work out, Shawn thought.

"Jack," Amanda's mother said, "this is Shawn Miller, the young man Mandy's been talking about." Amanda blushed. "So she's been talking about me." Thought Shawn. That's a good sign. He looked down at Shawn who was barely 5' 8" and weighed 140 lbs. Shawn felt intimidated. Jack wanted him to.

"I hope you kids have a good time. Young man, you have my daughter in this house by 9:30, is that understood?"

"Yes sir, I'll have her here by 9:25."

"Good," Jack smiled. "I don't want to come looking for you."

"Oh, Jack," said Amanda's mom, "don't scare the young man. You kids have a good time."

"We will," said Amanda. Amanda walked out with Shawn.

"You look nice tonight, Mandy."

"Thank you, Shawn." Then Amanda noticed the red mustang with the beautiful blond in the drivers seat. "Who's that?" she asked.

"Oh, that's my girlfriend. When I told her I had a date with another girl she insisted she go along. She's the jealous type." Amanda gave him that 'yeah right' look.

"Just kidding, that's my cousin Robin."

"She sure is nice to drive us."

"Well, I'll be paying for it tomorrow. That beautiful red car, I have to wash and vacuum it."

"Why, you'd do all of that for little old me?" Amanda said in her best Scarlet O'Hara imitation. They got in the car and Shawn introduced Amanda to Robin. Shawn sat in the back with Amanda. They arrived at Perry's Pizza Parlor. Robin told them she would be back at 8:00. Shawn and Amanda went in and were shown a booth for two in the corner. The waiter brought them two menus. Shawn just looked at the menu for several minutes. Finally Amanda spoke.

"Shawn, can I ask you a question?"

"Sure."

"Is this your first date?" Shawn looked at the floor and didn't answer right away.

"Why, am I doing something wrong?"

"Well, for starters, you could try talking to me a little. Otherwise, it's going to be a long hour and a half."

"I'm sorry, Mandy. Yes, this is my first date. I know you've probably had millions of them."

"Actually, you're my third."

"Who were the other two?"

"Well, my first date was to the eighth-grade banquet. I went with Jason Garlock. How come you didn't go?"

"I, uh, was sick with the flu." "Liar" he thought. He hadn't been sick. He'd been turned down three times.

"The flu really, in May. That's a little unusual."

"Is it? I had a rare kind."

"I didn't know there were different kinds." Mandy smiled. Shawn wasn't fooling her.

"So who was date number two?"

"Oh, that was Brad McKenzie. It was last year. We went ice skating. He still tells people I'm his girlfriend. I'm not. He's so arrogant I can't stand him." The waiter came. Shawn ordered a medium pizza with pepperoni, mushrooms, and sausage along with two cokes and an order of bread sticks. The waiter left.

"So tell me about your family, Shawn." Mandy was trying to get him to talk.

"Well, my dad died about six years ago and . . . "

"How did he die?"

"He died in a car crash."

"I'm sorry, go on."

"Well, my mom is a teacher and I have twin sisters who are twelve."

"What're their names?"

"Shannon and Sara. They're in the sixth grade." Their food came. Shawn divided the pizza making sure to serve Mandy before himself. While they ate, they talked more. They talked about school, TV, sports, friends, homework, cheerleading tryouts, football tryouts, family, sisters taking too long in the bathroom and a host of other subjects. They had a good time. They laughed and joked and the time flew by. Before he knew it, he looked up and Robin was standing at the door waiting for them. They got up, Shawn left a tip and they left with Robin.

Shawn wanted to take Mandy out for ice cream. There was a Baskin Robbins just down the road. They stopped and Shawn got his favorite, chocolate. Mandy got her favorite, mint chocolate chip. For another half an hour they sat and continued the conversation they had begun at the pizza parlor. They finally left at 9:00. Shawn wanted to make sure he kept his promise to Mr. Thomson. He didn't want him to come looking for him. It was a fifteen minute drive to Mandy's house. They got there exactly at 9:20. Robin drove a little slower than usual. Shawn walked her to the door.

"Mandy, I had a good time. Thank you for going with me." Mandy turned and looked at him. She smiled. Boy, was she beautiful when she smiled.

"I really enjoyed myself, Shawn. Thank you." She thought for a moment. "You know, you're nothing like what I thought you would be."

"What do you mean?"

"Well, you're so quiet in class, I thought you would be really boring, but I had a good time." Shawn smiled. He felt wonderful inside.

"You should smile more often. You have such a nice smile." She turned, pulled the key out of her pocket and unlocked the door.

"Good night, Shawn."

"Good night, Mandy, and don't worry, I won't tell anyone you went out with me."

"I don't mind if you tell people. Just don't get all cocky and brag about it like Brad did." She started to shut the door, then she turned, "And I'm NOT your girlfriend!"

Shawn didn't tell anybody about the date. He figured if he did, they would tease him and Amanda and that would turn her off. Instead, Shawn looked for opportunities to be alone with Amanda. He knew if others got wind of their friendship it would be the death of any chances of dating her. As it turned out, Shawn got his opportunity. Shawn was very good at history and Amanda was very good at English and Literature. They struck up an agreement. Shawn would help Amanda with history and she would help Shawn with English. Once a week one would go to the other's house and they would study together.

This went on through their sophomore and junior years of high school. Shawn did not ask Amanda out during that entire time. He didn't need to. He saw her every week. He figured if he asked her out, then she would turn him down and that would end their arrangement. What did happen is that Shawn and Amanda struck up a very close friendship. They were each other's best friend. In all this time their relationship never turned romantic. Amanda went out with other guys. In fact she even had a boyfriend for a while, but every week she still met her friend Shawn and they studied together. Shawn didn't have many dates; in fact, he only had one, and it was a disaster. He took a girl bowling and he locked his keys in his mom's car while she was out of town. They had to get someone to open the car door, it started raining so they got soaked, and he was an hour late getting the girl home and her parents were not happy with Shawn.

Shawn and Mandy's second date was to the senior prom. That's when there was the first hint that their relationship might become more than just friends. Amanda had just broken up with her boyfriend two weeks before, and Shawn saw his opportunity. Shawn had been noticing Amanda for years, but finally Amanda began to look at Shawn as more than a friend. Shawn had grown two inches. He would grow another inch his senior year. His face had cleared up from acne. He had also started working out and was quite muscular. Other girls had started to notice Shawn and Amanda noticed other girls noticing Shawn. Her study partner was becoming quite the hunk.

Shawn was nice looking, but he wasn't gorgeous like Amanda. Shawn didn't stand out in a crowd. Amanda did. But Amanda realized that there was a depth to Shawn that the other boys she dated lacked. He was more mature, and he liked her for more than her pretty face. They were voted the best-looking couple of the senior prom, and it was that night that Shawn kissed Amanda for the first time. It was just a peck on the cheek when he dropped her off at her house. She was absolutely beautiful in a full length blue dress, her hair done up. Shawn didn't look too bad, either. He was wearing a black tuxedo with a white cummerbund and bow tie. They were a handsome couple.

Both of them graduated with honors from high school on May 28, 1988. Unfortunately, they were headed to different colleges. Shawn was going to the University of North Carolina at Chapel Hill where he majored in Elementary Education. Amanda went to East Carolina University where she majored in office administration. Neither of them dated other people much. Both of them instead were very focused on their studies. Both would come home on weekends sometimes and, occasionally, they would see each other and go out to dinner. They sometimes even called each other just to talk. "I just need a friend to talk to," was a phrase Shawn heard often. Neither Shawn nor Amanda could pinpoint a time that they actually started dating. All they knew was they were calling each other more often and their talks became longer each time. Soon, they were not going home on the weekend to see their families. They were going to see each other.

The summer between Shawn's junior and senior year of college, he took a month long missions trip to Peru. The night before he left, he and Amanda went to Perry's Pizza Parlor and sat in the same booth they sat in five years before. They arrived at the restaurant at 5:00. They stayed until 11:00, when the restaurant closed. It was there that Shawn poured his heart out and told Amanda he loved her. He had loved her for five years. It was there that Amanda realized that she, in fact, too loved this man. He had been her friend through thick and thin. Through every trial she had been through for five years her friend Shawn was there for her. Kind and caring. How could she have ever been so fortunate to have found a friend like him? Yes, she too was in love. Not the silly kind of infatuation that junior high kids have. Their relationship was much deeper than that. They both knew that one day this relationship would lead to the marriage altar.

That day came only one year later. On June 18, 1992, Amanda and Shawn were married at Amanda's church, Oak View Baptist Church. Shawn played golf the morning of the wedding. He did that so he would always remember his anniversary, the 18th His best man was his Uncle Henry. The maid of honor was Amanda's sister. Shawn was so nervous, he didn't know what to do. He just didn't want to pass out before the wedding. As the organ played and Shawn watched Amanda walk down the aisle with her father, 'beautiful' was too trite a word to describe how Amanda looked to him that day. An angel from heaven could not have been more lovely than Amanda. This was the happiest day of his life. Shawn couldn't remember two words the preacher said, but he would never forget how beautiful his bride had been standing next to him.

They honeymooned in the Caribbean. Jack Thomson's wedding present to his daughter was a week-long cruise. They visited Mexico, Belize, and Honduras. They came back smiling and suntanned.

Mr. and Mrs. Shawn Miller moved into an apartment the week they got back. Shawn had gotten a job at Mountain View Elementary School teaching fifth grade. Amanda got a job working as a secretary for a law firm. They lived in their apartment two years before they bought a brand-new house. A beautiful, three-bedroom, two bath house with a fence. It had blue trim and a bay window. It was truly their dream home. They spent months planning their home down to the last detail. They had saved for two years to have enough for the down payment. Amanda had a talent with interior decorating, and she had worked hard to make their home attractive and comfortable. She had always been a great homemaker.

The second happiest day of Shawn's life came on February 16, 1998. That was when Heather Rose Miller was born. She was beautiful. She had big blue eyes like her daddy, but she had her mothers' good looks. Amanda stayed home for two years after Heather was born. Living off of one income took out some of the luxuries, but to Shawn and Amanda, their child's well- being came first.

Amanda went back to work in the fall of 2001. Things seemed to be going great. They were happy, they both had good careers, they truly loved each other, and then it happened. It was Christmastime of 2002. Shawn first noticed something was wrong when Amanda would trip and fall for no apparent reason. She would come home tired, more tired than usual and she had dizzy spells. She complained of headaches, severe headaches, like she had never had before.

The doctors decided to do a CAT scan, and that's when they found it. A tumor, right in the center of her brain. It was inoperable. The doctors decided to try radiation and chemotherapy, but all that managed to do was make Amanda's last few months even more miserable.

Amanda lost her hair; that beautiful long brown hair was gone. She had always kept herself physically fit, but she gained 65 pounds. At the time of her death she weighed almost 200 pounds. Nothing in Shawn's life could have ever prepared him for this. His wife, his lover, his friend was dying and there was nothing he could do about it. Shawn prayed every night for God to heal his wife, but his wife got weaker and weaker. Shawn took some time off work and was at the hospital every day. On the few days she felt a little better, they would play card games or talk. On days she didn't, he would read to her or play music on the tape player. It was agonizing for Shawn to see his beautiful wife deteriorate right before his eyes. The end finally came in August of 2003. Her hair was gone, and her body was swollen, but to Shawn, she was as beautiful as that night he picked her up for their first date and she came down the stairs in her jeans and pink sweater. She was as beautiful as the night of their prom when she wore a blue evening gown and as beautiful as the day she walked down the aisle in her wedding gown and Shawn saw a glimpse of heaven. He held her hand in his. It was just the two of them in the room and her last words were in a very faint whisper,

"I'm so blessed to have had you."

Losing his father was hard, but Shawn had gone on. Losing Amanda was devastating. Going back to that house they lived in was horrible. Everything he saw reminded him of her. The couch they sat and watched movies, or read their Bible, or talked, the bed they slept in, the kitchen where she made so many wonderful meals, the back yard where she spent many wonderful hours playing with Heather. All these memories of her, and now she was gone.

Heather took it hard too, though not as hard as her daddy. She would wake up at night crying and asking for mommy and asking why was she gone. Shawn did his best to comfort her and let her know that he was here and he was not going anywhere. His family helped all they could during these difficult months. The last few weeks of Amanda's life, Heather spent almost every night at Becky's house. Becky, Sara, and her husband Jeff did all they could to help Shawn and Heather. On nights when Shawn was totally exhausted, one of them would stay with Amanda in the hospital. One thing Shawn did not do was become bitter. He was brokenhearted, but he never blamed himself, and he never blamed God. In this, his mother was a wonderful encouragement. She was the one person in the world who knew the pain he felt. She had that same loss twenty-three years before. Shawn and his mother became even closer.

CHAPTER EIGHT

Shawn pulled into the parking lot of Mountain View Elementary School. The rain was still coming down. He opened his umbrella and then opened the door for Heather to get out. She was in kindergarten. It worked out nicely that she went to the same school that Shawn taught. He didn't have to stop at a day care or babysitters. She just went with him. Heather grabbed her backpack and swung it over her shoulders.

"Let's go, Sweetie." The two held hands and jogged to the front door. Shawn shook out his umbrella. "Go on to the cafeteria." The kids all met there in the morning before school. The teachers would pick them up from there. Heather knew the way very well. She had been a kindergartner for nine months now. She was in Mrs. Brown's class. Mrs. Brown was a wonderful teacher and Shawn had requested her for Heather.

As he made his way down the hall to the lounge he smiled and spoke to some of his students. Lori Price was the school secretary. She and her husband Stan were good friends of Shawn. Stan and Lori went to the same church as Shawn, and Shawn had known Stan since they were in the same youth group in high school. Stan and Shawn often played golf together, though Shawn had not had much opportunity to play the last few months. Lori was talking to some other teachers when Shawn entered the lounge.

"Hi, Shawn, did you swim to school today?"

"Just about. I keep my life raft in the trunk just in case. How's

Stan and the baby?"

"Fine. Listen, are you still coming over tonight?"

"Tonight? Oh yes, tonight, right, yes I'll be there." Shawn had completely forgotten that last Sunday, Stan had invited him over for dinner. He had told them then he would be coming. "Yes, I'll be there. What time?"

"Well, is 5:30 okay?"

"Sounds great. See ya then." Lori left and Shawn's friend and fellow teacher Veronica came in along with a new fourth grade teacher named Angela Bierman. Veronica was an old friend of Shawn's and had been working closely with Angela for the past year under the Teacher Mentoring Program. The program was started several years ago and had been an outstanding success. First year teachers were matched up with veteran teachers. The two would meet for half an hour twice a week and talk about teaching ideas as well as any problems the new teacher had. Veronica and Angela had developed a close working relationship as well as a good friendship over the past year.

"Hey, big guy, how's it going?" said Veronica.

"Awful."

"What's wrong?"

"I'm in a real jam. Stan and Lori invited me over tonight and I completely forgot about it. I don't have a babysitter for Heather. Veronica, dear sweet Veronica, old friend, is there any way you could . . . "

"No way, I've got a date tonight."

"You're kidding, I thought you gave up dating decades ago."

"Just because there's snow on the roof," she said pointing to her graying hair, "doesn't mean there's not a fire in the hearth."

"Who's the lucky man?"

"Donald Winston, he's in town visiting. He's in the Navy. His mom is a friend of mine. Oh, Shawn, he's tall, handsome, and he made my heart beat a little faster."

"How old is he?"

"I'll have you know he's one year older than me."

"So that would make him eighty-five?"

"Try forty-nine. Why don't you ask your mom or sister to watch her?"

"I can't. They're going to Raleigh to shop and Jeff's taking Jeremy to see a movie."

"I can watch her if you want," said Angela, speaking for the first time.

"Are you sure, I mean it's such short notice?"

"Oh, I'd love too. Just drop her off at my house and we'll have a blast."

"Thank you. I really appreciate it." Angela left.

"That's one sweet girl." Veronica said.

"Sounds like it. I hear she's an excellent teacher too."

"She is. She ought to be my mentor. Go look at her classroom sometime. I've never seen such creativity in a first year teacher."

"I thought she'd been teaching for several years."

"Nope, this is her first year."

"How old is she?"

"She's twenty-eight. She worked a while before she went to college. Any particular reason you're asking?" Shawn gave her a cutting look.

"Just asking. She's as cute as she can be."

"She's very attractive, but I . . . "

"I know, I'm sorry Shawn, sometimes I speak before I think."

"It's all right. Speaking of dates, where is Donald Duck taking you tonight?"

"Winston, his name is Winston."

"Sorry, where is Winston Duck taking you?"

"The Olive Garden."

"The Olive Garden? Well, he has style. You with a sailor, I'll be listening to the news tonight. If I hear of any drunk and disorderly, I'll know who it is."

"He's not like that at all."

"He's not the one I'm worried about." Veronica gave him a playful slap on the shoulder. Just then Mrs. Ann Jones, the principal of Mountain View came in.

"Oh Shawn, I need to talk to you today when you have a minute."

"What did I do wrong this time?"

"Nothing, I just need to talk for a minute."

"Sure, after school?"

"No, I can't after school. When's your prep time?"

"10:00. My kids go to music then."

"Good. Come see me then."

"I'll be there."

At precisely 10:00, Shawn was standing outside Mrs. Jones' office. She was on the phone. Through the doorway she waved Shawn in. Shawn came in. Mrs. Jones pointed to the chair.

"All right Mrs. Schultz, we'll see Tommy on Wednesday then. Bye." She hung up. "That was Mrs. Schultz. Tommy was in another fight yesterday. This time I gave him a three-day suspension." Tommy had a reputation. "Shawn, I called you in here to ask you something."

"Yes ma'am."

"Mr. Ford is retiring from the Middle School."

"I heard he was thinking about it."

"Yes, as you know he teaches history. I know you are certified to teach history up through 8th grade, and you had expressed to me once your desire to teach it. Before we hired someone new, I thought we'd give you a chance to take it if you wanted it. I don't need an answer right now, but tell me by Tuesday."

"Mrs. Jones, I appreciate the offer but I'm happy right here. I have no desire to move."

"Are you sure? You were so adamant two years ago."

"I know, but I like where I am. Thanks anyway."

"Shawn, would you come walk with me for a minute? I need to check on our playground equipment. We might be getting new equipment next year. If I can talk the board into it."

Mrs. Jones got up and walked out of the office with Shawn. Mrs. Jones had been the principal for two years. She had spent the previous twenty in the classroom. She, too, had trials in her personal life. Her husband of twenty-two years had left her for a younger woman just a year ago. She had gone through a messy divorce and her children were dividing their time between her and her ex-husband. Through it all she had remained an excellent principal. She was kind but somewhat distant from her teachers. She was a professional and she kept an air of professionalism about her.

She expected her teachers to be professionals. She reminded them at least once a week in case they forgot. The two walked outside to the playground equipment.

"This playground equipment's older than you are, Shawn."

"I believe it. Think we'll get some more?"

"That's totally up to the board. You know the governor cut our budget, so I don't know. Shawn, I know I'm not exactly the warm and fuzzy type, but despite what you hear, I do care about my teachers. You've been an excellent teacher but lately you've seemed distracted. I've even had a couple of parents say something . . . "

"What did they say?"

"Oh, nothing bad, just that you don't seem to be at your best. Is there anything I can do to help you?"

"I'm sorry Mrs. Jones, I will try to do better, I've had a hard time the last few months."

"I know. That's why I haven't said anything. Don't think I haven't noticed. I know when someone's hurting inside and I care, I really do. I just hope it doesn't hurt your classroom performance. You're too good a teacher for that to happen."

"Thank you, Mrs. Jones. I'd better go pick up my kids from Mrs. Daniels." Shawn walked back to his classroom. As he left, Mrs. Jones could not help but feel sorry for him. In a way she understood his pain, having gone through a divorce herself. She liked Shawn. She had recommended him for principal or at least assistant principal. However, the idea was shot down. There was only one person Ann knew in the entire school district who disliked Shawn, Colin Daniels.

Colin Daniels was the assistant superintendent of Wilson school district. He was a man who carried a lot of weight, literally and figuratively. He was 6' 3" and weighed 250 pounds. He did most of the hiring and firing. He had turned down Mrs. Jones suggestion that Shawn be put in administration. He and Shawn had a run in a couple years back that had soured their relationship. It was during the Christmas pageant three years ago. Some students were left unsupervised and one of them ended up falling off a chair and getting hurt. Mr. Daniels had a great fear of lawsuits and he blamed Shawn for the mishap. Shawn tried to explain that another teacher was supposed to be watching them. The situation never was completely resolved, and both men agreed to disagree. Fortunately, the boy was not hurt too badly and the parents did not sue, but Mr. Daniels still blamed Shawn. Poor Mrs. Jones was caught right in the middle of the situation. She tried to defend Shawn, but at the same time she understood Mr. Daniel's concern

Shawn could live with a disagreement. What really bothered him, though, was when Mr. Daniels corrected him in front of the other teachers. Mr. Daniel was the kind of man who said what he thought. It was one thing to correct him. It was another to humiliate him. Mr. Daniels had accused Shawn of not having the responsibility "God gave geese." Shawn was very hurt by this. Even Mrs. Jones had to go to Mr. Daniels and politely tells he that in the future he might consider correcting his teachers in private.

To Colin's credit, he did apologize to Shawn for the way he corrected him. He still made it clear though that he was not happy with what he felt was Shawn's unreliability. To make matters worse, a couple of months later some valuable science equipment was ruined because it was left outside over night. Shawn was partly to blame for that, though. He and another teacher were using it with their classes and both thought the other one had taken care of returning it to its rightful place. The bottom line was Shawn and Colin didn't trust each other. Shawn thought Colin was uncaring and insensitive. Colin thought Shawn was irresponsible and unreliable. However, you would never know this to see them together. After that one incident, Shawn and Colin were always polite and respectful to each other.

Colin's wife, Ellen, taught music at Mountain View. She was the exact opposite of her husband. He was tall, well rounded, rather ordinary looking, and rarely joked or kidded around. She on the other hand was short, slender, and quite attractive. She was also a very vivacious teacher. The students loved her and always looked forward to her music class. Even Shawn could not help but like her. He got along with her much better than he did her husband. When he and Colin spoke, it was short and to the point. Ellen was one of those people who never met a stranger. She made a person feel at ease.

The only person Shawn ever openly criticized Colin with was

Amanda. He justified this by the fact that she was his wife. He called it "confiding" in her. Amanda was usually a patient person, but even she had her limits. It came to a head one Saturday about two years ago as they were driving to Wal-Mart. Shawn spent the entire drive blasting Colin Daniels. He concluded his remarks with "I don't know who put him in charge, but they ought to have their heads examined." Amanda had enough. She had listened and tried to understand, but she had all she could take. She gave him that look that meant she had something important to say and he had better listen.

"Shawn, I do not want to hear one more word about Colin Daniels. Is that clear?"

"Yes, dear."

"If you can't say something nice about the man don't say anything at all."

"Then we won't be talking about him again."

Amanda rarely got agitated, but this was one time she was.

"Shawn, has it occurred to you that maybe you've misjudged Mr. Daniels. He seems to get along with everyone else but you. Maybe if you were nicer to him, he might treat you differently. Would you like someone who had the attitude toward you that you have toward him?" Shawn couldn't help but laugh to himself. Did she have to be right all the time? Couldn't she be wrong and he be right just once?

"Maybe you're right. Maybe I have been too hard on Mr. Daniels."

As it turned out, she was right. Months later when Amanda was in the hospital, Shawn saw a side of Colin Daniels he had never seen before. The Daniel's sent flowers to Amanda while she was in the hospital and even visited her and Shawn. They came to the funeral and offered their condolences. Mrs. Daniels even made dinner for Shawn and Heather, and Colin brought it over. Shawn had to admit he had been wrong about Colin. Like so many other areas of his life, he was a better man for having been married to Amanda. As a result he and Colin developed respect and a good working relationship with each other. He felt so guilty about it that he finally went and apologized to the Daniels and made up his mind that in the future to be very careful about judging other people and their motives.

That afternoon, Shawn stopped by Angela's classroom. He had spoken to her briefly a few times but he had never been in her classroom. He was stunned. It looked like something out of a teacher's magazine. It had a nautical theme. Her ceiling had strips of blue tissue paper that looked like the ocean. She had cut outs of fish hanging from the ceiling. Her reading center had stuffed animal seats and all around the room were attractive posters encouraging reading.

"Wow. Your room looks very nice."

"Thanks." Angela looked tired and frustrated.

"Are you all right?"

"Yeah, I have two students that are driving me crazy. I've done everything to get them to behave and do their work, but they won't."

"I'm sorry. Listen, if you need a break from kids, I think I can talk my neighbor into watching Heather."

"No, I'll, I'll watch her, I'm actually looking forward to it."

"I really appreciate it. I need your address to drop her off."

"Oh, of course." Angela gave him directions to her house.

"I'm sorry about your students. Have you talked to their parents?"

"I've tried to talk to them, but they are very hard to contact."

"That may be the problem."

"I know."

"I'll have Heather at your house at 5:00. Is that okay?"

"Sure. See you at five."

CHAPTER NINE

S hawn arrived home at 3:30. On his way in he checked his mail. He had two bills, a letter from his in-laws and a letter from Global Travels. That was the one he had been waiting for. He opened it up. It was his itinerary. Last Christmas, Shawn's friend from college, Eric Meyers, talked him into going with him to Europe this summer. Shawn loved to travel. He had been to Europe before with his Uncle Henry. That was the summer before his junior year of high school. He went to England, France, Germany, Switzerland, Holland, and Austria. They had spent two weeks and Shawn absolutely loved it. As soon as Eric mentioned it, Shawn knew he wanted to go. It would be a sixteen-day trip. It was a tour that visited Italy, and Greece. Shawn talked to his mother and Amanda's parents about watching Heather. They all agreed. The Thomsons would watch Heather for a week, and Becky would watch her the rest of the time. They wanted Shawn to go, especially Becky. She knew it would be a trip he would enjoy, and after what he had been through the last year, he needed a vacation.

Shawn sat down and looked through his itinerary. He was getting excited just looking at it. He would fly from Raleigh to New York to Rome. They would spend three days in Rome, a day in Florence, two days in Venice, three days in Athens and five days on a ship in the Greek Isles. He would leave June 11 and be back June 27.

"Daddy, will you push me on the swing?"

"Sure, let's go." They went outside and Shawn spent the next half hour playing with Heather.

Shawn arrived precisely at 5:00 at Angela's house. She only lived three streets over from Shawn. He noticed Angela's silver Honda Civic in the driveway. He knocked on the door. Angela opened the door. Her blond shoulder length hair was in a pony tail and her brown eyes twinkled as she smiled.

"Hello!" Angela said in a friendly voice.

"Hi." Said Heather waving.

"She's already eaten. I brought her favorite video, 'Winnie the Pooh', and I brought some books you can read to her if you want."

"Oh thanks, we're going to have fun." Shawn gave a few last minute instructions and then returned to his car.

Stan Price was one of the best friends Shawn had. They had been buddies since high school and Stan had been a groomsman in Shawn's wedding. He was one of those people who would do anything for you and never ask for anything in return. However, in the past nine months Stan had proven just what a true friend he really was. As Amanda lay dying in the hospital, Stan and Lori had visited them or called them every single day. Stan was right beside Shawn as they lowered Amanda's coffin into the ground. He called Shawn almost every day after Amanda died just to see how his friend was doing. They had invited him over for dinner. They even cleaned his house for him just to be a help. They had sent notes to him telling him that they were praying for him. Now they were concerned about him. Shawn had always been fun to be around. He was always joking and having a good time. Some of the best times they had were with Shawn and Amanda.

Since Amanda had died however, the light had gone out in Shawn's eyes. He didn't joke as much anymore. He wasn't the same man Stan had known and he didn't know what he could to help him. God knows he had tried. Tonight they were having him over for dinner once again to try to be an encouragement to him. Stan decided they would have the best possible meal. He had gone and bought steak. They had baked potatoes, green beans, and coleslaw. Julie, Lori's sister, who was also coming was bringing some delicious homemade rolls and caesar salad. It was just going to be the four of them.

Julie was a secretary at a computer store. She had been engaged to Derek Matthews, the piano player at Shawn's church. Derek Matthews was the heartthrob of single society in Wilson. He was tall, handsome, and had an incredibly beautiful Bing Crosby like voice. He was an extremely gifted musician who had published several pieces of music. He performed with the local orchestra. Women would come from far and near to hear him sing. Julie was hopelessly in love with him. She chased poor Derek until he just got tired of running. They were engaged. They had the whole wedding planned out. The bridesmaid dresses had already been made, airline tickets purchased for family, presents purchased, music selected. Derek had even written a love song that he would sing. Two weeks before the wedding, however, he abruptly called it off. He went over to her house and with tears in his eyes said he could not marry her. He loved her but he did not feel they were right for each other and marrying her would be a mistake. He hugged her goodbye and that was the last time she saw him. Two days later he moved to Pennsylvania to teach music in a small Christian college. Julie was devastated. She was so broken up over losing Derek that her family began to worry about her emotional and physical well being. She wouldn't eat, she would lie on her bed and cry, she would rarely leave the house, and she nearly had a nervous breakdown. Her job suffered. She missed three days of work after the break up. Julie had always been an excellent secretary but she began to forget things and at times be short with people. Shawn had never been close friends with Julie like he had Lori and Stan, but he felt sorry for her. Six months later, Derek married one of his music students and the last anyone had heard, they were expecting their first child. Lori had taken it upon herself to try to help her brokenhearted sister. Lori was pregnant at the time and so she would take Julie with her to pick out clothes, decorate the nursery, and just spend time talking. This helped both women, but Julie would still break out into tears talking about her beloved Derek. Stan had privately told Shawn that he wasn't sure Julie would ever get over him.

Lori had a reason for inviting these two to dinner together. She wasn't trying to set them up. Both Shawn and Julie would not have liked that, but Lori was hoping for maybe a friendship. They both had suffered a loss, and she and Stan had taken both of them under their wings.

There was only one problem with this. They didn't like each other. They both felt sorry for each other, but beyond that they did not have much in common. Julie had become bitter toward any man she considered eligible, even Shawn. Shawn didn't care much for Julie for that reason. She was often condescending, and on occasion she would belittle him in front of others. "It's a shame," thought Shawn. She had been a sweet girl once, but losing her beloved Derek was a loss she still had not recovered from. It had been a year since the breakup, and Shawn knew the anger and bitterness was really her response to the grief she felt.

Stan and Shawn stood outside watching the steaks grill while Lori and Julie were busy in the kitchen. "Have you played any golf lately?" asked Stan, knowing the answer.

"No, I've been really busy with end of the year things, plus I've been trying to spend a little more time with Heather."

"We should play before you leave. I've been working on my swing. I was practicing chipping and putting in the living room until Lori caught me. It was not a pretty sight. I knocked over her favorite vase. She very lovingly and tenderly told me that either the clubs go or I go."

"What did you say?"

"I told her I was sorry to see our marriage end like this." Shawn chuckled. "No, I told her I would only practice outside in the yard." Stan was a great friend but a lousy golfer. He had nearly been thrown off a golf course when he almost hit a congressman in the head. The only thing he could say was, "Sorry about that, but what can I say? I'm a Republican."

The table was set and it was beautiful. Lori had worked hard to make the table look nice. Lori and Amanda had also become good friends, and Amanda had given Lori some tips on how to decorate the table. She would have been proud.

The four of them sat down and held hands as Stan prayed. He blessed the food and thanked God for a good friend like Shawn.

"So, are you excited about your trip?" asked Lori. She was always so positive and cheerful and it was sincere. Julie had been so negative lately that it was hard to believe these two were related.

"Yes, I am. I have always wanted to do a trip to Italy and Greece."

"Good, I think this trip will be good for you."

"Who's watching Heather?" asked Julie.

"My mom and Mr. and Mrs. Thomson."

"With your love of history, I know you will enjoy it." Said Stan. "Be sure to send us a post card." Said Lori.

After they finished supper and cleaned away the dishes, Stan got out the Rook cards. They played to 500 points. It was Stan and Shawn against Lori and Julie. The girls whipped them badly. Shawn couldn't believe how badly he and Stan had played. Julie was ecstatic. The men had been beaten and she was not above rubbing it in. She felt a tiny bit of satisfaction at beating them. She was getting even with men and it felt good.

Shawn left Lori and Stan's and drove to Angela's house to pick up Heather. When he knocked on the door, Angela opened it.

"Come on in, we're not quite finished." She went back into her kitchen.

"Finished with what?"

"We're making cookies, Daddy!" said an excited Heather. "We're making you some."

"Well, that's very nice of you, thank you. Did you have fun with Miss Angela?" Heather nodded and went back to flattening the cookie dough.

"These will be done in ten minutes, do you mind waiting that long?" said Angela.

"Not at all."

"Why don't you just have a seat in the living room?"

"Okay." Shawn went into Angela's living room and looked around. Her house was decorated very nicely.

"You have a nice house."

"Thank you." Said Angela from the kitchen.

"Did you do all the decorating?"

"Most of it. My mom helped and so did my sister."

"You did an excellent job."

"Thank you." Shawn noticed a well-worn Bible on the coffee

table and a woman's devotional opened to today's date. The devotion for that day was entitled "Deliver us from evil." Shawn noticed the photos on her mantle above her fireplace. One was a picture of Angela in a military uniform. The other was an old picture of a young blond haired Marine holding a machine gun and smiling. Behind him were piles of sandbags, and a jungle setting. Angela came in.

"We're almost done. Just five more minutes. Would you like a glass of tea?"

"That would be nice, Thank you." She left and returned with the tea.

"Were you in the military?"

"I was in the Air Force for four years before I went to college. It took me five years to finish and then I got hired at Mountain View."

"Where did you go to school?"

"University of North Carolina at Chapel Hill."

"Really? That's where I went to school."

"Did you major in Elementary Education?" asked Angela.

"I did."

"Wow, then I'll bet we had many of the same teachers."

"I'm sure we did." Said Shawn. "Tell me, who's this man in the photo here?" Shawn pointed to the picture of the young Marine holding his machine gun.

"That's my dad. He was in the Marine Corps."

"Was this in Vietnam?"

"Yeah, I think he was at Khe Sahn."

"My dad was in Vietnam also."

"Really, where?"

"He was a Navy pilot."

"My dad doesn't talk much about Vietnam. Only rarely will he say anything. What about your dad? Does he talk about it much?" asked Angela.

"My dad died when I was ten. He did tell me some stories about his experiences though." Just then the oven beeped.

"Let me get your cookies so you guys can go home." Angela left. She came back a few minutes later with a dozen cookies in a zip lock bag. Heather was right behind her.

"You ready to go, sweetheart?" Shawn asked.

"No."

Angela and Shawn laughed.

"Well, we've got to go anyway so Miss Angela can get some sleep. Tell Miss Angela thank you." Heather gave Angela a hug and said "Thank you."

"You're welcome. Come see me again, okay."

"Okay."

"Thank you again, Angela. I really appreciate it." Shawn shook her hand. He tried to hand her a ten-dollar bill.

"Oh, absolutely not. I should pay you. I had a blast." Shawn decided not to push it.

"Well, thanks again." Heather and Shawn walked out the door and toward the car. Angela turned on her porch light and watched as they walked to the car. When they got to the car, Heather tugged on Shawn's pants.

"Daddy?"

"What sweetheart?" Shawn leaned down to hear what Heather had to say.

"I like Miss Angela."

"I know you do. I do too, Sweetie."

"Daddy, can she come over to our house?" Shawn thought a minute. He looked back. Angela was still at the door.

"Why don't you go ask her if she'd like to come over for dinner on Saturday?" Heather walked back to Angela.

"Miss Angela, can you come over to my house on," she stopped, and looked at her father.

"What day was it Daddy?"

"Saturday"

"Can you come over to our house to eat on Saturday?"

"I'd love too, but I have plans on Saturday. I'd love to come some other time, though."

"Daddy," Heather said very loudly, though Shawn was only ten feet away and heard everything she said, "Miss Angela said she can't come on Saturday but she can come some other day." Shawn and Angela smiled. You'd think they were ten miles away.

"Ask her if she can come Friday night."

"Can you come Friday night?"

"I'd love to come Friday night. Thank you."

"Daddy," Heather said again very loudly, "She says she can come on Friday night." Shawn and Angela both couldn't help but laugh at how cute she was.

"Tell her Friday night will be fine."

"My daddy says Friday night will be fine."

"Okay, I'll see you on Friday." Heather gave Angela a big hug.

CHAPTER TEN

S aturday Shawn spent all day with Heather. It was just the two of them and they both enjoyed it. Shawn had always been a good father, but with Amanda gone, he tried to spend more time with Heather. They spent the morning watching cartoons. Heather enjoyed cartoons, and her favorite show was "Sesame Street." Shawn could sing right along with Ernie and Bert because he heard them almost every afternoon. After a peanut butter and jelly sandwich for lunch, they went to the mall for ice cream

Spending time with Heather brought back memories for Shawn. Memories of him and Amanda going to the mall with Heather, going to the park, and Shawn began to feel sad again. He missed her. Yes, he missed the intense physical attraction he had for Amanda, but he also missed his best friend. He missed being able to share his inner most thoughts and desires with someone who would not laugh or belittle him for it. For eighteen years she had been such a vital part of his life. Now she was gone and she wasn't coming back. He thought of Heather. She would only have a few childhood memories of her mother. What was it going to be like when she became older and needed a mother to talk to? A lump formed in his throat and his eyes watered.

"Daddy, you're not listening!" Heather apparently was trying to tell him something.

"I'm sorry, Honey, what do you need?"

"I said, can I please go ride the helicopter?" There was a little helicopter ride that Heather enjoyed. Shawn checked his pocket for change. He had two quarters.

"Sure, Honey, you can ride it." Shawn was thankful for the diversion. If he had sat there any longer thinking about Amanda, he would have started crying in front of his daughter.

Sunday morning Shawn rose early to get ready for church. He poured some cereal for Heather and himself. They both drank a glass of orange juice and Heather ate as Shawn read the newspaper. The usual articles: the President's new economic plan, Red Sox in the lead. However, one article particularly interested him. It was about the Libyans threatening attacks on the United States unless certain terrorists were freed. He remembered in high school when President Reagan bombed Libya and shut them up for fifteen years. Now suddenly they were making a fuss again. It was ridiculous. The new President was a no nonsense kind of President and he had already stated repeatedly that he would not bargain with terrorists.

Shawn told Heather to go play in her room for a few minutes while he got ready. He wore his new navy blue suit, with a white shirt and a pretty yellow tie his mother had gotten him for Christmas. Shawn was a sharp dresser. He had been known as the sloppiest dresser in high school. His mom was forever getting after him because he would go to school looking like he had just fallen out of bed. His shirt would be wrinkled, his hair a mess, holes in his pants, and his shirttail hanging out. That all literally changed over night. It was the day after he met Amanda. His mother never forgot that morning when Shawn came to breakfast with his shoes polished, his hair combed, and his clothes ironed. Amanda had done in one day what she could not do in sixteen years.

After he finished dressing, he took his Bible from the night stand and put it by the door and then helped Heather finish getting ready. For her he chose a cute little flowered dress. He also was becoming quite good at helping her put barrettes in her hair. When they finished, Shawn stared at her for a second. She was a pretty little girl and she reminded him of Amanda.

The Reverend Dr. James Hamilton was pastor of the North Hill Baptist Church. With six hundred members, it was the largest church in Wilson, North Carolina. He had been the pastor for eighteen years and was the first black pastor in the church's one hundred and twenty-year history. It was very unusual to see a black pastor of a predominantly white church, but then Pastor Hamilton was not your usual pastor. His congregation dearly loved him, and they knew he loved them. He was affectionately known as Pastor Jim. He was a man of God who could preach God's love and God's holiness with the same passion. He was a gifted speaker and an outstanding Bible teacher. He was one of the most intelligent men Shawn had ever met. He was occasionally asked by civil rights groups to speak at their rallies, but he never did. He felt politics and the church should remain separate.

The community respected him because he took a strong stand against sin, and yet he always cared about the needs of others. He often stated from the pulpit that the mark of a Christian is love. "By this shall all men know ye are my disciples if ye have love one for another." He had earned the respect of the community and his congregation.

Pastor Jim had a difficult time at the beginning of his ministry at North Hill. When the church was looking for a pastor, he had been highly recommended by several other pastors. After preaching at the church a few times and talking to the pulpit committee, the congregation decided they wanted him as pastor. There were, however, a few members who were opposed to him. Though they never came right out and said, "We don't want him because he's black," everyone knew that was the reason. One man in particular who had done everything he could to keep Pastor Hamilton away was the chairman of the deacon board, Henry Evans.

Ironically, Uncle Henry was known as a kind hearted man who would do anything for someone in need. He always bought Christmas presents for kids and every Christmas he would find a needy family and buy their children presents. Oddly enough, on several occasions he did this for black families he knew. He didn't hate blacks. He didn't mind going to church with a few black families. He had even hired a black man in his accounting firm. On more than one occasion he had helped blacks get jobs. What he absolutely could not handle, was a black man in charge of him or his church. He could not handle taking orders as a deacon from a black pastor. Of course he never said publicly that race was why he was so adamantly against Dr.Hamilton. The reason he gave for his opposition was Dr. Hamilton's age.

"Thirty-five is just too young to be a senior pastor of a church this size." Henry said. "We need a man of experience." He had gone around privately and encouraged people not to vote for him. The problem for Henry was that Dr. Hamilton was a man wise beyond his years. He had outstanding qualifications and when he preached, people were blessed, encouraged, and challenged to live godly lives. He had a way of speaking from the heart to the heart. Uncle Henry realized that despite all his efforts the people would probably vote him in. On the night of the vote, Henry got up before the church and told the congregation that the church would be ruined "if we allow this man in. He doesn't have the character or the backbone to pastor this church and I can assure you I will never vote for him." After Uncle Henry finished speaking, the church voted Dr. Hamilton in with 90% of the vote. The highest percentage any pastor had ever gotten.

The night Dr. Hamilton was elected the pastor, Uncle Henry went to Shawn's house and talked to his mother. He was irate. Shawn never forgot what his uncle said that night.

"Why do these niggers think they can run everything? Don't they know where their place is? Our church will never be the same. Aren't there enough nigger churches he could go to, without wrecking ours?" It was at that point that Becky stood up and asked Uncle Henry to leave. She was hurt and crying, but she stood firm.

"Henry, you are entitled to your opinion, but I must tell you that I disagree with you. You're right about one thing. Our church will never be the same, but if our church judges someone because he's black, then I don't want it to stay the same."

"You'll regret it, I promise you that, you'll regret it, and I'll be darned if I ever stay in a church that has a nigger pastor."

"Henry, I should tell you that we intend to stay there, and I'll thank you not to talk about him in our house. He's my pastor now."

Henry left the church that night and only returned one time. That was for Amanda's funeral. He was a bitter man. He had attended North Hill his whole life and now it was being lead by a black man. It only made matters worse when the church soon realized that Henry couldn't have been more wrong about Pastor Jim. He had both the character and experience and genuine love for his congregation. The church doubled in size, started a Bible study program on different college campuses, a prison ministry, nursing home ministry, singles ministry, vacation Bible school, and a bus ministry. Through it all though, Pastor Jim was still the same kind, humble, servant of God he had always been, and he never said one unkind word about Henry Evans.

Henry's attitude toward Pastor Jim broke Becky's heart. She loved her brother dearly; he had been such a comfort to her and especially to her children, particularly Shawn, when her husband died, but Becky knew he was wrong. God was "no respecter of persons" and Christ died for the whole world. To be prejudiced against someone because of the color of his skin went against everything Christ ever taught. She was brokenhearted about what her brother had done. He was not the same man. He had once been a kind, loving man, though opinionated, but now he was a much colder and harder man. Becky believed he knew he was wrong but refused to admit it. It hurt his relationship with Bonnie and Robin also. They didn't want to leave the church, but they dutifully followed Henry. Becky and the kids still visited with Henry and his family, but it put a definite strain on their relationship when Becky and the kids stayed in the church. They all knew there was one topic of conversation that was off limits with Uncle Henry, and that was Pastor Jim or anything to do with North Hill Baptist Church.

It also hurt his relationship with Shawn. Shawn still loved his uncle, but he too was ashamed of what he had done. At first, Shawn wondered if Pastor Jim might be a little apprehensive of the rest of the family, but he wasn't. As the years went by Pastor Jim proved over and over to be a caring and loving pastor. He and Shawn had a great relationship and even played golf together on occasion.

In fact, it had been two years ago, while they were playing golf one day that Pastor Jim asked Shawn about running for deacon. His name had been submitted and Shawn had declined. He did not feel old enough or wise enough to be a deacon, but Pastor Jim encouraged him to run. After praying and talking to Amanda about it,

Shawn decided to submit his name as deacon.

Shawn didn't get elected. He was a little disappointed but Amanda reminded him that deacons were servants.

"The church may not elect you a deacon, but they can't keep you from being a servant. Remember, you're doing this for the Lord, and as long as you're serving him, titles don't mean much."

The night of the church election Pastor Jim could read disappointment on Shawn's face when he announced who the new deacons were. After church that night he called him.

"Shawn, I just wanted to call and tell you how much I appreciate your willingness to serve. It means a lot to me as a pastor to know there are members like you who will serve when needed."

"Thanks, Pastor Jim."

"By the way Shawn, don't take it personally that you weren't elected. You are well respected in this church. It was a case of more good men than there were positions."

"I know."

"By the way, the real reason I called is because I'd like you to consider taking one of the adult Sunday school classes. Mr. Fryer told me tonight that he would have to quit teaching at the end of the month. The doctor has told him he needs to slow down some, so he's decided to cut back some of his responsibilities."

"I'd like that."

"Let me know this next week, but I think you'll do a fine job." Pastor Jim always had a way of making Shawn feel special. Shawn took the class. It was probably a good thing he didn't get elected anyway. It was only two months later that Amanda began to get really sick and Shawn would not have been able to fulfill his responsibility as a deacon.

In addition to preaching Amanda's funeral, Pastor Jim had gone to the hospital every week and prayed with Shawn and Amanda as she lay dying. He had visited Shawn several times after her death. He and Mrs. Hamilton had taken him out to dinner, invited him over for dinner and had sent him cards of encouragement. Next to his mother, Pastor Jim had been a greater encouragement to Shawn than anyone else had.

CHAPTER ELEVEN

S hawn had gone to this church since he was ten. His mother had wisely seen the importance of attending church and Shawn was in church the first Sunday of his life. Shawn had missed Sunday school only once. It was the day Amanda died.

The Sunday school class Shawn taught was very special to him. He had to miss several Sundays teaching when Amanda was sick but the class was faithful. As Amanda got weaker and weaker, Shawn was afraid to leave for long periods of time. The two Sundays before she died, the class met at his home so he could teach it and Amanda could be there.

Shawn's class focused on the Life of Christ. Shawn threw his heart and soul into the Sunday school lesson and would stay up late on Friday nights to prepare the lesson. It helped take his mind off her. Except for the class for young parents, Shawn's class had the most people, nearly thirty in all.

His lesson that morning was from Matthew 26. Jesus was in the Garden and the disciples fell asleep instead of praying. Jesus rebuked them. "What, could you not watch with me one hour. Watch and pray that ye enter not into temptation. The spirit is willing, but the flesh is weak." Shawn reminded his class of the importance of prayer. He must have said a dozen times during the lesson, "Don't forget to pray." The irony of it was that Shawn had forgotten to open the class in prayer as he usually did. He couldn't figure out what his class thought was so funny until it was over and they told him.

The sermon that morning was on Psalm 23. Pastor Jim focused on verse four. "Yea, though I walk through the valley of the shadow of death, I will fear no evil, for thou art with me." The choir sang "A Mighty Fortress Is Our God."

Every Sunday Shawn and Heather ate lunch at Becky's house along with Sara, Jeff, and Ashley. Today, they were having roast, potatoes, corn, salad, and apple pie for dessert. Shawn and Jeff helped prepare the table while Sara and Becky finished preparing lunch. Heather and Ashley were off playing with some toys that Becky kept in the house. Ashley was a year younger than Heather and the two were very close. After everything was set, they all sat down and Jeff blessed the food.

When lunch was finished, Heather slipped into some pajamas that they kept at Becky's house and she lay down for a nap in Shawn's old room. She slept on the bed that Shawn had when they moved into the house in 1980.

Shawn excused himself and said he would be back in an hour. Nobody asked where he was going because they all knew.

Shawn stopped at a grocery store and picked up a single red rose and headed for Woodlawn Cemetery and parked the car and walked over to the gray marble tombstone that read,

Amanda Lynn Miller
March 20, 1970 - August 1, 2003
Beloved wife and mother

For three weeks before she died, Shawn had brought her red roses to the hospital every Sunday. He would still occasionally bring them to her grave. The cemetery was well-kept which was one reason Shawn had chosen it. Amanda's grave was under a weeping willow tree and near a pond with ducks in it. The flowers around the cemetery were in full bloom and it was actually a beautiful place, if you could get past the fact you were in a graveyard.

When Shawn was a little boy, he wondered if God let the people in heaven watch their loved ones on earth and listen to their conversations. Though he seriously doubted she was listening, he sometimes found himself talking to her. He always made sure no one was around lest they think he was crazy.

"Amanda, I don't know if you are listening, but if you are I just want you to know I still love you. Heather is growing like a weed. She is such a pretty little girl, Amanda. She looks just like you. The other day she prayed and said, " . . . dear Jesus, please tell my mommy 'hi' if you see her and tell her I 'miss her.' That goes for me too. I feel so lonely without you. There are so many times I wish I could just sit down and talk to you about Heather. I feel so inadequate in trying to raise her. I know if you were here, everything would be all right, but since you're gone, I have to get along the best I can." Shawn's eyes swelled up with tears but no one was around so he figured it was all right to cry. He thought of the day she had died. He had spent the night in the hospital because he was afraid if he went home, she might die while he was gone. She lost all her hair and was swollen, but he loved her just as much as the day they married.

Shawn laid the rose on her grave and just stood there a moment. "By the way, I'm taking a trip to Europe in a couple of months. Don't worry about Heather, she's staying with your parents and my mom while I'm gone. It's only for two weeks. I hope you don't think I'm a horrible father leaving her like that, but it won't be for long." Shawn's eyes swelled up with tears but no one was around so he figured it was all right to cry. "I wish you were going with me. I know we'd have a blast together, like when we went to Jamaica that one time."

After church that night, Pastor Jim asked Shawn if he could talk to him for a few minutes. Pastor Jim spoke to a few people and then made his way to his office with Shawn. Shawn liked the way Pastor Jim had decorated his office. One wall was filled with books. Another wall had his four diplomas, along with several photos of Pastor Jim's family. One wall had a window overlooking the church parking lot and right behind his desk was a large painting entitled "The Good Shepherd." He motioned for Shawn to have a seat across from his desk.

"Shawn, I wanted to talk to you for a minute if I could."

"Yes sir."

"I've been a little concerned about you. How have you been lately?" There was a sincerity in his voice. He genuinely cared about how Shawn was doing.

"My mother's been talking to you again hasn't she?" Pastor Jim smiled.

"I never reveal my sources. Seriously, Shawn, I only ask because I care. I only want to help, but if you don't want to talk I certainly understand."

"I know you care." Shawn paused, his voice got quieter. "I miss her." He started to cry. He usually could control his emotions but for some reason now the tears just flowed. He said nothing for a minute.

"I'm sorry, Pastor Jim."

"Shawn, there's nothing unmanly about weeping for the loss of someone we held dear." His voice was calm and reassuring.

"Pastor Jim, if I ask you a question, will you not think badly of me?"

"Of course not. I'll help you anyway I can."

"Why did God take my wife? Why her? Why now? Why when I need her so much?" Pastor Jim could see right through him. This was not a man angry or bitter at God, but rather a young man in love who had suffered a great loss and was now looking for answers or at least encouragement. He came to the right place.

"Shawn, you are not the first person who's been in my office and asked that same question. I must be honest with you. I don't know why God took your wife home to be with him. From a human point, I wish I did. I wish I could tell you exactly why this happened. I can't. God, in his wisdom has chosen not to reveal everything to us."

"I know. It's just there are mornings I wake up and I still expect her there and when I have that awful realization that she's not, I just wonder, why? Did I do something wrong? Is God punishing me for not being a good enough husband?"

"Shawn, I don't know a man anywhere that was more loving to his wife than you." There was another pause, and Pastor Jim's voice took on a fatherly tone.

"I can't answer your question about why, but may I share something with you that may help you? A personal experience that I had?"

"Yes, sir." Pastor Jim looked at his ceiling. For a moment he was lost in thought. His mind far away, remembering an event long past.

"Shawn, you know my wife and I have no children of our own."

"Yes sir."

"My wife and I were married thirty-years ago next month, right after I graduated from Chicago Theological Seminary. Anyway, we hoped to have children. Both of us wanted children very much. For ten years we tried to have a child. We prayed many nights for God to give us a child. We visited doctors, had friends pray and still no children. We had all but given up hope. We resigned ourselves to the fact that God's answer was 'No.' It was a very painful experience and many nights I would hold my wife as she would weep. Many nights I wept, but God's answer seemed to be 'No.' Then one day, ten years after we had been married, I was in my study working on my doctorate. My wife came home from the doctor and her face was beaming. It was the happiest I had ever seen her. There were tears of joy in her eyes as she told me that she had just found out she was pregnant." Shawn listened in amazement. He had never heard this before. Pastor Jim went on. "We called all our friends, family, church members and told them the good news. God had answered our prayers. The doctor had warned her that her pregnancy would not be easy. He also warned us that this would probably be the only child she would ever have. She was a high risk but we believed this child was an answer from God. People began to call my wife a modern day Hannah.

Our son, James Hamilton Jr. was born in April of 1985. I was so excited. I could hardly see straight. That afternoon, the doctor called me into his office and told me some shattering news. He said that my son had been born with a serious heart defect and that he might not live. I couldn't believe it. I thought surely there must be a mistake. There was no mistake. I had to tell my wife this devastating news." Now Pastor Jim's eyes watered. "Once again I prayed and asked the Lord to please spare the life of my child. Once again, my friends and family prayed with me. I stayed awake all night begging God to please let my boy live. The next day, my son went to heaven." Tears streamed down Pastor Jim's face but he continued. "Shawn, I've lost a father, mother, brother, sister, and many friends, but my soul has never been so anguished as the day we buried my son, knowing we would never have another. That night, I got down on my knees and I wept as I have never wept before. I asked the Lord the very question, you just asked me, 'Why.' Why my son after all the years and the prayers, why." Shawn was starting to get choked up again just listening to him. Pastor Jim continued, "Then Shawn, a miracle happened. In that still small voice which God uses to speak to the heart of one of his children, the Lord said to me, 'Jim, I know the sorrow you feel. Remember, My only Son died too. I gave Him to die because I loved you.' For a very brief moment, I got a tiny glimpse of the greatness of God's love, because I realized how much God must love us, if he were willing to make that kind of sacrifice. Shawn, it changed my life and the blessings that I have received, Shawn, only heaven will tell. That happened twenty-years ago, and God has used that incident to allow me to lead twenty precious souls to him. Twenty people were added to the kingdom of God, two of whom are already with the Lord because of that. People who were faced with a great crisis and I shared that story with them."

"That's amazing." Said a stunned Shawn.

"I take no pride in that. It was all of God, and as you know I got a double blessing. The next year my wife and I were in Brazil. While we were there, we visited an orphanage and we were able to adopt the twins who were less than a week old."

"Nicki and Michael." They were Pastor Jim's adopted children, juniors in high school.

"That's right. That was totally unplanned. God brought them to us."

"I have heard your testimony about that, it was right after you became pastor here."

"You see, Shawn, God took my son but he gave me a son and a daughter in return, and he used this tragedy to bring people to him."

"Pastor Jim, you are amazing."

"No, God is amazing. I'm humbled every time I think about how he blesses me so much." Pastor Jim grabbed a tissue and wiped his eyes. "Shawn, I said all of that to say this, God may use this tragedy to bring great blessing in your life. The Bible is filled with people who endured great hardships and received great blessing because they allowed God to use them. Daniel in the Lion's Den, Joseph sold into slavery, Paul and Silas in prison. I can only encourage you to not become bitter. Let God use you, and don't miss out on the blessings He wants to give you." Shawn smiled.

"Thank you Pastor Jim. I needed that."

"By the way, I don't mean to suggest that it's in any way wrong to grieve. Even the Lord himself grieved at the loss of his friend Lazarus. I still miss my son. I only knew him two days and I still love and miss him. As you can see, I still get a little emotional sometimes. My wife to this day cries whenever we talk about little James."

"I can only imagine."

"It's particularly hard on her whenever she's around children that would be the same age as our son would have been."

"Really."

"Yes, you know how we honor the high school graduates every year during a church service?"

"Yes sir."

"Last year, my wife cried during the entire service. I had a lump in my throat the whole time, too. We couldn't help but think that our son if he had lived would have been sitting on the front row with the rest of the graduates. He's buried in Memphis, Tennessee, my hometown. Every year when we visit my family, we go and visit his grave."

"Pastor Jim, I never knew this about you."

"We don't advertise it, but we tell people when they ask and occasionally I tell people when I'm counseling them as a way to relate to their situation. Let me show you something." Pastor Jim pulled out his wallet and took out a picture. It was a twenty-year-old picture of a much younger Pastor Jim smiling and holding a little newly born baby in his arms. "I've had this in my wallet for twenty years. It was taken the day little Jimmy was born. I never go anywhere without it. I keep it to remind me of him. To remind me that I have a child in heaven and one day I'll see him again."

"I guess you really haven't lost a child at all. He's just somewhere else."

Pastor Jim smiled. "That's a good way to look at it. There are two ways I could have accepted this. I could have been bitter at God for taking my child, or I could have thanked him for bringing a precious soul into my life, even if it was only for two days."

"I guess that puts everything in perspective."

"Can I share a secret with you? Only my wife knows this."

"Sure."

"Sometimes, when we're in Tennessee, I'll go to his grave alone, and I'll talk to my son like he's standing right in front of me."

"That sounds familiar" thought Shawn.

"What do you say to him?"

"I just tell him how much I still love him, and miss him, and I can't wait to meet him again."

Shawn rose to leave.

"I really appreciate you talking to me. I needed this. You've helped me put things in perspective."

"Anytime I can be an encouragement, let me know."

"You have been, more than you'll ever know." Shawn stood to leave. He gave Pastor Jim a hug.

"By the way, your mother also tells me you're leaving for Europe in a couple of months."

"Yes sir."

"Will you be gone over any Sundays?"

"Yes sir."

"I'd like to give you a couple of sermons on cassette to listen to. Will you have a tape recorder?"

"Yes sir, I have one I travel with."

"Good, they'll be my gift to you." Pastor Jim had started a tape ministry with his sermons. Many people in his congregation would buy his sermons on cassette and listen to them in their cars or at home. His sermons were so popular that people who weren't even members began ordering tapes. The church even had a web site that allowed people to order them. The church had to hire a part time secretary just to handle the sermon tapes. Even after paying the secretary, the church made nearly a thousand dollars a year. Pastor Jim was entitled to a percentage of the money. He refused to take a cent. The entire amount went to the church benevolence fund. This was money used to help needy church members as well as people in the community. Pastor Jim often said he would not make a profit off of someone's desire to hear the gospel.

"Thank you, Pastor Jim." As Shawn was leaving, he smiled and turned to Pastor Jim. "So it was my mom who talked to you."

"Oops. Well, you didn't hear it from me."

CHAPTER TWELVE

For the first time in nine months, Shawn had a full eight hours of uninterrupted sleep. When he woke up, he felt like a new man. Normally Shawn had to leave by 7:15 in order to get to school by 7:30. Today he left at 7:00. He arrived at Mountain View at 7:15 and after dropping Heather off at the cafeteria, he was in his room by 7:20. Shawn had much to do in the next couple of weeks. There were only four weeks of school left and he had several major events going on until then. The one most pressing right now was the end of the year choir and band concert. The concert was next Thursday night.

At 10:00 Shawn dropped his students off with Mrs. Daniels and made his way to the teachers lounge. He had two parents to call. Two of his students had been fighting in the hallway. This had not been the first time, and Shawn had enough. As he walked in, he saw Angela sitting on the couch reading a Reader's Digest magazine. Apparently the article she was reading was funny, because she was laughing as she read it. She looked up at Shawn as he came in.

"What are you reading?"

"Oh, you've got to read this some time, it's hilarious."

"What is it?"

"It's called 'If Men Had Babies, The Human Race Would Die Out."

"I believe it." Shawn went to the water cooler and got a cup of water. He sat down on the opposite end of the couch from Angela.

"So, what would you like for dinner on Friday?" asked Shawn.

"I'm not particular. What do you make best?"

"Reservations. I do make a mean spaghetti sauce but I've always been told never eat spaghetti on a first . . . " Shawn stopped himself before he finished his sentence.

"My mom told me the same thing."

"What's that?"

"You know, never eat spaghetti on a date." Now Shawn felt awkward. Angela gave him a curious look. "And is this a date, Mr. Miller?"

Shawn couldn't tell if she was joking or being serious. He decided to what any red blooded man would do in this situation. He would evade the question.

"Of course it is. I go on a date every week with my daughter. This week she wants a chaperone."

"Speaking of your date, I just want you to know, you have the sweetest daughter in the whole world. This morning she stopped me in the hallway and gave me a hug."

"Yes, I know."

Angela looked at her watch. "Oh my goodness, I've got to run, my kids were supposed to be out of band five minutes ago."

"See ya. Oh, one more thing."

"Yes?"

"What's your favorite meal?" Angela thought a moment.

"Chicken Cordon Bleu."

"One Chicken Corduroy coming up on Friday night."

Mondays were the days that Mountain View had staff meetings. They started exactly at 3:00. Mrs. Jones had a standing promise. If everybody was on time, the meeting would only be one hour long. Today she would have to break that promise because there were several things she needed to talk about. Heather would go to late stay until 4:00 on those days.

About halfway through the meeting, Mrs. Jones talked about the upcoming choir and band concert. Shawn's mind was in Venice. These meetings were always so boring. He was thinking about his trip to Europe.

"Mr. Miller? Mr. Miller?" Shawn awoke from his daydream. Everyone was looking at him.

"Yes ma'am."

"I was asking if you had the flyers ready for the concert next Thursday. You promised last week you would have them today."

"Uh, I'll have them in everybody's boxes first thing tomorrow morning. I have a final few finishing touches to make on them." There was the sound of quiet laughter in the room. He heard Veronica say, "He probably hasn't even started making them." Mrs. Jones continued.

"One more thing before we go on, we need some more chaperones to stay next Tuesday night until 6:00. As you know, it's the whole 4th through 6th grade. That's about a hundred and fifty kids. So far we only have three chaperones. It would be nice if it were one of their own teachers. As a little incentive, I will provide dinner for whoever stays. Any volunteers?" Shawn raised his hand.

"Okay, Mr. Miller, thank you. We could probably use one more. Anyone else willing to stay?" No one else raised volunteered immediately. Finally someone volunteered.

"Okay, Miss Bierman. Thank you. The practice ends at 5:30, so warn your students their parents need to pick them up then."

Shawn had to stop at the grocery store on his way home. Heather loved going to the store because Shawn would usually get her a little something. Today he got a half gallon of low fat chocolate chip ice cream, which he promised her after she ate her dinner.

They didn't get home until 5:45. Fortunately, he had two containers of left overs from his mother's lunch on Sunday. He stuck them in the microwave to warm them up. He and Heather sat down, prayed and began eating. Just as Shawn put the first spoonful of potatoes to his mouth the phone rang. It was his sister, Shannon.

Shannon lived in Raleigh. She was a physical therapist. She had just gotten married last December to a prominent young attorney, Todd Landon. Two years ago, he had been elected to the state House of Representatives. He had done very well in his legal practice and in his blossoming political career. He had talked about running for Congress in 2006. Shawn liked him. He was a nice guy and he took good care of Shannon. He and Shannon had dated for four years before they finally tied the knot.

"Hey, big brother."

"Hello. It's been awhile."

"Yes, it has." Shawn and Shannon talked for a few minutes, then she asked,

"Shawn, what are you doing next Friday?"

"Having dinner with the President. Want me to cancel?"

"Smart aleck."

"I don't have anything planned. Why?"

"Well, Todd's taking some of us to the play Phantom of the Opera. He has a friend visiting from out of town. He's bringing along his girlfriend and the four of us were going to dinner and then the show. Well, when he ordered the ticket, they sent five tickets instead of four. We called and they said we could keep the extra ticket. We were wondering if you would like to come?"

"Sure, I think I can talk Sara or mom into watching Heather. What time?"

"You know the Olive Garden just off of I-64 in Raleigh?"

"Yeah."

"We're going to meet there at 5:00. The show starts at 7:00, so make sure you're on time."

"Okay, sounds like fun. Who's the other couple coming?"

"You might know them. They're from Wilson. It's Todd's friend Scott Hughes. He's in Florida right now. He gets back on Monday. He's bringing his girlfriend but I don't know her name. Do you know them?"

"The name doesn't sound familiar but I might recognize him when I see him. We know half the town."

"I guess he's serious about this girl. He wants us to meet her."

"Okay, well, I'll be there."

"See ya, bro."

CHAPTER THIRTEEN

Shawn had to consult his mother on how to make Chicken Cordon Bleu. "Whoever heard of blue chicken." Said Shawn. His mother finally dug up a recipe for it. On Thursday afternoon he and Heather went shopping again, and he got the ingredients for the meal, along with a cherry pie from the frozen food section and some whipped cream. Heather was so excited that she could hardly stand it. All week long she talked about when Miss Angela was coming to visit. She told Becky about it twice. In her mind, Miss Angela was her visitor, her daddy was just going to be there because he happened to live in the same house. Shawn spent Thursday night cleaning up his house. Shawn was a reasonably good housekeeper, but his home definitely lacked a woman's touch. He finally had his home presentable by 10:00 that night. He then went into the kitchen and got out all his bowls, spoons, and recipe book and laid them out on the counter. He double checked to see that he had all the ingredients he needed in the refrigerator. Chicken Cordon Bleu was not going to be easy, but he would succeed.

Shawn avoided Angela on Friday. He did say 'hi' to her once in the hallway, but that was the extent of their conversation. He left right after school was out. As soon as he got home, he started on dinner while Heather watched 'Barney.' He had three hours until Angela was coming. He was all of five minutes into preparing his meal when he got stumped. He picked up the phone and called Becky. Fortunately, he had a cordless phone with an ear and mouth piece that fit over his head. For the next hour his mother talked him through the preparation. Finally, he had the chicken in the oven cooking. He made some iced tea, cleaned up the kitchen, and looked at his watch. It was 5:30. He had a half hour. He went to his room and put on a long sleeved blue polo shirt and khaki pants.

The doorbell rang at 6:00. Shawn opened it and there was Angela. She was wearing blue pants, a white turtle neck, and a beautiful vest. Her hair was all curled and she looked very pretty. Heather came running up behind Shawn.

"Hi, Miss Angela!"

"Hi, Sweetie." Heather grabbed Angela's hand.

"You want to come see my room?"

"Sure."

"While she's giving you the ten-cent tour, I'll get dinner on the table." After Shawn finished getting dinner on the table, he went into Heather's room. Angela was having 'tea' with Raggedy Ann, Barney, Winnie the Pooh, and Heather.

"Daddy, do you want some tea?"

"In such distinguished company, I'd love a cup." Heather took her little plastic kettle and pretended to pour some tea into a tiny cup. Shawn pretended to drink it. "You two ready for dinner?"

"But Daddy, we're not finished."

"I tell you what honey, after dinner, we'll play Candy Land with Miss Angela." Heather loved Candy Land.

"Okay." They all went to the dinner table and sat down as Shawn prayed to bless the food.

Heather dominated the conversation during dinner. She had so much she wanted to tell Angela that Shawn couldn't get a word in. She talked about school, her dolls, her cousin Ashley, her grandparents, recess, the boy who pulled her hair today, Winnie the Pooh, and her new bicycle her daddy had gotten her for Christmas. Through it all, Angela just listened and smiled. She would occasionally say "Wow" and "That's really neat." Shawn didn't say much.

Heather wanted to play Candy Land right after dinner, but Angela said she wanted to help her daddy clean up. Heather went off to her room while Angela and Shawn cleared the table and put the dishes in the dishwasher.

"My daughter sure had a lot to say tonight."

"I enjoyed it. I love talking to little kids. They're so honest." They finished and went to Heather's room. Heather had already gotten out Candy Land. They played three games. Heather won two and Angela won one. Heather was so proud of the fact she had beaten them. Shawn looked at his watch. It was 8:15.

"All right, it's time for a certain little girl to go to bed."

"But Daddy . . . "

"Don't 'but daddy' me. Put on your pajamas and brush your teeth."

"Will you read me a story?"

"Sure. You pick one out and I'll read it."

Angela spoke up. "I should probably go."

"No." Shawn said this with a little too much emphasis. "I mean, if you need to go, it's fine, but if you'll indulge me for fifteen minutes, I'd love to sit and talk." Shawn smiled, "Someone else was hogging the conversation during dinner."

"You sure?"

"I am. Why don't you make yourself comfortable in the living room, and I'll be there in just a few minutes." Angela made her way to the living room while Shawn helped Heather get ready for bed. He read her "The Tale of Peter Rabbit" and the two prayed. Heather then asked if she could tell Miss Angela good night. She and Shawn went into the living room where Angela was looking at a photo album of Shawn's. Heather went over and gave her a hug.

"Good night, Miss Angela."

"Good night, Sweetheart."

"Where's my hug?" said Shawn. Heather gave her daddy a hug. "All right, off to bed." Shawn sat down next to Angela on the couch

"Your daughter is such a cutie."

"I know. I have her mother to thank for that." Angela looked at the photo album. She pointed to a photo of Shawn, Amanda, and Heather. It was taken three years before.

"This is your wife?"

"Yes."

"She was very beautiful."

"Yes, she was."

"Is it hard for you to talk about her?"

"Oh, no. Sometimes people hesitate to ask me about her. I guess they're worried it's too emotional a subject for me to talk about. But I don't mind talking about her. In fact I like talking about her."

"How did she die?"

"She died of a brain tumor last August. The hardest part was watching her suffer. The headaches, the severe depression she had because of the medication, and all the while trying to work and take care of Heather and explain to her about mommy. It was hard on all of us, but God saw us through it all."

"I remember when I was hired, I interviewed with Mrs. Jones. She told me a wife of one of the teachers was very ill. I asked Veronica about it and she told me Amanda had cancer." Angela looked back at the photo album. She flipped threw a few more pages of photos. She stopped at one large black and white photo that filled one whole page. She looked at it for a moment.

"Is that who I think it is?"

"It sure is. That's John Wayne."

"Who's that next to him?"

"That's my dad. That was taken while he was at the Naval Academy." There was a little card beneath the photo. Angela read the inscription out loud.

"To my good friend, John Miller. May you always serve our country well. Best wishes. John Wayne."

"So he got to meet the Duke."

"Actually, his nickname was Duke. People said he reminded them of John Wayne." Angela stared at the photo again.

"I can see why they would say that." The photo on the next page was John Miller standing in front of a fighter plane.

"So your dad was a pilot."

"Yes, he served in Vietnam." She flipped the page and looked at another photo.

"Who's that?" It was a photo of John Miller receiving a medal.

"That's the Secretary of Defense."

"So your dad won a medal. Which one?"

"Actually he won four of them. The one he received there was the Navy Cross. He also received two purple hearts, and the silver star." Shawn walked over to his mantle and pulled down a wooden box with a glass front. There were four medals laying on a velvet background. "Here they are." He handed them to Angela. She studied them for a moment.

"Wow. Your dad was a hero."

"He was my hero, that's for sure."

"You said your dad died when you were young?"

"I was ten years old."

"Did you say he died in a car crash?"

"That's the official version." Angela looked up at Shawn.

"The official version. You sound skeptical. You don't think he died in a car crash?"

"Oh, I know he died in a car crash, it's just what caused the crash that I don't believe." "I hope you don't think I'm being too nosy. I just find this interesting."

"Not at all. The official version says he was killed because he was driving under the influence of alcohol."

"You don't believe that?"

"My dad had not touched liquor in fourteen years. There's no way in this world he had been drinking."

"Do you mind if I ask what you think happened?"

"That's the question I've wondered for twenty-four years. I know as sure as I'm sitting here he wasn't drinking. He may have fallen asleep at the wheel. That had happened before. He may have been speeding and lost control, but he wasn't drinking. Don't laugh, but I've sometimes wondered if he wasn't murdered."

"I would never laugh at something like that. What makes you think it might have been murder."

"Oh, I don't know if it was. It probably was just an accident, but there were some strange things going on right before he died."

"Like what?"

"Well, I could always tell when something was bothering my dad. Something, I don't know what, was going on at work. We lived in Norfolk at the time and my dad was serving in the fleet command there. Anyway, the Monday before he died, his commanding officer was brutally murdered." Shawn flipped the page and pointed to a picture of his Little League baseball team.

"That boy there." He pointed at one of the players. "His name was Rusty. He played on my team." Angela scanned the photo and pointed to another little boy, one with blond hair and blue eyes.

"Is that you?"

"Yes."

"You were cute."

"Thank you."

"I'm sorry. I didn't mean to interrupt you. Please continue. I find this very interesting."

"Okay. Anyway, that boy," Shawn pointed at Rusty again. "It was his family. They were all murdered." Angela shuddered.

"Were you close to Rusty?"

"I only knew him from my baseball team. He played first base and I played outfield. He was a nice kid. Very likeable."

"Why would anyone murder a whole family?"

"I have no idea, but it gets even weirder. The next night the house we were living in burned to the ground."

"How awful."

"Then my dad told us to go stay with my Uncle Henry for a few days. The next night was when he was killed." Angela was spellbound.

"I can see why you wouldn't believe the official version. Did you or your mom look into it?"

"That's another strange thing. To this day my mother will not discuss it at all."

"She won't talk about your dad?"

"She talks about him all the time and we have talked about his death, but the few times I've ever brought up that his death was not what it appeared to be she will change the subject. One time I pressed her on it and she told me flat out not to talk about it with her."

"So you never looked into it?"

"Once when I was a teenager I suggested we look into it. Maybe write the Navy or something."

"What happened?"

"My mother absolutely refused, told me not to and left the room."

"Why would she respond that way?"

"I think she's afraid; in fact, I know she's afraid."

"What's she afraid of?"

"I think she's afraid of what she'll find out."

"You think your dad might have been involved in something illegal."

"I highly doubt it but I suppose it's possible. I don't know. I have to admit I'm stumped, but it didn't satisfy my curiosity."

"What did you do?"

"My sisters and I decided to investigate on our own. Unfortunately, I had to go behind my mother's back. If you ever meet her, don't tell her what I'm about to tell you."

"I would never betray the trust of a friend."

"Well, when I was in college, we wrote the Navy and asked for some information. They gave us some, but nothing that was different from the official story. They said they didn't know any more than we did. They suggested we ask the police department. We did. I interviewed one of the policemen who responded to the accident. He told me to my face that all the evidence pointed to my dad driving drunk. He told me a man fitting my dad's description left a bar twenty minutes before the accident and was reported in a car like the one my dad drove. He even showed me the police report."

"I hope you won't be offended if I ask, but do you think it's possible your dad was drinking when you and your family weren't around?"

"No, I don't mind you asking. I asked myself the same thing. The big problem is timing. The man left the bar a little after 10:30. The call reporting the accident came at 10:48. That's eighteen minutes. The accident happened 35 miles away and there was some construction on the road that night. My dad would have had to been driving over 120 mph. That's nearly 70 miles over the speed limit. My dad had never had a speeding ticket in his life. The fastest I ever remember him driving was 10 miles over the speed limit. He was driving a 1969 Oldsmobile that recently had engine trouble. I might also add whoever saw him go over the cliff would have had to call on their car phone the second they saw him go over because the closest pay phone was five miles away."

"That is very strange."

"Another thing, whoever called never left their name or number. They just reported the accident and hung up." Angela just shook her head. "One more thing, the bartender was never even sure it was my dad he saw. He only said a man in a Navy uniform about six feet tall, and brown hair came in at 10:00 and ordered several drinks. He went to a booth, sat by himself, finished his drinks and left a little after 10:30. You have to remember, the Navy base was not far away. Guys came in all the time."

"I can certainly understand why you would be skeptical. Did your dad hit another car or what?"

"No, he went over a cliff and down an embankment. The car caught on fire. His body was so badly burned, they had to identify him with his belongings. We had a closed casket funeral."

"Did you tell the officer all this?"

"I did."

"What did he say?"

"He said he understood where I was coming from, but it wouldn't be the first time a Navy officer drank, or drove fast when his family wasn't around. He said he could appreciate my desire to protect my dad's reputation, but he had to look at it from a policeman's point of view. He admitted that it was all very strange but it still was not out of the realm of possibility. 'Stranger things than that have happened,' is what he told me."

"What about your mom? Does she believe your dad was driving drunk?"

"Do you know in twenty-four years I have never heard her say she did believe it. I've never heard her say she didn't believe it. That subject is off limits with her."

"Do you think you'll ever find out the truth?"

"I hope to one day."

"You've lost both your dad and your wife. How do you cope?"

"The Lord has seen me through it all. I could never have made it without him. We've been talking about me way too much. Can I ask you a question?"

"Sure."

"I noticed a Bible and a devotional in your house. Are you also a Christian?"

"Yes, I am. I accepted the Lord when I was in the Air Force. I was stationed on the little island of Guam. A friend of mine invited me to a large Baptist church there and that's when I came to know the Lord."

"That's great, where do you go to church?"

"I go to Heritage Bible Church."

"I've heard of it. Who's the pastor there?"

"Dillon Matthews. I really enjoy it. The only thing I don't like is that there aren't many people my age there. Most of the church is older. There are only a few singles and most of them are in their forties or fifties."

"Well, I'm not trying to recruit another shepherd's sheep, but our church has a large single's ministry. Maybe you could visit sometime."

"I'd like that." Angela looked at her watch. It was 10:15.

"I'm sorry. I've got to go." She stood up. Shawn walked her to the door. "I had a very enjoyable evening. Thank you for dinner and the conversation."

"Thank you for coming. I'll see you Monday."

"Bye." Angela walked out into the darkness toward her car. Shawn watched until she got in and drove away.

CHAPTER FOURTEEN

The following Tuesday afternoon was the day of the choir and band concert. Shawn woke up feeling more tired than when he had gone to bed the night before. Today was going to be a very long day. It was near the end of the year. That's the time of year when teachers are the most tired and every day seems like an eternity. People who have never taught sometimes have a misconception of what teaching is like. At first glance it seems to be an ideal job. You only work nine months out of the year. You start work at 7:30 and are home by 4:30. What many don't realize is the tremendous amount of energy that a good teacher puts into teaching. It wears you out, and Shawn was worn out. He loved teaching and wouldn't do anything else, but he was ready for a break. He left for work at 7:00 and he would not get home until 6:30 at the earliest. That made for a long day. He also had a science experiment he was doing with his class in which he modeled the water cycle. Shawn's students loved him because he was a fun and interesting teacher. He had spent an hour last night getting his materials ready and doing a run through the experiment. His kids would love it, but it would add one more thing to do to an already busy schedule.

To make matters worse, when Shawn got to school, he found out he would have no prep time today. Normally he got a forty-five minute prep from 10:00 to 10:45 when his students went to music. Mrs. Daniels would not be in today until 12:00, and Mrs. Jones was unable to find a substitute. The first thing Shawn did when he got to school after dropping Heather off was to check his box. There was a note from Angela. "Dear Shawn, thank you for dinner on Friday. I had a wonderful time. I have enjoyed getting to know you and your daughter. I hope you have a great rest of the year. Angela." Shawn smiled. Reading that note somehow made his day a little brighter.

School ended at 2:40. Shawn left school with Heather at 2:45. He had permission to leave early because he had to take Heather to Sara's house. She had agreed to watch her while Shawn was staying for the dress rehearsal. He was back at school by 3:15. He met Angela in the hallway on their way to the Cafetorium.

"Hey, where have you been all day?" said Angela.

"Running my head off. I didn't get a prep today so I've been scrambling to get everything done."

"Oh, I'm sorry. Anything I can help you with?"

"Thanks, but it was a science experiment I was doing with my students. We did it this afternoon." The two walked into the Cafetorium. Mrs. Daniels was directing students here and there, arranging music stands, and barking orders to whoever could hear. She looked a little flustered. Shawn was her next victim.

"Mr. Miller, you're five minutes late, but that's okay."

"Actually, I'm ten minutes early but whose counting."

"Mrs. Jones said you had to be here at 3:15; it's now 3:20."

"Actually, Mrs. Jones said 3:30."

"She did."

"I can vouch for him. She told me the same thing." Said Angela.

"Oh, well, sorry I falsely accused you."

"It's okay. Where do you need me?"

"Shawn, you go and make sure the guys are behaving themselves in the changing room and Angela if you could do the same thing with the girls, I'd appreciate it. Make sure they aren't goofing off too much." Shawn and Angela went off in separate directions.

The rehearsal went an hour longer than it was supposed to be. Mrs. Daniels was in tears before it was over. The students messed up on several pieces, the kids weren't coming in on cue, her star solo had laryngitis and everyone was sure the whole thing was going to be a disaster. Shawn reminded her that a lousy rehearsal usually meant a great performance.

"Then this one ought to rival the premiere of Beethoven's Fifth Symphony."

For a moment she even considered cancelling the whole thing. Her husband reminded her she couldn't do that.

As if the extra hour wasn't bad enough, Mrs. Jones didn't order enough pizzas for everybody. After the students finished eating the pizza there was nothing left for the teachers. She finally told them to go get a meal and bring her a receipt. She would reimburse them up to ten dollars. Everybody was gone by 7:00. Shawn was starving. He hadn't eaten a thing since 11:30 when he ate lunch. As he walked out into the parking lot, he saw Angela going toward her car.

"Hey Angela," Shawn jogged toward her.

"I'm glad that's over," she said as she unlocked her car door.

"Have you eaten yet?"

"No."

"Since Mrs. Jones is buying, want to grab a bite?"

"What about your other date? Do you think she'll mind you being out so late?"

"Heather's with my sister. I just called and told her I would be late."

"Okay, where would you like to go?" said Angela.

"You decide."

"Applebee's is right down the road. Want to meet there?"

"See you there in five minutes." Shawn got into his car and followed Angela's Honda Civic out of the parking lot. The two met in the parking lot of Applebee's.

There wasn't much of a crowd, so the two got a seat almost immediately. The waiter brought them each a menu and some water. They both looked at their menus for a minute.

"They have a really good chicken salad here," said Angela.

"I know. I also like their soup." The waiter appeared again. Angela ordered the chicken salad and a bowl of vegetable soup. Shawn ordered a chicken dinner and a bowl of vegetable soup. The waiter left.

"I have to tell you, Friday night we spent so much time talking about me and my family we never talked much about you."

"What would you like to know?"

"Oh, I don't know. What kind of hobbies you have, what books do you read, what your family is like; you know, the basics."

"My hobbies, let's see. Well, I like to cook. I like to hike. I like to go camping up in the mountains. I love to travel."

"Where do you travel to?"

"When I was in the Air Force, I was stationed for a year in Guam and a year in England. While I was in Guam, I went to Australia, the Philippines, Korea, and Japan. While I was stationed in England, I went to France, Germany, Holland, Switzerland and Belgium."

"Wow. You're quite the world traveler. Why did you join the Air Force?"

"Well, it was a good opportunity. If I stayed in four years I would have my college paid for and I really wanted to be a teacher. Also, my dad had been in the Marines, and I have a brother in the Army."

"You come from a military family. We have something in common."

"And we're both teachers." Said Angela smiling.

"And we're both carbon-based life forms." Said Shawn. Angela laughed. Suddenly, out of the corner of his eye Shawn saw a man leaving the restaurant. It was a face he knew. A face he had seen many times. The man was just walking out the door.

"Excuse me, Angela." Shawn jumped up and walked very quickly toward the door. He went outside in the parking lot but the man disappeared. He had only gone out a few seconds before. It was like the man completely vanished into thin air. There wasn't a soul in the entire parking lot. Shawn walked back in. He stopped the waiter.

"Pardon me, ma'am. Did you see where that man went?"

"What man?"

"The man that was just here a minute ago?"

"I'm sorry. I don't know who you're talking about. What did he look like?"

"He was around fifty, about 5' 10." He was just here a minute ago. You didn't see him?"

"I'm sorry. I didn't wait on anyone like that tonight." Angela came walking up.

"Shawn, is everything okay?"

"Yea, everything's fine." Shawn went back to his seat and sat down. His face was white and his palms were sweaty.

"What's wrong?"

"Nothing."

"Shawn, don't tell me nothing when we both know something is seriously bothering you. What is it?"

Shawn took a deep breath. He said nothing.

"You don't trust me. I understand."

"No, that's not it at all. Of course I trust you. It's just that if I tell you this, you really will think I'm crazy. I'd hate to have someone as nice as you thinking I'm looney tunes."

"Shawn, if you don't want to tell me I really do understand, but I will believe whatever you tell me because I know you to be an honest person."

"If you think the story Friday night was bizarre, wait until you hear this one." The waiter brought their food. They thanked him and he left.

"Once again, you have my attention." She said as she sipped her soup.

"I saw a man leave this restaurant that I have seen at least a dozen times in my life."

"Okay."

"I've never met him. He just shows up in the most unusual places."

"Like Applebee's?"

"No, well," Shawn stopped and looked down at the table in thought for a moment. "Any time something significant happens in my life I see this man. I've seen him in everything from jeans and T-shirts to a tuxedo. Sometimes his hair is different but it's always the same face."

"All right, I'm officially spooked."

"Well, the first time I saw him was at my dad's funeral. I didn't say anything because there were many people I didn't know there. Then I saw him again one day at a school play when I was in the fifth grade. I had a major role. I asked my mom about him but she had never seen him. I saw him again at a basketball game in junior high. I've seen him twice at the airport. Once when I was in high school, I was traveling to Israel with my Uncle Henry and his family. The other time I was going to Peru on a mission's trip. I saw him at my high school graduation, college graduation. I saw him at my wedding. I even saw him in the hospital the night Heather was born. I saw him at Amanda's funeral and then finally tonight. It's strange. I get just a glimpse of him and then he disappears before I can ever speak to him. No one ever seems to know who he is or what he's doing. Tonight I saw him. I went out into the parking lot and he was gone."

Angela just looked at him.

"All right, go ahead, tell me I'm crazy or paranoid or schizophrenic."

"I believe you 100%"

"Really?"

"That's too crazy not to be the truth. No way you'd make something up like that. I'd never believe it." Angela looked like she had a question on the tip of her tongue that she was afraid to ask.

"Go ahead. Ask whatever it is you're afraid to ask."

"I was just wondering," she said slowly. A smile came across her face. "If he only shows up during special moments in your life," Angela gave him a sly look. "Well, what's special about tonight?"

CHAPTER FIFTEEN

For the next two days Shawn could not get the question Angela had asked him out of his mind. He had not answered her question, but the obvious answer was her. She was the reason he was there. There was something special about her. Shawn didn't need a mysterious stranger to tell him that, but why had he shown up that night at that restaurant? He now found himself wondering more about why he showed up than he did the man's identity. Did this man know something he didn't? The more Shawn thought about it the more frightening the answer became. This man, whoever he was, knew something Shawn was just now beginning to realize himself. He had definite feelings for Angela. He liked her. She was pretty, she was kind, she was intelligent, and she shared his faith in Christ. How could he not like her? She was the kind of person you couldn't help but like. He wouldn't have been human if he didn't like her. As if that wasn't enough, his daughter loved her. Now the question in his mind was, did she like him. Oh, he knew that she probably liked him as a fellow teacher, but did she have any real feelings for him. He wished he could ask his mysterious friend if he knew.

Once again Shawn deliberately avoided Angela the next two days. His heart and his mind were having a very heated debate. His mind was telling him the only woman he ever truly loved, he buried a year ago. The girl he had loved since he was a pimple faced high school sophomore, the girl who had given him a beautiful child, and for eighteen years, had seen him through all of life's trials and triumphs. She was gone, and no one could ever take her place. It would be an act of cruelty for him to expect anyone to take the place of Amanda.

His heart was telling him that Amanda was in heaven and he wasn't. He had fulfilled his vows "until death do us part." God never intended for a man to live his life alone. He needed someone. He was lonely. Here was a kind and compassionate individual whom he genuinely liked. He was attracted to her for many reasons. No one expected her to take Amanda's place, but should he be lonely and miserable the rest of his life simply because no one would ever be exactly like Amanda?

His heart and mind were still arguing with each other Thursday night when he went to the choir and band concert. Both Heather and his mother were with him that night. Shawn had not told Becky or anyone else about his dilemma. The concert started at 7:00. They arrived at 6:45. Shawn spent a few minutes backstage talking to his students and encouraging them. His mom and Heather found a seat. Shawn joined them. There was an empty seat next to him. He was leaning over whispering something to his mother when he heard a familiar voice.

"Mind if I join you?" He looked up at Angela. She looked incredible. She was wearing a lavender dress and her hair was done up.

"Hi, Miss Angela," said an excited Heather. Angela sat down next to Shawn. Shawn introduced them.

"Angela, I'd like you to meet my mother, Becky Miller. Mom, this is Angela Bierman. She's a friend of mine and also a fellow teacher."

"It's nice to meet you, Mrs. Miller."

"Please, it's Becky and it's nice to meet you."

"Nonnie," said Heather, using her name for her grandmother. "Miss Angela came to my house for dinner."

"She did? Did you wear her ear out?"

"Just about," said Shawn.

"She also beat me twice in Candy Land." Said Angela. Just then Mrs. Jones showed up.

"Miss Bierman, I need to speak with you." Angela got up and left. After she had gone, Becky leaned over and said in a low voice so Heather could not hear,

"And who is that attractive young lady?"

"She's just a friend, Mom. Nothing more."

"And how many 'friends' do you cook chicken cordon bleu for? In fact how many friends have you cooked anything for? In fact, how many times have you cooked chicken cordon bleu for me, your own mother, who spent nine hours in labor bringing you into the world, and eighteen of the best years of her life raising you, spent many nights comforting you when you were sick, and how many times have you ever cooked . . . "

"All right Mom, she's a good friend, but she's only that."

"Well, she seems very nice."

"By the way, if you're not doing anything next Friday night, your granddaughter and I would like to have you over for chicken cordon bleu."

Angela returned. The lights were dimming and Mrs. Daniels came to the microphone. Shawn leaned over and whispered in Angela's ear.

"What happened?"

"Some of my students left their instruments in my classroom. They needed to get them."

Shawn had been right about if the rehearsal was bad the performance would be great. It was outstanding. The children outdid themselves. Shawn was very proud of them. Almost half his class was in either the choir, the band, or both. At the end everyone gave Mrs. Daniels a standing ovation. She was crying again, but this time they were happy tears.

Angela was not at school on Friday. Mrs. Noah was the substitute in her class. Mrs. Noah was an older black lady who had taught in the district for thirty years and retired only last year. She now occasionally subbed. She was a dear sweet lady whom the children loved. More than one had asked her if she was married to the man who took all the animals on that boat. Shawn stopped her during his prep time.

"Excuse me, Mrs. Noah."

"Oh, yes Shawn, what can I do for you?"

"I know you're subbing for Miss Bierman. I was just wondering if she's sick today?"

"I honestly don't know. She called me yesterday and asked me to sub for her today. She didn't tell me why." "She didn't seem very sick last night," thought Shawn. Mrs. Noah smiled.

"I'll tell her you were concerned though."

"Oh, that's not necessary."

Shawn felt a little guilty dropping Heather off at Sara's again. It seemed she was staying with someone at least once a week. He was leaving for Europe in a month and she would be staying with relatives for over two weeks. If he hadn't promised Shannon and Todd he was going, he would have canceled, but he hadn't seen his sister and brother-in-law in over a month. He promised Heather he would to take her to the mall on Saturday.

Shawn arrived at the Olive Garden exactly at 5:00. Shannon was seated at a table. She waved Shawn over. He walked over to their table and gave her a hug.

"It's good to see you, bro," said Shannon.

"Thanks. It's good to be seen by you. Where's Todd?"

"In the little boys' room. He'll be here in a minute."

"What about his friend?"

"Oh, he called a few minutes ago. He said he would be ten minutes late. Traffic accident on I-64."

"Oh yeah, I got caught in it. Fortunately, I left earlier than I needed to. So who is he again?"

"Scott Hughes. He's a friend of Todd's from way back. Todd hasn't seen him in over a year and he wanted to get together. The real reason he wants to get together is he wants us to meet his girlfriend. He's been dating her and Todd thinks they're about ready to tie the knot. Speaking of lady friends, who is this girl I've been hearing about?"

"Is nothing sacred in this family?"

"Of course not. Now give me the full scoop. Who is she? Where's she from? Is she pretty? How serious is this?"

"I think those are personal questions."

"Of course they are. They're the best kind of questions."

"Well, since I can't get out of this gracefully, her name is Angela and she's a fellow teacher. Her family is originally from Tennessee, she's very pretty and right now we're only friends so you can tell Mom not to start planning the wedding yet." Just then Todd came toward them. He was with a tall man in a gray suit who looked like he could be a model in a men's fashion magazine. Next to him was a beautiful young lady in a navy blue dress.

"Scott, I want to introduce you to my wife and brother-in-law. This is Shannon and Shawn." Scott shook Shawn and Shannon's hand.

"And this is Scott's girlfriend, Angela Bierman."

CHAPTER SIXTEEN

This was without a doubt the most awkward moment of Shawn's life. He shook hands with Angela. She was every bit as surprised as he was but she hid it well.

"It's nice to meet you, Shawn," she said. "Oh great," he thought. "She's pretending like she doesn't even know me." They all sat down. Todd and Scott sat across from each other as did Shannon and Angela. Shawn sat next to Shannon and across from Angela. Scott began to talk about his recent trip to Florida. Todd and Shannon listened attentively. Angela wouldn't even look at Shawn. He couldn't tell if she was embarrassed or angry. Shannon spoke to Angela.

"So how long have you two been dating?" Shawn felt himself sinking lower into his chair.

"About a year and a half."

"That's great. How did you meet?"

"We met while I was in college. Scott was speaking in one of my classes."

"That's right. She was the pretty girl on the front row asking all the hard questions. I knew right then, I had to go out with this girl."

"So you asked her out right then?"

"No, we continued talking after class, and I asked her if she would like to have a cup of coffee with me and we could continue our conversation, and we've been dating every since."

"By the way, Shawn," Todd said smiling, "Mom's been telling

us that there's a pretty teacher you've been spending a lot of time with lately." Shawn would have gladly died right then to avoid the embarrassment he felt. Todd was oblivious to Shawn's reaction. "So, what's her name?"

"Angela." Said Shannon. With this Angela buried her head in the menu.

"Would you excuse me for a minute? I need to use the restroom." Shawn quickly left the table. He stood just outside the men's room and called Sara on his cell phone. It rang twice before she answered.

"Hello."

"Sara, this is Shawn. I need you to do me a big favor."

"Sure, if I can."

"I want you to call me in five minutes on my cell phone and ignore everything you hear me say."

"Is something wrong?"

"Do you remember that time you went out with that red headed guy in high school? The one with all the freckles and was always blowing his nose."

"Yeah, what about it?"

"Remember how you called me pretending to be sick and I came to your rescue?"

"Yes, I remember."

"You said you owed me one. Well, now I'm collecting, and Sara, remember I never told anybody about this. I expect the same courtesy."

"Whatever you say." Shawn went back to his table. The others were in the middle of ordering. The waiter asked what he wanted.

"I'll just have soup and salad." Just then his cell phone rang.

"Hello?"

"Hello. This is the Sisters of Mercy Hospital. We have the results of your brain scan. We didn't find a thing."

"Sara, hey is everything all right?"

"That's 'goddess' to you."

"What happened?"

"Well, it all started a long time ago. You see I was born at an early age."

"Really, all over the carpet."

"Come to think of it, it is getting pretty deep in here."

"Well, have her lay down and I'll be there as soon as I can. You might want to keep a trash can near by."

"Now I think I'm going to be sick."

"I hope it's not contagious."

"Her illness or your insanity?" Shawn hung up.

"I've got to go. I'm sorry, guys."

"Is Heather sick?" asked Angela. Shannon looked at Angela with a curious look.

"How did you know his daughter's name was Heather?" Angela's face turned bright red.

"I must have mentioned her before I went to the restroom." Shawn quickly interrupted. "Well, got to run. It was nice to meet you, Scott and Angela. I hope you all enjoy the play."

Shawn quickly left the restaurant and went to his car. He arrived an hour later at his sister Sara's house. He rang the doorbell. Sara answered. She was wearing an apron and had a spatula in one hand. Heather and Ashley were behind her.

"Daddy!" She gave her daddy a hug.

"Come on in." A delicious aroma was coming from the kitchen where Sara was baking a cake. "You have to wait until the cake is finished. I promised Heather a slice." She turned to Ashley. "You and Heather go play in your room for a few minutes. I'll tell you when the cake is done."

"Okay." Said Ashley.

"All right," she said. "I'm waiting."

"Waiting for what?" asked Shawn.

"An explanation perhaps." Shawn really didn't want to explain, but he figured he owed it to Sara. Besides, it might be nice to get it off his chest.

"As long as you give me a slice of cake when I'm finished."

"Agreed." For the next fifteen minutes Shawn explained the whole story to her. He left nothing out. He was very close to Sara and he knew their conversation would be confidential. Jeff was working late so it was just the two of them and the kids.

"I'm sorry, Shawn. Don't blame yourself though. I'm sure she never meant to embarrass you."

"I know. I just feel like such an idiot."

Two slices of cake later he took a protesting Heather home. They got home and Shawn helped her get ready for bed. He read her a story and put her to bed. It was 9:00. The only bright spot of the entire evening was that he had taped two episodes of "Murder, She Wrote." This was one of Shawn's favorite TV shows. He changed into a comfortable pair of jeans and got himself a coke from the refrigerator.

The second episode had just ended when Shawn heard a knock on the door. He looked at his watch. It was 10:55. Who in the world would be knocking on his door at this time of night. He looked through the peep hole. It was Angela. "Oh, no." He said out loud. He opened the door.

"Hi," said Angela. "I have some rotten vegetables in my car you can throw at me if you wish."

"What do you need, Angela?" There was more than a hint of coldness in his voice. Angela's face took on a serious look. She could read the hurt look in Shawn's eyes.

"Shawn, I know you're probably upset at me and I certainly don't blame you. I saw your light on and I really need to talk to you."

"You know Angela, Heather's sleeping. This really isn't a good time. I will give you call tomorrow. I promise."

"Shawn, if I don't talk to you tonight. I won't be able to sleep." Angela had a pleading look in her eyes. "Just give me five minutes and I'll go. I'll leave you alone. I'll even let you throw me off your porch if it will make you feel better. You're such a sweet guy and I don't want you to hate me forever."

"I don't hate you."

"I know. I've not been totally honest with you and I'm genuinely sorry. I certainly never meant to embarrass you or hurt you."

Shawn sat down on the porch swing and motioned for her to do the same.

"Let me explain about Scott. We broke up tonight. I have been dating him for a while. We had . . . "

"Wait. You broke up with him tonight?"

"Yes, I'm trying to explain why. Anyway, we had been dating for over a year and a half. We had reached a point in our relationship where we had decided to either get married or break it off. Before he left for Florida, he asked me to give him an answer when he got back. I agreed. After praying about it and seeking some counsel from my family and my pastor, I decided I could not marry him."

"May I ask why?"

"A number of reasons. One, he's married to his work. I could never compete with his job. Second, he doesn't want to have children. I do, and he expects me to be a doormat, which I refuse to be."

"Why did you go with him tonight?"

"He had planned this quite awhile ago. I had already promised to go with him so I felt I needed too. I had already planned to break up. It was just a matter of timing. I didn't say anything to you because I already knew I was going to end the relationship, but I felt after nearly two years together, I owed it to him to tell him first face to face." Angela's eyes watered a little. "The truth is, I love him. I really do love him but I am absolutely sure that marrying him would be a disaster. Anyway, I knew that I had to tell him tonight. I had it all planned out how I was going to tell him. I was hoping to inflict as little pain as possible. Of course, I had no idea my now ex-boyfriend was best friends with your brother-in-law." Shawn said nothing.

"I should tell you one more thing. Scott did ask me if there was someone else. I told him I wasn't dating anybody else, but that I had met someone and we were just friends but I wasn't sure where it was headed." Shawn looked at the ground. "I'm talking about you." Shawn looked up.

"Really? But look at your friend. I mean, he's incredibly handsome and . . . "

"Yes, he is, but he's not the one for me. Besides, don't be so hard on yourself Shawn. You are a very attractive man and what is more important, you're a gentleman. You know how to make a girl feel special."

"Thank you. You really broke up with him tonight?"

"I did. I just came by to tell you this and now I'll go and leave you alone." Angela turned to leave.

"Wait."

"Yes?"

"What if I don't want you to leave me alone?"

"What do you mean?"

"I mean, I've been alone for almost a year now. I hate being alone. Being alone stinks."

"I know. I've been feeling very alone lately too."

"Well, since we're both alone, why don't we be alone together sometime?"

Angela smiled. "Are you asking me out?"

"Yes, I believe I am."

"Well, that was the worst line I've ever heard and believe me I've heard some bad ones."

"Well, I thought about slipping you a note during English class, but maybe I'll try the direct approach. Angela, will you go out with me sometime?"

"I would love too." Then as an afterthought she said, "Anywhere in particular?"

"Well, how about the Olive Garden, the one here in town, Friday night perhaps?"

She smiled a devilish smile. "Perhaps."

CHAPTER SEVENTEEN

The following Sunday was Mother's Day. It was Heather's first Mother's Day without Amanda. Shawn had always tried to make it special for both his mother and Amanda. On Amanda's first Mother's Day as a mom, Shawn bought red roses for her and wrote a card. He signed it with Heather's name. He continued the tradition. As Heather got older, she would color a picture and they would stick it to the refrigerator. He would also make breakfast for her and serve it to her in bed. Mother's Day a year ago had not been a pretty sight. Amanda was home, but she was extremely sick and in a great deal of pain. Her body was bloated and she was very dizzy. Shawn had to help her sit up. She didn't say much but she smiled when they brought her flowers. They did make some breakfast for her, but she was so sick she couldn't eat any of it. Because of the medication she was on, she was extremely thirsty all the time. The only thing that seemed to quench her thirst was carrot juice. Shawn got out their wedding china and brought her carrot juice in one of their nicest cups. He included a chocolate mint with it. Angela was right about one thing, Shawn knew how to make a girl feel special.

Shawn and his sisters had always tried to make Mother's Day special for Becky. They had bought flowers for Becky and cooked breakfast for her in bed. In fact this is where Shawn got the idea for Amanda. Becky would still get tears in her eyes as she thought about Mother's Day 1983. Her children had worked extra jobs so they could buy her a nice dress for Mothers Day. They got Uncle

Henry to take them to J. C. Penney's and Aunt Bonnie had discreetly found out her dress size. Shawn and his sisters spent nearly $100 on a dress and a nice pair of shoes for Becky. They had worked for four months to earn the money. The dress was a nice one, but it was the love that went into buying it. Her children spent many hours working to buy that dress. The dress still hung in her closet. It was old and she had long since stopped wearing it, but she would not sell it for any amount of money. That dress was her most prized possession because it reminded her of the love her children had for her and how much she loved them.

This Mother's Day would not be so dramatic. The kids still brought flowers, and this time they decided to take their mother out for lunch to her favorite restaurant, the Italian Garden. They each had a present for her. Sara and Jeff gave her a book entitled "A Mother's Love." Shannon and Todd, who had driven down from Raleigh for the day gave her a gift certificate to Bed and Bath, and Shawn gave her a beautiful set of candlestick holders. It was a special day and Becky once again felt blessed that she had such wonderful children.

Shawn and Heather did not go over to Becky's house after lunch. They usually spent Sunday afternoon there, but this Sunday they had another visit to make. Shawn and Heather left the Italian Garden at 2:00 and stopped at a florist to pick up some flowers. He then drove to Woodlawn Cemetery and parked the car. Heather had been there several times, so this was not new to her. The two held hands as they walked past the graves and stopped at the familiar headstone. The two just stood there for a minute holding hands and thinking.

Shawn's mind went back to the day of the funeral. Amanda's funeral was on a Thursday. Shawn had asked the choir to sing a special song for Amanda. Pastor Jim was worried because most of the choir members had jobs, and he wasn't sure they would be able to get off. The day of the funeral, the choir was completely filled. Not one choir member was absent, except of course Amanda. The song they sang was entitled "It Sounds Like Home to Me."

> Somewhere just across the Jordan River,
> Is a place of everlasting joy and peace.

Where the tree of life is blooming there forever,
And a crown of life is waiting there for me,
And it sounds like home to me,
Right where I want to be.
There'll be no tears to fill our eyes again,
The hills will echo with the story,
As we sing of his grace and glory,
Where the saints of God will be.
That sounds like home to me.

Pastor Jim preached from the verse "Precious in the sight of the Lord is the death of one of his saints." He spoke of her kindness and the fact that she was an encouragement to others.

"We must mix tears of sorrow with tears of joy. For though we will miss our dear sister and we grieve with our dear brother Shawn and his family, we must never forget the example of Christ-like love she was to all of us. We weep for ourselves, but rejoice for her. She is in the presence of the Lord and has heard those words all Christians long to hear the Savior say, "Well done, thou good and faithful servant." The congregation sang, "It is Well with My Soul."

"Daddy, why do mommies die?" The question caught Shawn off guard.

"Well honey, sometimes God takes our mommies home to heaven to be with him." He wished he could explain it better but that was the best he could do on the spur of the moment.

"I don't like God."

"Honey, you shouldn't say that. God still loves Mommy and he still loves you. Sometimes He does things we don't quite understand." This explanation was lost on Heather. Shawn bent down to where he was eye level with her.

"Sweetheart, it's okay to be sad about mommy being gone and it's okay to want her to still be here. I'm still sad and I still wish she was here but remember God has given you other people who love you very much. Nonnie loves you and so does your Aunt Sara and Uncle Jeff and Ashley." Heather butted in.

"And Aunt Shannon and Uncle Todd."

"Yes, they love you, too and you're forgetting someone else."

"Mrs. Brown?" Heather worshiped her teacher Mrs. Brown. Shawn smiled.

"Well, yes Mrs. Brown loves you too but I was thinking of someone else."

"Jesus?"

"Yes, of course Jesus loves you, but I was thinking of one other person." She thought a minute.

"I don't know." Shawn playfully slapped her forehead.

"Me you silly goose. I love you very much."

"Daddy, are you going to die?"

"Not anytime soon I hope." Shawn gave her a big hug. "Sweetie, I love you so much it hurts."

"Well, Daddy, you're hurting me." Shawn had hugged her a little too hard. He let go.

"See what I mean? Heather, would you like a little ice cream?" There was an ice cream and yogurt shop just around the corner. An excited Heather responded quickly.

"Yes!"

"All right, I'll race you to the car. Last one there gets to pay." Heather took off toward the car. When he finally got there, Heather was smiling.

"I beat you. I beat you."

"You sure did. I guess today is my treat." They got into the car and headed to the ice cream shop.

CHAPTER EIGHTEEN

Monday afternoon Shawn stopped by Veronica's classroom. Veronica was the best teacher Shawn ever knew. She was the only teacher who had more requests from students' parents than Shawn. She had won many awards for Outstanding Teacher. It was for that reason Mrs. Jones chose her to mentor Angela. She was also the best friend Shawn had in the educational profession. Though she was fifteen years older than Shawn, she was a kid at heart. Perhaps that's the reason she and Shawn got along so well. She had been a valuable help to him his first two years of teaching. She had been over to Shawn's house several times and became good friends with Amanda. She, like so many others, had visited Amanda while she was in the hospital. After the funeral, Veronica had cooked meals for Shawn and Heather many times. Shawn could not remember how many times he had asked her advice for everything from teaching, to family, to marriage. He would be asking her advice again today.

Veronica was sitting at her desk grading papers. She had a tired, frustrated look on her face.

"Hello," said Shawn. Veronica looked up.

"Hi."

"Are you busy?" Veronica rolled her eyes.

"I am so swamped. It's ridiculous. Don't tell anyone this but I haven't graded a paper in three weeks."

"Veronica. I'm so shocked."

"Well, with all this stuff we have to do at the end of the year, how am I supposed to do it all?"

"Can you talk and grade at the same time?"

"This wouldn't have anything to do with a certain beautiful fourth grade teacher would it?"

"So you two have been talking about me. Why am I not surprised?"

"Why, Shawn, I'm shocked you would think I would ever talk about you behind your back."

"I know what you girls do when you spend twenty minutes in the bathroom. You spend nineteen of it talking about guys." Veronica laughed. Shawn continued. "I haven't been on a date in quite a while. I would like to make a good impression. That's why I came to the love doctor."

"Oh please. If you only knew."

"By the way, I never asked how your date with Popeye the sailor man went."

"I don't even want to talk about it."

"That bad, was it?"

"The most embarrassing incident of my entire life."

"Surely it wasn't as embarrassing as the time we had the fire drill while you were in the bathroom and you came running out in your . . ."

"Okay, the second most embarrassing moment of my life." She was silent for a moment.

"All right. I'll tell you, but you have to swear you'll never tell a soul under any circumstances."

"All right."

"Well, he showed up an hour late for starters. He called and told me he had to pick up someone at the airport. He picked her up and brought her with him."

"He brought someone else on his date with you. Who?"

"His wife." Shawn bit his tongue, trying with all his might not to laugh.

"I can see where that would take the romance right out of the date. He didn't tell you he was married?"

"He sort of forgot to mention it."

"I'm so sorry."

"It's okay. Hopefully things will go better with you."

"What has she told you?"

"She really didn't tell me much. Just said you were going out to dinner. But if you really want to impress her, don't try to impress her. Just be yourself. Let her do most of the talking and remember to compliment her on her appearance and . . . What?" Shawn was smiling and shaking his head.

"I just had deja vu all over again."

"One more thing. Smile. You have such a pretty smile."

"Well, I'll try to remember that."

"Wear your royal blue shirt and khaki pants. You look really sharp in that."

"Thanks."

On Friday Shawn purposely avoided Angela. He was so nervous he was worried if he talked to her he would say something stupid and make a fool of himself. He did say 'hi' to her in the hall, but that was the extent of their conversation.

Sara had graciously agreed to watch Heather again tonight. Heather was always excited whenever she had an opportunity to spend time with her cousin Ashley. As Shawn was buttoning his shirt Heather came into his room as she often did to talk to him.

"Daddy, you look nice."

"Thank you sweetheart. You do, too." Shawn patted her on the head. Heather looked thoughtful.

"Daddy, don't kiss Miss Angela tonight."

"Don't worry, Sweetheart. I won't." Heather hugged her daddy. "You know. We may be having this same conversation in about ten years. Only it will be me telling you not to let the boys kiss you."

"Yuck! Daddy, I don't like boys."

"Good. Let's keep it that way for a while. If any boys come chasing you, you tell them you already have a sweetheart and he's the jealous type."

After dropping Heather off at Sara's house, he arrived at Angela's house at exactly 6:00. He couldn't help but feel nervous. He rang the doorbell. Angela opened it. She looked stunning. Her hair was curled and she was wearing a black dress and an olive coat.

She smiled as she opened the door.

"Hello."

"Hello. You look very nice tonight."

"Thanks, you do too." Their eyes met. For a second neither said anything.

"Shall we go?" she said.

"Sure. Our reservation is for 6:30." The two walked to Shawn's car. Shawn opened the car door for her.

They arrived at the restaurant five minutes early. The waiter seated them and handed each a menu. They both studied it for a minute.

"I remember they have a delicious chicken Alfredo," said Angela.

"Not to mention their lasagna."

"There's something I've been meaning to ask you and every time I see you I forget to ask," said Angela.

"Go ahead, ask anything you like."

"It's about your dad."

"That's fine."

"You said your dad was awarded the Navy Cross. I was wondering what he did to earn it."

"He was shot down over North Vietnam. His partner was severely wounded; in fact, he nearly died. My dad carried him out of the jungle to safety."

"Wow." The waiter came and took their order. After he left, Angela continued the conversation. "My dad's Marine division has a reunion every year. My dad has not missed one in thirty years."

"There's something about men who have been in combat together. They form a bond that is very strong."

"Usually the worse the combat, the stronger the bond," added Angela.

"That's very true."

"My dad remains close friends with all the men he served. How about your dad? Is your family still close to this man?"

"Actually, I've never met him. In fact I don't even know his full name. I only know his first name." said Shawn.

"How's that?" asked Angela.

"One time when I was eight years old, I heard my dad talking on the phone to a man he called 'Dave.' I distinctly remember that. Anyway, when he got off the phone I asked him who he was talking to. He said a friend of his. I asked him how they became friends. He said they had been in Vietnam together."

"Did your dad ever tell you his last name?"

"He may have, but I don't remember. Anyway my dad also told me his friend Dave lived in Washington, D.C. The night my dad was killed in the car crash, he was driving back from Washington, D.C."

"You think he went to see Dave?"

"He may not have gone there necessarily to see him, but I'm sure he would have looked him up while he was there. It's funny you should bring this up. After our conversation the other night, I was thinking how much I would like to find out who he is so I can talk to him."

"You'd like to pick his brain."

"He was a close friend. May I be brutally honest for a moment?"

"Of course."

"My dad didn't have many close friends other than family of course and this man Dave. I want to find out if my dad told him anything that might help me understand why he died."

"Well, if your dad was close to this man, surely your mother would know who he was." There was a pause. "Let me guess. She's not talking."

"Not a word."

"Do you think maybe your mom knows something and that's why she's not talking?"

"Possible but highly unlikely. I've spent hundreds of hours investigating this and turned up nothing. Unless my mom's turned into Becky Miller P. I. behind my back, I don't know what she could have uncovered that I haven't. No, I still think she's afraid of something. She doesn't want to look because she's afraid of what she'll find." Shawn's next statement was more to himself than Angela. "One day, I will find out the truth. I will find out what happened and then I'll be free of this nagging question, 'Why?'"

"You shall know the truth, and the truth shall set you free. May I give you some friendly advice?"

"Sure."

"Sometimes the truth can be an ugly reality. You idolize your dad. Are you prepared to deal with him not being what you've always thought him to be?"

"Maybe that's the real reason I want to know. Was he the kind loving father I knew him to be or was there more to him than met the eye?"

"Nobody's perfect, Shawn, not even your dad."

"If the worst thing he ever did was have a beer once when he was very stressed out, I'm prepared to live with that. I just want to know there's not more to it."

"Well, for whatever it's worth, I wish you the best."

"Thanks, lets talk about something more pleasant."

"Like what?"

"You for instance. Tell me about you."

For the next two hours Shawn listened as Angela told of her home in Tennessee, living in the same house her whole life, her brothers and sisters. Her dad was a retired businessman, her mom a nurse. Shawn was surprised to learn her mom had recently recovered from breast cancer. Angela told of her time in the Air Force, her college days and her first year as a teacher. After they finished eating, Angela said,

"I really appreciate dinner, Shawn. It was very good."

"Thank you. Would you like dessert?" Angela grinned.

"Actually, I was hoping you'd let me treat you to dessert and coffee." Shawn was a little surprised, but he was flexible.

"Okay." Shawn paid the bill and they left the restaurant. As they pulled out of the parking lot Shawn asked, "Where are we going?"

"Just a little ways away." They drove to the center of town and stopped at a little yogurt shop. Next door was a gourmet coffee shop. They both got a small yogurt and coffee. They sat down at one of the little outdoor tables.

"I have a confession to make," said Angela.

"Confession is good for the soul."

"Veronica told me about your conversation."

"I'm going to hang her up by her toe nails."

"Don't be angry. It's my fault. I passed by her room on Monday and saw you two talking." Angela looked down. "I eavesdropped."

"You didn't," said Shawn in mock surprise. "How much did you hear?"

"Enough to know that I was the topic of the conversation. I would have stayed longer, but Mrs. Jones was coming down the hall. After you left, I asked her about your conversation. She tried not to tell me, but I can be very persuasive when I want to be."

"And what did my dear friend Veronica tell you?"

"She said you were interested in me and that you wanted to make a good impression."

"And have I?"

"Yes, but you didn't need to."

"So what you're saying is I don't stand a snowball's chance in . . . "

"Oh I'd say you have at least a snowball's chance." She paused. "What I'm trying to say in my own sweet way is the feeling is mutual." Shawn looked at her with genuine astonishment.

"Really?"

"Shawn, do you suffer from an inferiority complex?"

"I asked my therapist that once."

"What did he say?"

"He said I didn't have an inferiority complex. I was just inferior." She laughed.

"That's another thing I like about you. I like a man with a sense of humor."

"So where do we go from here?" asked Shawn.

"You're the man. You're supposed to take the lead."

"Well, we're a little late for the prom."

"Too bad. I missed mine in high school," said Angela.

"Actually what I had in mind was us spending some time together getting to know each other and just seeing what happens."

Angela smiled,

"Sounds good to me."

"May I make one suggestion?" said Shawn.

"Sure."

"We should probably keep this under our hats. If we start

advertising that we're dating, people will start planning the wedding and naming our children."

"I wouldn't have it any other way."

"By the way," said Shawn, "Do you have any plans for tomorrow night?"

"Nothing I couldn't break."

"Would you like to come over and help me cook chicken cordon bleu?"

"You need help? You did a pretty good job last time."

"Well, I had a little help from Mom."

"She only offers help one time per customer?"

"Well, actually, she's the guest of honor tomorrow night. I can't very well ask her to help."

"I'd love to come, but are you sure your mother won't mind?"

"Not at all."

"Well, I'll try. I love to cook but I don't know how much help I'll be."

"I know a certain little girl who would take issue with that."

"Speaking of Heather, do you think she'll be jealous?"

"That's a good question. I don't know."

Shawn dropped Angela off at her house. He walked her to the door.

"I really had a good time tonight." She said.

"Me too."

"I enjoy talking to you."

"Thank you. It's nice to talk to someone about something other than Winnie the Pooh and Barney." The two gazed at each other for a moment. "Well, I'll see you tomorrow night."

CHAPTER NINETEEN

Saturday afternoon Angela came over at 2:00. She had 'tea' with Heather while Shawn went to the store to pick up some ingredients. By 3:00 they were working on dinner. It took a good two hours to make. Heather watched Veggie Tales. She came into the kitchen to get some milk. She gave her daddy a hug and went back into the living room.

"You know. I'm so jealous sometimes."

Shawn smiled. "She is a sweetheart, but you'll have your own children someday and you'll make a terrific mom."

"You misunderstand me. I'm not jealous of you having Heather. I'm jealous of Heather having you." Shawn's face registered complete incomprehension. Angela continued. "What I mean is, I'm jealous of Heather having such a loving father. You're not afraid to hug her or tell her you love her." Angela had a sad look in her eye. "I can only remember my dad telling me one time in my whole life he ever loved me and I can count on one hand the number of times he ever hugged me." She looked like she was about to cry. Shawn reached out and gently touched her arm.

"I'm sorry."

"Oh, it's okay. I know my dad loves me, but he comes from that generation of men who think that real men don't cry and don't show emotion because that's a sign of weakness." Angela's eyes watered slightly. "Remember, Shawn, your daughter needs to know you love her whether she's six or thirty-six, and don't ever be afraid to tell her so."

"You know Angela, losing the two most important people in the world has taught me a few things. Life is short, and not to take people for granted. I try to tell people I care about how I feel because who knows what lies ahead."

An hour later, while Shawn was putting the chicken in the oven, he noticed Angela taking a quick break and looking through his newspaper.

"So the space shuttle is supposed to take off tomorrow?" said Angela, looking at the headlines.

"It's supposed to. They say it will be the most publicized mission since the <u>Columbia</u> took off in 1981."

"Yeah, I heard about that. What's the big deal about it?"

"Well, there's a congressman from Florida who will be on board and they're also taking the first Israeli astronaut. In fact, it's the first time they've let a non-American citizen aboard the shuttle."

"Well, it should be interesting. What time will it launch?"

"I think around 6:30 in the morning."

Becky arrived at 6:00. Shawn had already called her earlier in the day to tell her there would be another guest at the table. Becky greeted Angela warmly. Becky had brought one of her best desserts, chocolate eclairs. She put them in the refrigerator and helped Shawn and Angela get the dinner on the table. Shawn turned down the lights, lit some candles, and put on some soft music. Over dinner Angela and Becky got to know each other. Once again Shawn was largely left out of the conversation, but he didn't mind one bit. Heather butted in a few times to say what she was thinking. Shawn made some coffee to go with dessert. That was one thing Shawn did very well.

After dinner the four of them played Candy Land. Becky left at 8:30. Angela didn't leave until 11:30.

Shawn woke up at 7:00 to the phone ringing. He groggily walked to where it was and answered it. It was Sara.

"Shawn, turn on the news."

"Why what happened?"

"Just turn it on." Shawn reached for the remote and turned the TV to NBC just in time to hear Tom Brokaw say, "For those of you just joining us, we have just received word that the space shuttle <u>Endeavor</u> exploded on take off today. We are now joined by Katie and Matt. Katie, tell us what happened."

"Well, Tom we have received an unconfirmed report that the space shuttle and its crew were the victims of a terrorist attack." Shawn dropped the phone. He quickly picked it back up.

"Sara, are you still there?"

"Yeah, I'm still here."

"Do they know who did it?"

"I was watching CNN and heard it might be al Jihad." Shawn hung up and listened some more. Tom Brokaw announced that the President would be addressing the nation at 3:00 that afternoon.

Al Jihad was without question the most feared terrorist organization in the world. They had a laundry list of terrorists' acts against the United States. The space shuttle was their latest and greatest. They blew up a federal building in Colorado and killed over 100 people. At least 60 Americans had died in embassy attacks in the Philippines, Indonesia, and Kenya. They had attempted hijacking American commercial planes. They had also blown a hole in an American aircraft carrier while it was in port at Yemen.

The leader of al Jihad was the most feared man in the world, Mohammad Azeim. He had been the FBI's most wanted man for 10 years, a record. They were currently offering thirty million dollars for him "dead or alive."

Mohammad Azeim was born to one of the wealthiest families in Saudi Arabia and indeed the world. His father was a billionaire from oil and it was his wish that his son would take over the family business. With that in mind, he saw to it that his son received the best education in business, economics, and politics and, of course, the Muslim faith. In 1973, Mohammad graduated from Eton, one of the most elite boarding schools in England. That fall he entered Cambridge where he graduated at the top of his class in business in 1977. He went on to Harvard and graduated in 1979 with a Masters in Political Science. It seemed that his father's wish would come true until Azeim's life took an unexpected turn. In 1980, he went to Libya to study Islam. While he was there, he was exposed to a very radical version of Islam. He was taught that since the Crusades, western civilization had existed for one purpose, to destroy the Muslim faith. He was taught that western culture and particularly the United States was the enemy of Islam and must be destroyed. The true followers of Islam must fight the enemies of Allah and, if necessary give their lives to defend their faith.

In 1981, Azeim started al Jihad. At the age of twenty-six, he was the CEO of an organization that would one day rival the great car companies of America, only his business was to destroy, not create. Azeim was as organized as Jack Welsh and as evil as Adolf Hitler. Many commentators said had Azeim turned his gigantic intellect to business, he would have been a billionaire in his own right. He was a brilliant organizer who oversaw everything, the purchase of weapons, recruiting and training, collecting money from sympathizers, and, of course, planning and carrying out terrorists attacks all over the world against the United States. He studied the United States, her strengths, her weaknesses, her psychology. He was slow and careful in his planning so that when he attacked, he would do it where it would do the most harm.

Azeim also had a genius for selecting people to work with him. He was very careful to whom he delegated authority. His first requirement was absolute and total loyalty to his radical Muslim faith. He had it. The men and women of his organization shared his fanatical hatred of the United States and all were willing to die to destroy it. His second requirement was that they be good at what they do. He had that, too. He had an amazing ability to find people from accountants to arms dealers who were willing to die for him. He also had everything compartmentalized so that on the rare occasion the Americans were able to interrogate a member of al Jihad, he usually knew nothing except his own mission. It would be all but impossible to shut them down. No more than ten people at any one time would know where Mohammad Azeim was, and most even in his own organization didn't know what country he was in.

Experts estimated that Mohammad Azeim's IQ was at least 160 if not higher and many believed he was the most organized CEO of any corporation in the business world or underworld. What was even more amazing than his intelligence or his organizational ability was how loyal his followers were to him and his holy war. The

CIA said there had been nearly 200 suicide bombings by his followers from Tel Aviv to Manila to Los Angeles. What had started out as a small network with a dozen recruits in 1981 had turned into the most feared group in the world with literally thousands of followers wholly committed to inflicting terror and sabotage on the United States. Today they had succeeded.

The attack was unusual in one sense. Normally, al Jihad tried to take out dozens if not hundreds of people in a suicide bombing. Today, seven died, only six of whom were Americans. However, al Jihad knew the pride America took in their space program and how devastating an attack on it would be. These six were some of the finest citizens of the United States. One was a freshman congressman from Florida, another a schoolteacher from Iowa, a doctor from California, two scientists from Harvard, and an Air Force pilot. The seventh member of the crew was an Israeli pilot who had become a hero during the Six-Day War. He was Israel's most decorated soldier.

Shawn was late for Sunday school that morning. Had he not been the teacher, he probably would have missed. He waited until the last minute to leave for church. Several people in his class were absent and he ended up not teaching at all. His class talked about what happened. Several women and even a couple of the men were in tears. They all knelt and prayed for their country. They prayed for the families and for the President.

During the morning service, the congregation sang "It is Well with My Soul." After they sang, Pastor Jim stepped to the podium. He asked for one minute of silent prayer for the country and the families of the Endeavor.

His sermon that day was from the passage "Come unto me all ye that labor and I will give you rest." His normally powerful voice was soft and reassuring. He sounded like a father comforting a frightened child.

Shawn stayed at his mother's house after lunch. He was glued to the TV. The news said the attack was definitely the work of al Jihad. What was truly amazing was how simple the whole operation was. The terrorists simply hijacked a patrol boat, smuggled a stinger missile on board, and fired from the harbor. They then set a bomb off on the boat and killed themselves. Four terrorists had single handedly shut down the mighty space program of the United States.

At 3:00 that afternoon the President spoke from the Oval Office.

"My fellow Americans, today our country has suffered a great tragedy. The space shuttle <u>Endeavor</u> exploded on take off. There were no survivors. What's even more tragic, this was no accident. We have learned that this is the work of al Jihad and its leader Mohammad Azeim." Shawn felt anger hit him. His country was under attack. How dare they? Heather tugged at him. She had been lying down in bed.

"Daddy, can I have a glass of water?"

"Just a minute, Sweetie. Go lie down and I'll bring it to you." Shawn's attention went back to the President.

". . .our thoughts and prayers are with the families of the crew. May God grant you grace and comfort in your time of grief." Shawn understood a little of their pain. ". . .rest assured those who committed this heinous act will be hunted down and brought to justice." The President talked for ten more minutes. He was always direct and to the point. Shawn liked this President. He didn't always agree with him, but he liked him. He was honest and direct. Shawn, as well as most Americans, trusted him. He was a good man. Shawn said a prayer for him that night.

CHAPTER TWENTY

That Monday, the space shuttle was all anyone talked about. The staff had a special meeting with Mrs. Jones before school began. She recommended that the teachers spend a few minutes talking about what happened, especially to the older grades, and reassuring the children that everything would be all right. Shawn didn't have to wait to bring it up in his class. His students were talking about it when they came in the class. Shawn spent thirty minutes talking about it with his students. A couple of his students asked if the terrorists would try to kill other people. Shawn was honest in his answer.

"They might. But remember we have thousands of people, policemen, soldiers, and others whose entire job is to make sure you are safe. These people work day and night to make sure you are safe. So you don't need to be afraid, because they are going to do everything they can to protect you. Not only that, your parents are going to do everything they can to protect you, and as long as you're in my classroom, I'm going to do everything I can to protect you." His children seemed satisfied with his answer. One little girl raised her hand.

"Mr. Miller, were you afraid when the space ship blew up?"

"I don't think I was afraid, but I was sad. I was sad for the families of the people who were killed and I must be honest, I was angry, angry that someone would hurt someone else like that." Another little girl raised her hand. "Yes, Amy."

"Mr. Miller, did it make you think of when your wife died?"

"I did think about it a little bit, but my situation was a little different. My wife was sick and I knew she was going to die before she did. The families of these people had no idea this would happen. Shawn heard someone at the door. He looked up. It was Angela.

"Class, excuse me for a minute." The mood of his class went from seriousness to hilariousness in two seconds. His students all in unison went "Ooooh, Mr. Miller."

"All right class, cool it." He walked to the door where Angela was leaning against the frame.

"Sorry to bother you but . . . "

"You never bother me."

"I was wondering if you would like to have dinner at my house tonight?"

"Sure, I'd love too. May I bring a date?"

"As long as she's not over four feet tall."

"So you know about my midget girlfriend." Angela playfully slapped him on his arm.

"What time?"

"5:30 okay?"

"Sounds great."

"By the way, I was listening to you just now. You handled this very well."

"Thank you."

When Shawn and Heather arrived at 5:30 that night, Angela was just taking the dinner rolls out of the oven. The rest of the meal was already on the table. It was roast with mashed potatoes and gravy, green beans, corn, and peach cobbler for dessert. The meal looked delicious and smelled even better. The three of them sat down and Shawn prayed.

"Angela, this is wonderful." Shawn said after his third mouthful.

"Thank you."

"Is it all right to talk about the recent tragedy in front of present company?"

"Yes, Heather asked about it, and we talked a little."

"We talked about what, Daddy?"

"Remember last night when you asked daddy what he was

watching? Remember what we talked about?"

"Oh yes. The mean people who live far, far away." She then looked at Angela. "But daddy says they won't hurt me because he won't let them."

"That's right. As long as you have your daddy, they won't bother you. Speaking of which, I know you follow the news more than I do. Have you heard anything more?"

"Just that it's definitely al Jihad and the President has said this is an act of war."

"Why do they hate us so much? What did we ever do to them?"

"They hate us because of who we are. They view us as a threat. Just remember, it's only a small group who are like this. I had several friends in college who were Arab Muslims. They were all fine, decent people. Remember this is the exception."

"Are you still going on your trip to Europe?"

"Of course. I wouldn't miss it for the world."

"Aren't you a little afraid? I'm not even going, and I'm worried about you."

"Honestly, I haven't even thought about it much since I learned about this whole thing, but now that I think about it. Yeah, I suppose I am a little nervous, but I'm still going."

"Daddy's going far far away, but he's coming back," Heather piped in.

"Daddy?" She looked lost in deep thought for a moment.

"Yes, Sweetie."

"If you're going far, far away, and the people who did the bad thing are far, far away, will they be mean to you?"

"No, Sweetheart, I'm not going to where they are, I'm going to a different place. In fact, one day when you're older, I'm going to take you far, far away. I'm going to a city where they don't have streets. Their streets are water and people don't drive cars. They ride around in boats." Heather's eyes got big. Angela joined in.

"What's more, the drivers of the boats, where funny hats and they sing as they drive you down the street." To Heather, this sounded like something from outer space. A city with no cars, and water in the streets and singing drivers.

"Daddy, can I go with you, please?"

"One day I'll take you."

"Can Miss Angela go?"

"Who knows? Maybe we'll meet her there." Angela laughed.

"Sounds like fun."

Shawn and Heather stayed at Angela's house until 8:00. Shawn would have liked to stay longer, but Heather's bedtime was 8:00 and she still needed a bath. By 8:30, Heather was bathed, brushed, and had selected her story for Shawn to read her, "If You Give a Mouse a Cookie."

The next morning, Becky called Shawn and asked if he and Heather would like to eat dinner with her. She cooked a wonderful meal and then asked Heather to go into the living room and watch TV. Shawn had an idea of what was coming.

"Shawn, I had a reason for inviting you over tonight."

"You mean, besides my charming personality."

His mother smiled. "You inherited that from me. I know you're a grown man and I certainly am not trying to tell you what to do."

"But . . . " There was a moment of silence. "It's okay mom."

"I know how much this trip your taking means to you. I know you love history and you want to see your friends again. If I were your age I would probably go, too, but this terrorist attack on the space shuttle has me worried. I wish you would reconsider." If Becky had any flaws as a mother, it was that she tended to meddle a little too much in her kids' lives and sometimes that irritated her children. This however, was not one of those occasions. Shawn could tell this was genuine motherly concern, and he was grateful for such a caring mother.

"Mom, I appreciate your concern, I really do, but I will be fine." Shawn put his arm around his mom.

"I know, but you're the only man I have left in my life and I want to make sure you're all right."

"I hope Todd and Jeff don't hear you say that."

"Oh, I love them, of course, but you're flesh and blood. I'm partial to you. There are some crazy people out there."

"I know. I'll be careful. To be honest, mom, I thought about canceling but I'm not, for two reasons."

"And they are?"

"One, these terrorists did this to scare us. They want us to live in fear. They don't want us to enjoy our lives. I am a little afraid. But if I give in to my fear, the terrorists have won. In a sense, they will have taken away my freedom. So I refuse to live my life in fear."

"And the other reason?"

"The trip's non-refundable."

"So when do you leave?"

"Two weeks."

CHAPTER TWENTY-ONE

Becky spent the rest of the week preparing for Saturday. A group of older ladies in the church, most of them widows, had started a prayer group. They met in a different lady's house one Saturday a month. This month it was Becky's turn. Each would bring food for breakfast and then they would pray. It had been started three years before, and it was the highlight of Becky's month. There were about a dozen ladies in all, though the numbers varied from month to month. Pastor Jim had often referred to them as the backbone of the church. While Amanda lay dying in the hospital, this prayer group had gone up there and prayed with her and had been a tremendous support to Shawn and his family. These ladies had a list of every member in the church which they divided up between them. Day after day every church member was prayed for by name. Many times from the pulpit, Pastor Jim used these ladies as an example of those who do what they can for God.

The lady who started the prayer group and unofficially headed it up was a dear friend of Becky's. In fact she was the closest friend Becky had in the world outside of family. Her name was Evelyn Pierce, whom everyone called Miss Eva. She was sixty-eight years old and had been widowed for ten years. She was without a doubt the most praying person Becky had ever known. Pastor Jim used to joke that "Miss Eva has a direct line with God. It seems like whatever she asks for, God answers." Each lady in the prayer group had a partner she was responsible to. Miss Eva and Becky were partners.

These ladies had the respect of the entire church. Often members would give these ladies requests to pray for at their meetings. They often shared burdens of their heart that they did not share with others. Becky had told them her concerns about Shawn's leaving and they prayed with her.

For breakfast the ladies had muffins, fruit, toast, and coffee. They always spent a few minutes eating and talking with each other. Several of the ladies were in their seventies and two were in their eighties. They did not get out often, and this was their chance to socialize and find out what was going on. After breakfast was over, the ladies made a circle in the living room. They spent a while sharing prayer requests. One request that was foremost on everyone's mind was the terrorist attack on the country. Along with that, Becky again asked prayer for Shawn who would be leaving for Europe in eight days. Other prayer requests were mentioned. People who were sick or in trouble. One member of the group tearfully told of her daughter who had just told her last week that she was getting a divorce. Another one's husband was going in for heart surgery on Thursday.

The prayer meeting started at 8:00. It ended at 10:30. Miss Eva was the last to leave. She stayed a few minutes to talk to Becky. She ended up staying for lunch. When she finally left at 1:00, Becky wished she could have stayed longer. Miss Eva was so kind and easy to talk to. She promised to pray for Shawn as he traveled.

CHAPTER TWENTY-TWO

It was the final week before Shawn left for Europe. So much had happened in the last few days that Shawn could hardly believe that his trip to Europe was nearly upon him. It was also the last week of school. Wednesday was the last day, and Friday was the last day for teachers. Shawn was leaving for Rome on Sunday night.

Through all he'd been through this year, Shawn had been blessed with a wonderful class. As any teacher will tell you, classes vary from year to year. This class had been his best yet. He had sent only two students to the principal all year, and that hadn't been until March. He would miss them even more than he usually missed his classes.

On Wednesday, Shawn and his class had an end of the year party. Many of the students' parents came. One of the parents brought hot dogs and chili, another brought ice cream, and still more brought sodas, chips, and cake. Many brought cards and presents for Shawn. Shawn had written a card for each of his students telling each of them know how much he appreciated them and would miss them. School dismissed at 11:00. Many of his students and even some of the parents gave Shawn a hug goodbye.

On Thursday Shawn spent the day in his classroom finishing his grades and cleaning his room. It felt strange sitting at his desk in an empty classroom. He was so used to having students talking and moving around that the quietness seemed odd. Mrs. Jones told them they could take lunch whenever they wanted, but they had to limit themselves to one hour. At 10:00, he went to Angela's classroom.

Shawn could tell she had been crying.

"What's wrong?" he asked.

"Oh, I was just thinking about my students. Some of them are leaving the district and I'm going to miss them."

"I know. Despite all the grief they give you sometimes, you just can't help but love them." Shawn walked over and tenderly put a hand on her shoulder. "Do you have any plans for lunch?"

"No, not yet."

"Would you allow me the honor of taking you out to lunch?"

Angela smiled. "That would be very nice."

"I'll see you in an hour." Said Shawn.

"Do you want me to meet you in your room?"

"Sure."

Shawn took Angela to Applebee's. The waiter seated them in a corner booth.

"So when do you leave for Italy?"

"Sunday night."

"Is your mom taking you to the airport?"

"No. My mom doesn't go to the airport to see people off. It's very hard on her emotionally to go to the airport. She prefers her goodbyes in more comfortable surroundings."

"So who's taking you to the airport?"

"Actually, I haven't worked that little detail out yet. I leave from Raleigh Durham, so I might ask Shannon to drive me down . . . no wait, I can't. She's leaving Saturday to visit Todd's family. I don't know. I'll find someone." Angela smiled.

"Consider 'someone' found. I'd be happy to take you to the airport."

"Are you sure? I mean, I'd really appreciate it but you would probably miss church Sunday night."

"That's okay. My pastor will understand."

"Well, thank you. I might be able to talk my mother into having you over for Sunday lunch. I'll need to leave by 3:00. My flight leaves at 6:30."

"I'm going to miss you while you're gone."

"I'm going to miss you, too."

"I'll be expecting a postcard. You know, I wonder if your mom would mind if I took Heather to McDonald's or to the mall one day while you're gone?"

"She'd probably welcome the break and I know Heather would enjoy it."

"Take plenty of pictures."

"I will."

On Friday morning, Shawn went to the office to hand in his grade book, attendance book, and report cards to Mrs. Jones.

"Have a wonderful trip." Lori Price said cheerfully.

"Thank you."

Shawn had brought Heather to school with him that day. She played in his classroom and read books while Shawn finished up his work. He left at 2:00. He and Heather went to the mall. There was a bookstore Shawn loved to visit. He and Heather had dinner there at the food court. After they were done, Shawn took her to the Disney store and bought her a shirt with Winnie the Pooh on it and a Tigger video.

On Saturday Shawn took Heather with him to Wal Mart, and bought a few items for the trip. He bought some snacks, a nice backpack to take as his carry on, a journal, pens, and a few medicines in case he got sick. He spent the rest of the day at the park with Heather.

When Shawn woke up Sunday morning, he realized this was his last night in his house for over two weeks. He had already packed his suitcase and his backpack. He dressed in his suit for church but took an extra set of clothes to change into at his mother's house. He put his suitcase in the car and he and Heather left for church.

After church, Pastor Jim stopped him.

"Shawn, I have something for you before you leave." Pastor Jim handed him three cassettes. They were the sermons he had promised.

"Thank you, Pastor Jim."

"I'll ask what you thought about them when you return." That was Pastor Jim's way of letting him know he was going to be checking on him.

Lunch on Sunday was baked chicken, potatoes, green bean casserole, and apple pie. Angela arrived a few minutes later than the rest. Her pastor was a little long winded that morning.

Shawn helped clean up and then went and changed for his trip.

He spent a few minutes with Heather. He read a story to her and played one game of Candy Land. He looked at his watch. It was 2:45, time to go. He went downstairs and started saying his goodbyes. He hugged Sara, Jeff, Ashley, and his mother. When Shawn hugged his mother goodbye, she started to cry.

"What's wrong, Mom?"

"You know me. I hate goodbyes. You just be really careful." She hugged him again.

"I will, Mom. Take care of my little girl." Heather was not going with Shawn and Angela to the airport. They felt it would be better if she said goodbye from more familiar surroundings. Shawn leaned down and hugged her.

"Goodbye, Sweetheart. I love you."

"I love you, Daddy. Daddy, when will you be back?"

"I'll be back before too long. You be good for Nonnie, okay?"

"Okay." Shawn and Angela got in the car and drove away. Shawn waved to everyone as he left.

When they arrived at the airport, Shawn pulled up to the curb and got out. Angela wasn't going into the airport with him. They would say goodbye here. Shawn got out his suitcase and threw his backpack over his shoulder. Angela got out and stood in front of him.

"Take care of yourself, Shawn."

"Thanks, I will. I'm going to miss you while I'm gone."

"You'd better miss me." She put a hand on his face and smiled.

"I'm so glad I've gotten to know you," said Angela. Shawn leaned over and kissed her on the cheek. They gave each other a hug. He grabbed his suitcase and rolled it toward the door. He turned and waved to Angela. She waved back. Shawn went to the counter. He was flying to New York first, then on to Rome. Fortunately, he had arrived early enough so that there was not a long line. He checked his luggage all the way to Rome. The lady asked for his passport and ticket.

"Would you like a window seat?"

"Actually, I would prefer an aisle seat all the way to Rome." The lady typed on the computer.

"Are you checking in just one bag?"

"Yes ma'am." She grabbed his bag and put it on the conveyer

belt. She typed a little more and then waited for the boarding passes to print out.

"Your bags are checked all the way to Rome. You have aisle seats on both flights. Here are your boarding passes. You are seated in seat 23C. Your flight departs from gate 15. Boarding time is 5:45."

"Thank you." Shawn looked at his watch. It was 4:30. He walked through the security check. They examined his backpack, frisked him, and sent him on his way. Security was much tighter since the terrorist attack on the space shuttle. Shawn walked past all the little shops in the airport. He went into a little bookshop. He browsed the newspapers, and finally went to the section that had bestsellers. In his rush to get his things packed, he forgot to pack a book to read. Oh well, if that was the worst thing that happened on this trip, it would be all right.

Shawn purchased the latest John Grisham book. He had seen it advertised and had wanted to read it. Now he would have a chance. He stopped and got a coke, then he walked to his gate, sat down, and began his book.

The flight to New York was smooth and quiet. After dinner was served Shawn read two chapters of his book. He would have read more, but he was getting tired. He had gone to bed late, woke up early, and now it was catching up with him.

He had barely dosed off when the pilot announced that they would soon be landing. Shawn felt a little irritated. He would have liked a longer nap. His next flight though, would give him plenty of opportunity. It was an eight-hour flight to Rome. Shawn looked at his boarding pass. His layover in New York was short, forty five minutes. He would have just enough time to get to his gate before leaving.

When the plane landed, Shawn waited a moment to let the other passengers off. He hated crowds. After the aisles cleared a little, he left the plane. The pilot and flight attendants were standing by the door to thank them for flying. Shawn smiled and kept walking.

As Shawn reached his next gate, the attendant at the counter was making an announcement.

"Would Shawn Miller, please come to the ticket counter, Shawn Miller, please come to the ticket counter?" Shawn walked up to the counter.

"Hello, is something wrong?"

"Are you Mr. Miller?"

"Yes, is everything okay?"

"We have a little problem. Apparently there is another S. Miller on the flight. The agent at the ticket counter gave him your seat."

"So, are there any more available."

"Well, Mr. Miller, this is your lucky day. All the economy class seats are full. The only seat we have available is a first class seat, so you'll be flying first class today."

"That's great." Shawn had never flown first class in his life. This would be a flight he would not forget.

The people in first class got to board first, along with handicapped passengers and passengers with children. Shawn noticed one man with a cane walking down the ramp in front of him. It was a metal cane and Shawn guessed it was aluminum or titanium. The man also had a bag slung over his shoulder.

Shawn was seated in seat 3C. The man with the cane was in seat 1A. His cane was on the floor. Shawn sat down in the leather seat. He wanted to see how far back the seats went. They lay down almost like a bed. A very attractive flight attendant put her hand on his arm.

"Excuse me, sir. Would you mind straightening your seat for take off?"

"Yes ma'am."

"By the way, may I get you something to drink? We have beer, wine, or soda."

"I would like a coke." The flight attendant poured a coke in a glass with some ice and handed it to Shawn along with a bag of peanuts.

"My name is Jessica. If I can be of any service, please let me know."

"Thank you, Jessica." Seated next to him was an older English gentleman named Mr. Smythe. Across the aisle was his wife Mrs. Smythe. Shawn offered to switch with her but the plane was starting to move. He promised to switch once the plane was in the air. Shawn felt excited. It hadn't really hit him until now that he was headed for a wonderful vacation. It was only eight hours away.

The plane went to the end of the runway and waited for five minutes before taking off. Shawn looked out the window and saw the landscape fly by. Soon the nose turned up, and the ground was disappearing from the window. Butterflies were dancing around in Shawn's stomach. He couldn't wait to get to Rome and see his friend Eric and start his trip. For a few minutes the plane continued its ascent into the heavens. It turned a few times and then headed off into the wild blue yonder. Shawn reached into his backpack and retrieved the Grisham novel he had started. He opened it to the third chapter and began to read. Something caught Shawn's attention. The man with the cane had gotten up and apparently was going to the bathroom. The seatbelt sign was still on, but the plane was starting to level out some. Shawn noticed that the two passengers in the seat behind him seemed to be watching him closely. Maybe they were traveling together. Oh well, when 'you gotta go, you gotta go.' Shawn did think it strange that he was taking his toiletry's bag with him. Why would a man need to brush his teeth ten minutes into the flight? Maybe there was some medicine or something in there he needed. Shawn's attention went back to the book.

Fifteen minutes later, the man with the cane came out of the bathroom. One of the men in the seat behind him went into the same bathroom, and when he came out the other man went into the same bathroom. By now Shawn was beginning to think this was unusual. The other bathroom was empty. Why didn't they just go in there? He didn't have time to think to much about it. Suddenly, without warning, the man with the cane began to go into violent convulsions. At once, the whole first class was on their feet. The man was shaking violently and fell to the floor. His eyes were rolling in his head and white foam was coming out of his mouth. The attendant was there almost immediately. Shawn heard one lady yell, "Oh my, he's having a heart attack." Another flight attendant said, "We need a doctor!" The man who was sitting in the row behind the man in the cane jumped up.

"I'm a doctor!" He went over to where the man was and began looking into his eyes and feeling his pulse. "I do think this man is having a heart attack. We must get him to a hospital quickly or he will die!" The flight attendant knocked on the cockpit door. A man opened it. The doctor jumped up and in one very quick motion pulled something out of his jacket, pushed the flight attendant away, and put a gun to the pilot's head. At that same moment, the man who supposedly had been having a heart attack and the man who had been sitting next to the 'doctor' both jumped up, pulled guns out of their coats, and were standing in front of the cockpit door. A cold shiver went down Shawn's spine. His heart started beating very fast and his palms were sweaty. Two thoughts raced through Shawn's mind at that moment. One, this was the work of al Jihad and two, Heather would soon lose a parent for the second time in a year.

CHAPTER TWENTY-THREE

The whole first class turned chaotic. Women screamed and cried. One man made the horrible mistake of trying to grab one of the hijackers. The hijacker put a gun to his head and blew his brains all over the floor. Shawn got a glimpse of the man's severed head and blood running from his body and he immediately grabbed the bag in the front of his seat pocket just in time to throw up. The woman across the aisle from Shawn passed out, and Shawn instinctively got up to help her. As he did, he realized this was probably a mistake. He was right. From behind him came a tremendous blow that hit him so hard he nearly blacked out. He fell to the floor in excruciating pain. He felt the back of his head and found that he was bleeding. As he lay on the floor, he looked up only to see the barrel of a gun aimed right between his eyes. In broken English he was told that if he moved out of his seat again he would be shot dead on the spot. With the gun pointed he painfully got back in his seat. As fate would have it, Mrs. Smythe had a few alcohol swabs in her purse that she always took when she traveled. She handed them across the aisle to Mr. Smythe who cleaned the wound with the swabs. Shawn hoped the terrorists would not care. The hijackers walked up and down the aisles screaming and cursing in both English and Arabic. One woman who was crying and nearly in hysterics was hit so hard that she was knocked unconscious.

A thousand thoughts filled Shawn's mind in a matter of seconds. He wasn't particularly afraid of dying, but the thought of never seeing his precious little girl again was terrifying. Then there was Angela, just when things between them were getting interesting. Where might things have gone? His mind turned to the terrorists. What were they up to? How long before they were all killed?

Shawn was right about it being the work of al Jihad, but he was wrong about them killing everybody on the plane. He was not going to die, at least not today. One burning question on many passengers minds was, how did they do this? It was common knowledge that al Jihad hated Americans, but how with the most advanced security system in the world had the hijackers smuggled guns onto the plane?

The answer was so simple it would almost be humorous if it weren't so tragic. First of all, the Americans had underestimated their enemy. They had underestimated the powerful motivation of hate. Americans have a history of underestimating their enemy. They underestimated the Japanese before Pearl Harbor, they underestimated the will of the North Vietnamese, and now they grossly underestimated the determination of Mohammad Azeim and al Jihad.

The terrorists had spent months planning the attack. They had specially made titanium bullets hidden inside the hollow part of the cane. The bullets were the same color and material as the cane and were especially made so that the head of each bullet fit into the end of the other. To an X ray scanner, it would appear as a titanium rod inside the cane to reinforce its strength. The springs for their gun were hidden inside pens in the terrorists coat pocket and the gun itself was made out of plastic. The pieces were disassembled and hidden inside regular toiletry items. Shaving cream, hair spray, and cologne bottles were especially disguised so that to all outside appearances, they were what they seemed. The bottles even sprayed shaving cream, hair spray or cologne. Hidden inside them, were the pieces of the gun. The three terrorists spent many hours practicing assembling and disassembling the weapons blindfolded until they could do it in their sleep.

The last part of the plot was of course the most tricky. Timing was essential. Once the plane took off, the terrorist with the cane would go to the bathroom and take the bullets out of his cane and hide them in the paper towel holder. He would also assemble his gun. The other two would go into the bathroom, assemble their guns, and take their bullets hidden in the paper towel holder. After all three had their weapons ready and hidden in their coat pockets, the terrorist with the cane would fake a heart attack. When the other terrorist posing as a doctor told the flight attendant the man was going to die unless they got him to a hospital, she would predictably need to tell the pilot to turn the plane around. Once that cockpit door was open, the rest was history. All three terrorists were trained pilots. The beauty of the plan was, they didn't need a flight crew. What was worse, the cockpit door was reinforced so that hijackers wouldn't be able to break the door down and take over the plane. The problem was, once the hijackers got into the cockpit, no one could get in there to stop them.

This time however, al Jihad's mission was not to kill the hostages. They needed them alive as a favor to a friend. Mohammad Azeim was a man without a country. The Saudis had denounced him and he lived on the run for twenty years. He finally found a home in Libya and a friend in Qaddafi. "Birds of a feather . . . " as the old saying goes. They were kindred spirits. Qaddafi, too, hated the United States and was very willing to host her number one enemy. Qaddafi though, also had problems of his own. The Americans had recently learned that he was building nuclear weapons and would soon have at least one operational. He had publicly denied it. The United Nations had sent in weapons inspectors who, of course, found nothing, but there were a few places they were not allowed to look. The President of the United States had stated publicly that Libya was strongly suspected of building nuclear weapons, and if the Libyans did not allow the weapons inspectors free access, the United States would use "any means necessary" to end Libya's weapons program. For several months there was debate after debate in the United States Congress, the United Nations, the TV talk shows about what the Libyans really had, who were the real warmongers, and on and on it went. The latest polls showed that 60% of Americans, including Shawn, agreed with the President that the Libyans could not be allowed to keep their weapons' program.

What no one knew, not the President, the Congress, the United Nations or anyone outside of Libya, was how close the Libyans were to the finished product. Their goal was not necessarily to start a nuclear war with the United States, which they knew they would lose, but rather to blackmail the United States back to the Stone Age. They would ask for billions of dollars, as well as terrorists released. Qaddafi figured he would be untouchable to attack by the United States because he could always retaliate against them. Qaddafi and his team of experts who were building the bomb only needed an estimated three months to have a working atomic bomb.

The problem was that the Americans, especially their President, were getting very impatient, and Qaddafi knew he would not wait three months to launch an air strike on Libya. The Americans had already done it once in 1986 when Ronald Reagan was President. What Qaddafi needed was time, not much, just enough to finish the job. He needed something he could bargain with. Something that would make the Americans, especially their crazy President hesitant to attack them. In a flash of inspiration, an idea came to him. Hostages. He needed hostages. A plane load of American hostages. If they could take a hundred or so hostages, they could dangle them in front of the Americans with vague promises of releasing them long enough to keep their President at bay. They could finish the job, return the hostages unharmed and have their bomb working.

It was brilliant. The Americans would never attack unless they felt diplomacy had failed. If they thought diplomacy was working, they would wait. Qaddafi might even release some of the hostages early in order to give the appearance of good will. Allah willing, he would hold the Americans back long enough to finish his nuclear weapons' program, and then he and not the Americans would be calling the shots.

For this job, Qaddafi turned to his old friend and fellow terrorist Mohammad Azeim and his al Jihad organization. It was time Azeim paid rent on his stay in Libya. He told Azeim he needed a plane load of hostages alive so he had something to bargain with. Mohammad Azeim was only too happy to oblige.

CHAPTER TWENTY-THREE

Seconds seemed like years. Shawn could only guess how many minutes he had left to live. Fifteen, thirty, maybe an hour at the most. Shawn began to pray. His thoughts were not mainly on himself. He thought first of Heather, then his mom and sisters and, of course, Angela. He was going to die. How would that affect them? Then he thought of the other 150 people on board the plane. What about their families? His thoughts were interrupted by the speaker. Shawn heard one of the terrorists speak, in heavily accented English, in a conversational and almost pleasant tone as if he were talking about the weather.

"Ladies and gentlemen, we represent the freedom group, 'Liberation of the Islamic faith."

"Better known as al Jihad," whispered Shawn to no one in particular.

"We apologize for the inconvenience . . . "

"Inconvenience?" Shawn whispered to Mr. Smythe. "He's got to be kidding."

"He doesn't strike me as the humorous kind," whispered Mr. Smythe.

"...as the American government has continued to kill our brothers, desecrate our lands, and destroy our faith, we have no choice but to defend our homes, families, and our faith. Like your forefathers, George Washington, Thomas Jefferson, and Patrick Henry, we too must defend our freedoms from a tyrannical and oppressive government."

"I don't recall Washington and Jefferson killing hundreds of unarmed civilians," Shawn whispered.

"You can't reason with these people. They are so brainwashed they'd kill their own mothers for the cause," said Mr. Smythe.

"It's not their mothers I'm worried about right now."

"...do as you are told. Stay in your seats, and you will not be harmed. Any attempt to stop us will result in the instant death of you and one other passenger."

The plane flew for several hours and Shawn was constantly looking at his watch. An hour went by, then two. The terrorists were letting people go one at a time to the restroom. On through the night the plane flew. Daylight came. Shawn looked at his watch. It had been eight hours since the plane had taken off. Strangely enough, Shawn fell asleep. He wasn't sure how long he slept but he woke up to Mr. Smythe nudging him.

"You'd better sit up young man. I think the plane is landing." Sure enough, Shawn could feel the plane descending. It took half an hour for the plane to finally touch down. Shawn wished he could look out the window and see where he was, but he couldn't. The terrorists had ordered all the window shades pulled down, even after the plane landed.

Once the plane was on the ground, the hostages stayed in their seats for another hour. Finally, they were told to get their passports and travel documents and walk out in a single file out of the plane. Anyone who attempted to resist would be killed. All but one did as they were told and no one said a word. Shawn's blood ran cold as he saw an old man who did not move when they were told to leave. He had not moved since the plane landed. A guard went over and kicked him. He fell to the floor, dead of a heart attack. "What a sad way to die," thought Shawn. He followed the British couple out of the plane. As he walked out he could feel the heat as if he were walking into a sauna. He descended the stairs and looked around. It was a desert landscape. He looked up to see a solid green flag over one of the buildings and he knew exactly where he was. "Welcome to Libya," he said quietly.

CHAPTER TWENTY-FOUR

After Shawn had left, Becky cleaned up the house, cooked dinner for her and Heather, and then put Heather to bed. After Heather was asleep, she went into her room, read her Bible, prayed, and then went to sleep. That night was a night she would never forget. She woke up at 4:00 in the morning out of a dead sleep and immediately knew something was terribly wrong with Shawn. She sat there in the darkness at first trying to ignore it but the feeling overwhelmed her. His life was in great danger.

Becky's mind went back thirty-two years. There was only one other time in her life she had this overwhelming feeling that someone she loved was in great danger. It was the morning of December 22, 1972. She found out later her husband, John Miller had been shot down over North Vietnam. She even remembered where she was. She was feeding little Shawn breakfast and suddenly she knew she needed to pray for her husband. Now that little boy was in trouble. She didn't know what. Maybe his plane was . . . no, no. She wouldn't allow herself to think that. The feeling was getting more intense. Shawn was in grave peril. The only thing she knew to do was call Miss Eva. She picked up the phone and dialed.

"Hello," came a surprisingly alert voice.

"Miss Eva," Becky's voice was trembling. "I'm so sorry to bother you at this time, but I need your help. It's Shawn. His life is in great danger."

"What's wrong? What happened?"

"I don't know. I don't even know for sure where he is. I just woke up a few minutes ago and I had this intense feeling that his life is in jeopardy. Call it 'mothers' intuition."

There might have been some who would have told her that she was imagining it, not to worry, and to just go back to bed. Not Miss Eva. She had known her friend too long to know that she would not have called if she did not firmly believe her son's life was in danger. She didn't need to be convinced anymore. Besides, she had four children and nine grandchildren of her own. She knew something about mothers' intuition.

"Have you called the other ladies in our group?"

"No, I'm not sure that I should."

"You should. You call Betty and Orphah, and I'll call the others. Don't worry, Becky, we'll put this in the Lord's hands. It's the safest place your son can be right now."

Becky hung up and immediately called the other ladies. She apologized for waking them up and explained why she called. Within an hour, over a dozen people were praying for Shawn Miller. Not one of them knew what was wrong, but none of them doubted Becky's feeling. Miss Eva actually came over to Becky's house to pray with her. After praying awhile, Becky and the others felt a peace that God was going to take care of Shawn. Becky still felt fear, but she knew her Shawn was still alive.

At 1:30 that afternoon, Becky heard a knock on her door. She opened it to find four well-dressed gentlemen and a lady. She immediately recognized the one in the middle. She couldn't believe he was standing at her front door. He was United States Senator Michael Graham of North Carolina, a very popular and, of late, very famous senator. He was young, only 46, energetic, well- spoken, and very good looking. He was often compared to John F. Kennedy.

"Are you Mrs. Rebecca Miller?"

"Yes."

"Mrs. Miller, may we come in? We need to speak to you." Becky opened the door all the way and motioned for them to come in. They all sat down. Senator Graham introduced his colleagues.

"Allow me to introduce, Mr. Jerry Elben, he's one of my assistants, and Miss Dana Carmichael. She's a counselor." He didn't introduce the other two men, but Becky figured out they were secret service agents.

"This is about my son, isn't it? What happened?"

"I'm afraid we have some bad news," said the senator. "Last night your son was on a plane from New York to Rome. I'm afraid it was hijacked by a group of terrorists from Libya. We don't know much. A few passengers were killed, but I don't think your son was one of them."

"He wasn't," said Becky. Her heart sank to the pit of her stomach. "How long ago did this happen?"

"About fifteen hours ago." Becky's eyes swelled up with tears, but she was remarkably calm under the circumstances.

"Who did this? Where have they taken him?" The senator's heart went out to her. He was a compassionate man.

"I honestly don't know. I only found out myself six hours ago."

"What are you going to do?"

"As near as we can figure, they will probably be going to make some kind of demand. They may want something in exchange for the hostages. When we find out what they want, then we can negotiate, but we just don't know yet. I do think for the moment they are safe."

"Are you going to give them what they ask for?"

"It depends on what they want. I promise you when we find out more, we will be sure to contact you immediately."

"I appreciate that," Becky said as she wiped her eyes with a tissue.

"Mrs. Miller, for whatever it's worth, I am truly sorry, and I promise you I will do everything I possibly can to see to it your son comes home safe," Miss Carmichael spoke up.

"Mrs. Miller, do you have any family we can contact?"

"My daughter is coming over in a little while. She's bringing her daughter and my other granddaughter with her. They went to the park and got some ice cream."

"Would one of them be Shawn's daughter?"

"Yes, her name is Heather."

Senator Graham only stayed an hour. Becky was surprised at how kind and sympathetic he was. He seemed genuinely concerned. He was almost like a minister. He even prayed with her. She could see why he was so popular. People were drawn to him. He was the kind of man you couldn't help but like.

Becky agreed to let Dana stay with her until Sara arrived with the kids. Dana was a psychologist who specialized in traumatic events. After the senator and Jerry left, Dana and Becky talked for a few minutes. Though Becky was still crying, Dana couldn't believe how composed she was. Suddenly the phone rang. Becky picked it up.

"Hello?"

Dana couldn't hear who was on the other line.

"Dave . . . " there was a few seconds of silence. "...no, actually I'm very glad you called. I just found out a little while ago." Becky began to cry again. "Dave, would you excuse me a moment." Becky put a hand over the receiver and spoke to Dana. "Miss Carmichael, I have an old and very dear friend on the phone. I don't mean to be rude but I would like to talk to him privately for a few minutes if you don't mind."

"Not at all. I'll just step outside and take a look at your beautiful yard."

"Thank you." Becky returned to her conversation.

CHAPTER TWENTY-FIVE

S hawn looked at the rundown airport where they had landed. There was a small terminal with several hangars and soldiers everywhere. Shawn looked around the perimeter of the airport and saw a heavily barbed wire fence with guards every fifty feet all the way around. At least forty soldiers escorted the hostages to one of the hangars. The passengers had to walk with handcuffs around their wrists. One man stumbled as he walked to the hangar. Shawn quickly ran and helped him up. A soldier came and angrily yelled at the two of them, and Shawn half expected to be shot right then, or att the very least to be hit again. The soldier did not do that though. He just pointed toward the line indicating for them to get back in it. Shawn wondered why the guard had not struck him. Was it because he was helping the man or maybe because Shawn expected to get knocked down again? He may have been playing a mind game. Shawn walked up to the man he had helped.

"Thank you, young man. You may have just saved my life," he whispered.

"No problem, any time."

"My name is Jack Warren, nice to meet you," he said as he awkwardly stuck out his cuffed hand.

"I'm Shawn Miller, it's a pleasure to meet you," He said as he shook his hand.

"Silence!" yelled one of the guards. Their conversation ended. They had already seen what happened to those who broke the rules, and they were not eager to see it again. When they got to the hangar, they formed a single line, and for the next three and some half hours, they were separated into two groups. One consisted of Americans, British, and Canadian citizens. There were about a hundred. The other group consisted mostly of Italian, but also Swiss, Portuguese, Polish, and Russian.

"What are they going to do with them?" whispered Mr. Smythe, who standing next to Shawn.

"Probably let them go."

"But why?"

"They don't have a bone to pick with them." Then he realized Mr. Smythe may not know what he was talking about. "It's mainly the Americans they don't like."

"Well, they probably don't care for us much either. Our Prime Minister has backed your President all the way."

"Our governments are a threat to them."

"Why take us hostage? That's what I can't figure out. They must want something, I just don't know what," said Mr. Smythe. Shawn's heart sank once again. He knew the President would never give in to the demands of terrorists no matter what. He had always agreed with that policy but now it was different with their lives on the line.

After all the hostages were searched, they were finally given water to drink for the first time in ten hours. They boarded two buses that had no windows. The buses had to be at least thirty years old and had not been well-taken care of. It was hot and dark inside. There was no air circulating in the bus and the only light was through a grilled window in the front. There were no guards inside the bus. They were not needed. The hostages each had their hands and feet handcuffed to a chain that connected to a metal rod on the floor.

Shawn was sitting next to a young African-American lady who was about his age. She was crying and Shawn always hated to see women cry.

"Ma'am, are you all right?" he asked.

"Yes, I'm sorry. I was just thinking about my children back home. Their daddy left us a couple of years ago and I'm all those children have got."

"What are your children's names?" he asked hoping to comfort her.

"I have a boy and two girls. My oldest is Jermaine. He's nine. Lakisha is six, and Quanisha is four, and when I think that I might not ever see them again . . . " She could not finish her sentence and she started sobbing.

"Your children are very fortunate to have a mother that loves them so much. I'm sure that's something they can never forget."

She smiled through her tears. "I'm Crystal, Crystal McGregor," she said.

"I'm Shawn Miller. Pleased to meet you, Mrs. McGregor. Are you Scottish?" Several people laughed, and he realized how dumb that must have sounded.

"I'm sorry, Mrs. McGregor, I guess I wasn't thinking. I've had a bad day." This time everybody laughed including Mrs. McGregor.

"That's okay. Mr. Shawn Miller. Tell me, are you Irish?"

"My grandfather was. I guess this disproves the theory about the Irish being lucky."

"So, a nice man like you has to have a wife and kids somewhere." Shawn looked at the ground.

"I had a wife, but she died almost a year ago. My little girl Heather is six."

"I'm sorry."

Most of the people were in their late forties or fifties. Some were younger though. They rode for an hour and sweat poured off Shawn's face. Several passengers became ill on the way over. All of them were tired, hungry and extremely thirsty. As they got out of the bus the brightness of the sun hurt Shawn's eyes. He looked around again and guessed that they were at some sort of army base. There were soldiers everywhere walking in and out of a number of buildings. There was a thirty-foot electronic fence with barbed wire and guard towers all the way around it. At least thirty guards escorted them to a large building at the center of the base. As they came to the entrance of the building, a handsome Arab in an army uniform came out the meet them. He spoke perfect English.

"Good day to you all."

"It hasn't been," thought Shawn.

"My name is General Omar Siad and you are now the prisoners of the nation of Libya." He paused for dramatic effect. "Each of your countries has wrongfully and illegally charged victims with crimes for which they are innocent. We have sent requests to each of your governments demanding that these innocent victims be released at once. If they are released, you will be sent home unharmed. If not, you will die. The nation of Libya will not be intimidated. In the meantime you will remain here. If you do as you are told, you will be treated well. If not, you will be punished."

Shawn felt butterflies in his stomach. He knew the United States would never give in to terrorists. Something didn't make sense in Shawn's mind. Anyone who knew anything about the President or his administration could tell you that he would not yield to their demands. If they did kill the hostages that would mean war. It sounded like they were cutting their own throats. Surely the Libyans weren't that stupid. Once again, fear began to creep up as he realized how hopeless his situation seemed.

For some strange reason, Shawn's mind wandered to Angela. If only he could see her again. He could picture himself going into her classroom, pulling up a chair and having a chat. He also thought of one of Pastor Jim's sermons on the twenty-third Psalm. "Yea, though I walk through the valley of the shadow of death, I will fear no evil for thou art with me." Shawn realized once again that his future was in God's hands. Why was it so difficult for him to accept that? God does not make mistakes. He would hope for the best and prepare for the worst.

They were marched into the building and Shawn figured it must have been an old military prison. There were enough cells for each hostage to have his own. They were all marched into their cells and told to wait there. Shawn looked around his tiny cell. Though not much, it was actually more than he would have guessed it to be. He judged it to be about ten feet long and eight feet wide. There was a bed, sink, a small mirror, and a toilet. There was a small empty shelf above the bed. Shawn took off his shoes and lay down on the bed. He was asleep as soon as his head hit the pillow. After two hours a guard woke him up. The guard gave him two complete sets of clothes, a toothbrush, toothpaste, a razor, shaving cream, soap, shampoo, a towel, two pairs of socks, and a pair of brown leather shoes. He was told that a guard would escort him to the shower in ten minutes.

Shawn examined the walls of the room. They were a dull gray color and the door was solid steel. There were no windows except a small window about four inches square on the door. Shawn looked out, but there was nothing to see. He took off his watch and wedding ring and laid them on the sink while he washed his hands and face. He was curious as to why they allowed him to keep them. He figured they would take all his personal items away. He was grateful, however, that they, for whatever reason, had allowed him to keep them. His wedding band was the only thing he had to remember Amanda by and then it dawned on him that he had not thought of her since he had been hijacked. The watch had been a Christmas present from Todd and Shannon. It was a silver Titanium watch that was worth over a hundred dollars.

Shawn found a list of "rules" and began reading them as he waited for the guard to escort him to the shower. They were allowed a five minute shower twice a week. Their clothes would be washed once a week. Their meal schedule was basic. They would eat three meals a day: breakfast was at 7:00, lunch at 12:00, and supper at 6:00. The guards would come and escort them to the dining area ten minutes before the meal, and they must stay one full hour. They were to attend whether they ate or not. Since meals and showers were the only times they would be allowed out of their cells, Shawn figured he had better get used to it, since he would be in his cell twenty hours a day. It was not the Waldorf-Astoria, but it was better than what he expected. Shawn knew what the Libyans were doing. They wanted to keep them in decent shape in the hopes that it would convince America of their humanitarian intentions.

The guard came and opened the huge steel door and escorted Shawn down the hall. The shower had a little area right next to it to change in. The guard stood outside as Shawn showered and changed. The pants were an olive colored pair that looked like army pants. He was also given a white long sleeved shirt. He put it on. He put on his black socks and what looked like tan hiking boots. This was his first shower in thirty-six hours so he actually felt good, all things considered.

CHAPTER TWENTY-SIX

The President called an emergency meeting of his cabinet on Tuesday morning. After reading the Libyans' demands to release certain prisoners, it took the President and his advisors all of ten seconds to realize they were bluffing. The Libyans couldn't have cared less what America did with these prisoners.

It took them another ten seconds to realize what the Libyans were really up to. They were stalling for time. They needed time to finish building their first atomic bomb, and the latest intelligence reports said it would take four months or less.

Oddly enough, the Libyans building a nuclear bomb was not what worried the President the most. Every credible intelligence report said the bomb was not operational, and even if it had been, the Libyans would have a difficult time delivering it. He had already put the entire military on alert. He had one aircraft carrier off the coast of Libya and another on the way. If he wanted to, he could order air strikes and wipe out their nuclear weapons' program before the day was over, but that would mean the instant death of more than one hundred Americans. Yet if he waited too long, he would be playing right into the Libyans hands, doing exactly what they wanted him to do.

Most days the President enjoyed his job. If the truth were known, he hadn't really wanted to run for President. After a long and very distinguished career in the military, he and his wife were looking forward to retirement. He had even bought a home in

Winter Haven, Florida where he planned to spend the remainder of his days, playing golf, hiking, and fishing. He even had plans to write a book. Then fate stepped in. Nearly eight years ago, his predecessor, a popular Democrat, was overwhelmingly reelected as President. The day after the election, the newly reelected President asked him if he would serve as Secretary of State. This took many people by surprise, including him. He was a moderate Republican, a veteran soldier, being asked by a Democrat to serve as the nation's chief diplomat. He agreed. He was an American first, a Republican second.

For four years, he again served his country with distinction. He traveled the world, spoke to many heads of state and earned the respect of people everywhere. His country loved him. He was a legend in his own time and by far the most popular figure in the previous administration. However, he kept his home in Winter Haven, Florida.

When his predecessor finished out his second term, he was asked by many people, Republicans, Democrats, friends, family, and total strangers to run for the nations highest office because they believed he could make a difference. He had never run for a single office in his life. He had not even been elected class president of his high school. He had said 'no' many times, but he finally had given in. It was not a sense of pride, or a desire to be famous that caused him to run. It was his duty. He felt he owed it to his country. He was a soldier, and a soldier never shirked duty. He loved his country. His country which had done so much for him now needed him. He sold his home in Winter Haven and was overwhelmingly elected President of the United States.

Most days he loved his job. He loved helping people, righting wrongs, making the country more free. Most days he loved the cheering crowds, the fanfare, the excitement on people's faces when they met him. Today, he would gladly give it all up and switch places with the janitor. Americans everywhere were afraid. They had lost the space shuttle just a month ago to al Jihad and now this same group had hijacked a plane and was working hand in hand with a country who was building a nuclear bomb that they would threaten to use on America. The President felt as if the weight of the whole world was falling on his shoulders. His country was afraid and looking to him for answers. One thing was sure though, he would not let them down. He was a soldier, and his country was at war.

CHAPTER TWENTY-SEVEN

Angela had a week off beginning with the week Shawn left. She would be working summer school the following week. Driving home from the airport, she came to a startling reality. She was in love with him, hopelessly in love with him. She had tried to convince herself otherwise. He was just a good friend that she cared about very much. Sure, she was attracted to him. His smile and charm were irresistible, but she wasn't fooling anyone but herself. It didn't make sense she told herself. He was several years older than she. He was a widower with a child. He was still in love with his wife. Why did she have to fall in love with him? There were plenty of other attractive single men around, why this one?

The hostage situation was all over the news by Monday afternoon. Angela was visiting her grandmother in Winston-Salem on Monday night. Her parents and she had just finished eating dinner. Her father was watching the evening news. The leading news story was the plane being hijacked. Angela was in the kitchen baking cookies with her grandmother and her niece.

"Angela!" her father called from the living room. "Come here, quick!" Angela came into the living room.

"Again we repeat, American Airlines flight 396 from New York to Rome was hijacked this morning. The passengers have been taken to Libya." The blood drained from Angela's face.

"What flight was your friend on?" her dad asked. Angela had an itinerary in the glove box of her car. She had planned to pick Shawn up when he returned, and he had made her a copy. She ran to her car, tore open the door, yanked open the glove box and grabbed the itinerary. Her heart sank as she looked at it. Raleigh Durham to New York- American Airlines 128, New York to Rome-American Airlines 396. She ran back to the house. The whole family was glued to the TV. No one had to ask when she came in if the plane hijacked was the one her friend was on. Her face said it all. She started to cry. Her mom and grandmother came over and put their arms around her.

"Sweetheart, I am so sorry," her mother said.

Becky didn't tell Heather right away when she came home. Sara, Ashley, and Heather arrived at Becky's house at 4:30 Monday afternoon. Becky asked Heather and Ashley to go in the back and play for a few minutes. Sara could immediately tell something was wrong with her mom. She had obviously been crying.

"Mom, what's wrong?"

"It's Shawn." Somehow she was able to maintain her composure. "Last night his flight to Rome was hijacked." Sara gasped.

"What happened to him?"

"He's still alive, but he's being held hostage in Libya."

"When did you find out?"

"About an hour ago." Becky looked down. "I have to tell Heather. She deserves to know."

"You're right mom. I'll take Ashley and go."

"No, why don't you stay here. I need family with me right now."

"Okay Mom, I'll do whatever you need me to do."

"Why don't you take Ashley out and talk to her? She's very fond of Shawn also. I'll talk to Heather."

"Okay." Sara called Heather and Ashley to the living room. She told Ashley she wanted to take her for a walk. When they were gone, Becky called Heather over to the couch.

"Heather, I need to talk to you." There was a seriousness in Becky's voice.

"Nonnie, I'm sorry." Heather was about to cry. "Are you going to spank me?"

"No, Sweetie, why would I spank you?"

"Because I broke your vase." Becky was taken a little by surprise.

"What vase did you break?"

"The one in your guestroom. I'm sorry, Nonnie. It was an accident." Heather was referring to a little blue vase Becky had in her guest bedroom. She had paid five dollars for it at a garage sale.

"It's okay. I know you didn't mean it. I need to talk to you about your daddy." Heather's big blue eyes looked up at Becky. Becky put her arm around Heather.

"Last night some bad people on daddy's plane took it somewhere besides where it was supposed to go. Your daddy's okay, the bad people haven't hurt him, but he won't be coming home when we thought he would. We need to pray that God will bring him back home to us soon." Now Heather started to cry.

"Will the bad people hurt my daddy?"

"We hope not, but we have to pray that God will protect him."

"Did daddy do something bad?"

"No Sweetie, your daddy didn't do anything wrong. We just need to pray that God will take care of your daddy."

"Will the bad people hurt us?" Heather was truly scared.

"No, they will not hurt us at all. We are safe here." Just then Sara came in with Ashley. She was talking on her cell phone to Shannon.

"...yes, let me ask mom."

"Mom, Shannon and Todd want to come over tonight. Is that okay? Todd heard about Shawn from one of his friends in the legislature."

"Tell them to come on over."

After Sara hung up she came over and hugged Heather. Seeing a little girl who had already lost her mother, and now crying her eyes out because the person she loved most in the whole world was now in danger was enough to melt the heart of anyone. Her little world was turned upside down.

"I went ahead and called Jeff. I hope you don't mind. He said he'll be over in an hour. He's with a client right now."

At 7:30 that night, Becky's daughters and their husbands were sitting around talking about what had happened when they heard a knock on the door. Becky went and opened it. Standing there were Uncle Henry and Aunt Bonnie. Henry hugged his sister as she wept. He kept saying over and over, "Becky, I'm so sorry."

"I know." She finally replied. "I know how much you love Shawn." Becky motioned for Henry and Bonnie to come in. They came and sat on the couch with the rest of the family. The girls each gave them a hug and Henry shook hands with their husbands.

"Are they doing anything to try to get him out?" asked Uncle Henry.

"We haven't been told much. I think they're waiting to see what the Libyans want. As far as I know they're all unharmed," said Sara.

"That's good. I listened to the President's speech this afternoon," said Uncle Henry.

"I missed it," said Jeff. "What did he say?"

Becky answered "He didn't say much except that the plane was hijacked by al Jihad, the hostages were being held prisoner in Libya, and the U.S. would do everything we can to get them out."

"Do you believe him?" asked Aunt Bonnie.

"I do. I really do believe he will do everything possible to get my boy home. If I didn't believe that, I would probably go crazy." She had a far off look in her eye. "I already lost one man I loved. I can't lose another."

CHAPTER TWENTY-EIGHT

After Shawn had showered and napped, the guard came in and shook him awake.

"Wake up. It's time to eat." He said in a gruff voice. All the guards here must speak English, Shawn thought. He wanted to go back to sleep, but he knew he did not have a choice. He sat up, put on his shoes and followed the guard down the hall into the dining area. It could have passed for a small run-down school cafeteria except, of course, for the twelve guards with machine guns standing around the room. They had no choice of food. They were given rice, pears, and some kind of beef stew. There were about two dozen tables which could seat six people. They were allowed to sit in any one of the seats, so Shawn sat with Crystal, Mr. and Mrs. Smythe, and Jack Warren, who were already seated when Shawn came.

"Shawn please come and join us," Crystal said in a feeble attempt to be cheerful. Shawn sat down and without saying a word he bowed his head and silently prayed.

"What are you thanking Him for?" said Jack.

"Well, for starters the fact I'm still alive. There were some who weren't so fortunate."

"Pray that we will get out of here alive," said Mr. Smythe.

"I already did. How are you doing so far Crystal?"

"I'm doing better, Shawn, thanks for asking."

"I don't understand these people," said Mr. Smythe. "They beat us and kick us around until they get us here and then treat us decently. Why?"

"They want us in good shape to exchange us or bargain for us," said Jack. "Will they really kill us if our countries don't hand over the prisoners?"

"I can't think of a single reason they would want to kill us. As long as we are alive, they can bargain for us. If they kill us . . . " Shawn stopped. He had everyone's attention.

"If they kill us what?" asked Mrs. Smythe.

"Well, if they kill us, Tripoli will become a big hole in the ground."

"I could see your President doing that," said Mr. Smythe, a bit enthusiastically.

"He seems like a decent man," said Mrs. Smythe. Jack spoke up.

"Yeah, I'll admit it. I've changed my mind about him. I didn't vote for him, and if I live long enough to get out of here, I'm not sure I'd vote for him the second time, but he's no coward."

"It's in God's hands whatever happens," said Shawn. "May I suggest we talk about something else?"

"Amen," said Crystal.

"I have an idea," said Mrs. Smythe. "Why don't we each tell a little about ourselves?" Everyone nodded in agreement.

"Why don't you go first, Mrs. Smythe?" suggested Shawn.

"Okay." She nudged her husband. "I'll let you do the honors."

"Well, I'm Charles Smythe and this is my wife Helen. We have been married for thirty-one years. I own a men's clothing store in London and my wife works at home. We have a son and a daughter. Our son is an officer in the Royal Navy and is stationed in the Falkland Islands. Our daughter is a school teacher in Sheffield." Crystal was next.

"I'm Crystal McGregor. No, I'm not Scottish. I'm a single mom with three wonderful children whom I love very much and I hope to see again." She choked up and could not continue.

"I'm sure you'll see them again." Shawn said as he patted her hand. Jack was next.

"Well, I'm Jack Warren. My wife died about ten years ago. I have a daughter, but I don't see her much. She's twenty-eight and lives in Richmond, Virginia." Shawn expected him to say more but he didn't. Then he realized it was his turn.

"I'm Shawn Miller. I live in Wilson, North Carolina. My wife died about a year ago. I have a daughter who is six years old named Heather."

After they finished eating, they were given thirty minutes to walk around a little courtyard and talk. Shawn made a point of introducing himself to as many of the hostages as he could. There were forty-eight all together. Most of them appreciated his friendliness and quickly introduced themselves. One man, an American, was very unfriendly. He seemed almost angry with Shawn. He did manage to mutter his name, Harry Corman.

They were all escorted back to their cells at 7:30. A guard came around at 8:00 and offered some old books for them to read. Shawn was surprised to see some old Louis L'amour books. He took two, "The Cherokee Trail" and "The Last of the Breed." He couldn't help but wonder how they got there.

CHAPTER TWENTY-NINE

The very Sunday night Shawn's plane was hijacked, Pastor Jim and Mrs. Hamilton left for Greenville, South Carolina. The twins were leaving that Monday for a week at a Christian camp in Brevard, North Carolina. They were spending the night with some friends from the youth group who were also going.

The conference in Greenville was for three days. After the conference, Pastor Jim and his wife were going to spend two nights in a cabin in the mountains of Tennessee. It was a much needed vacation for Pastor and Mrs. Hamilton. He tried to go to at least two conferences a year, though this was the first one he'd been to in a year and a half. This particular conference had more than sixty pastors from six states. He had been looking forward to this meeting for some time. Many of the men in attendance were personal friends of his, and all of them at least knew of each other by reputation. It would be a wonderful time of fellowship. Few people really understand the burden of being a spiritual shepherd. It had been a difficult year for Pastor Jim and his family. Shawn was not the only member who had suffered a loss. Two other members of the church had died within the last year, though both of them were older. One lady had cancer, another member had a stroke and several members had either lost jobs or had some family problems. Dealing with other people's problems began to take its toll on Pastor Jim and especially his family. His son had been suspended from school for cheating, and his wife had severe bouts of depression. People began to notice how tired and worn out Pastor Jim looked.

Fortunately, the deacons at North Hill Baptist Church understood that a pastor gives and gives and gives and eventually needs to have his batteries recharged. They had decided years ago to send their pastor to conferences or retreats for his and ultimately the church's own good.

The pastors had just finished their first afternoon session. They were taking a ten minute coffee break. Pastor Jim was with a group of other pastors who were all laughing at a golf joke that one of them had told when the manager of the hotel walked up.

"Excuse me, is one of you Reverend Hamilton?"

"I'm Pastor Jim Hamilton."

There was a serious look on the man's face.

"We have an emergency call for you."

The mood of the group changed immediately.

"If you'll follow me, sir."

The men all assembled for the next session entitled "Church Finances." The speaker was Dr. Bill Jones, the head of the conference. He had been preaching for over fifty years. During that time he had been a missionary to Africa, South America, had pastored two churches, and had just retired from being president of Southwestern Baptist College. He was also a close personal friend of Pastor Jim.

"Gentlemen, by now you've all heard about the great tragedy our country is facing. I'm afraid this time its hit a little closer to home. Our dear friend Pastor Jim Hamilton has just learned that one of the hostages on that plane is a member of his congregation. He's not with us right now. He is leaving immediately to go back and be with the family. He has asked us to remember the young man in prayer. We will continue this session, but before we do, let's all take a few moments and pray silently for our country, our President, and the Miller family at this time."

Pastor Jim and Mrs. Hamilton did not get back to Wilson until 7:45 that night. They drove straight from the airport to Becky's house. It was almost 8:00 before they arrived. Becky opened the door. She shook Pastor Jim's hand and hugged Mrs. Hamilton. Tears rolled down both cheeks as the women embraced.

Seated in the living room were Shannon, Todd, Sara, Jeff, Henry, and Bonnie. Heather and Ashley were in the back bedroom sleeping. Pastor Jim went around the room greeting each person and giving them his condolences. Becky felt a little uneasy when he finally got around to Henry. The two men had only spoken to each other a couple of times. Pastor Jim warmly shook his hand.

"Henry, I'm so sorry."

"Thank you, Pastor . . . uh Jim."

"Shawn sure thinks a lot of you," said Pastor Jim. "He talks about you all the time." At that point, Henry broke down and cried. Becky looked at her brother in utter amazement. She had not seen Henry cry in thirty years. Bonnie was the most surprised of all. She had rarely seen her husband cry, and never like this. Pastor Jim gently put a hand on his shoulder.

"Whatever else I may have done, I truly love that boy." He was sobbing like a baby.

"He knows it. He loves you like a father. He's told me so many times."

This was a sight Becky and her family, and especially Bonnie, never thought they would see. Their Henry, sitting on a couch, pouring his heart out to a black pastor.

Pastor Jim only stayed an hour. He spent some time reading scripture and then prayed with the family. His visit was like a breath of fresh air for Becky. Again she felt a peace that her son was in God's hands.

Two days of having her son as a hostage in another country was physically and emotionally draining for Becky. She tried to stay strong for Heather's sake. Though only six, Becky knew Heather was old enough to know something was wrong with daddy. Last night she heard her crying in her room. She went in to check on her. "I miss Daddy" was all little Heather could say.

The next morning Becky was making breakfast for herself and Heather.

"Nonnie, can I go get my doll? I left it in on the porch swing."

"Sure Sweetie, go ahead." A few seconds later Heather came running back in with the newspaper in her hand.

"Look, Nonnie. It's Daddy! It's Daddy!" Becky looked at the

front page of the Wilson Tribune. The headline was LOCAL TEACHER TAKEN HOSTAGE. There was a small color picture of Shawn. She recognized the picture as one of his pictures taken for the yearbook last year. There was her boy, wearing a blue shirt and yellow tie and smiling. She read the article about Shawn. It was well written. The article told a little about his background. He had graduated from Wilson High School, gone to college at the University of North Carolina, and had taught for ten years. It did mention that he was a father of one and that he was the son of Mrs. Rebecca Miller who was also a teacher. She felt a sense of pride sweep over her as well as sorrow. She turned away so Heather wouldn't see her eyes moisten. Her son was in danger, but at least everyone knew whose son he was.

All the next week, Pastor Jim saw to it that different people checked on Becky and Heather. He or his wife called her every day to see if there was anything they could do to help and to let her know that they were still praying for her and the family and especially Shawn. He and the deacons had arranged for an all night prayer meeting on Friday night. Starting at 10:00 p.m. and going until 6:00 a.m. members, and even some non members, agreed to come for one hour blocks. Each hour one deacon would be in charge of the group for that hour. Pastor Jim had divided the church up, and each deacon called during the week to make sure that everyone who said they were coming would come. Well over half the church had committed to at least one hour of prayer on Friday night and many had committed for more than that.

At 9:45 on Friday night Pastor Jim showed up to begin preparing for the prayer meeting. He would lead the 10:00 to 11:00 group. They would start out singing a few hymns and he would give a short devotional on prayer. They would then divide up into different groups and go to different rooms to pray. Most people got there a few minutes early and were sitting quietly talking to each other before the meeting started. At exactly 9:59 though, everyone's eyes were focused on who walked through the door. Henry and Bonnie Evans came in. He came down the aisle and sat next to Becky, Sara and Jeff. The first person to greet him was Pastor Jim. He walked up, shook Henry's hand and told him he was glad he had come.

When the groups separated, Henry and Bonnie stuck with the family. Becky didn't feel like going to church. In fact she was strongly tempted not to. She was worried people would come up to her and ask her questions that she did not want to answer, and she might not be able to keep her emotions in check. However, Pastor Jim had graciously passed the word around the church not to ask too many questions about the situation. A simple note or word of comfort was all she really needed. He did ask her if it was all right for him to mention it from the pulpit.

CHAPTER THIRTY

On Sunday morning, the congregation at North Hill was unusually quiet as they came into the service. There was some sense of disbelief that one of their own was involved in the international crisis. Pastor Jim began his sermon by dealing with the issue.

"Dearly beloved, I know by now all of you are aware of the crisis our country is facing. You are also aware that one of our own friends and fellow members, Shawn Miller is one of the hostages. It is a shame that those who do not love God and his word have set themselves to destroy all that we hold sacred and dear. This has taken us all by surprise, and maybe some of you are not sure how to deal with this, but I will remind you that God was not taken by surprise. The Scriptures tell us that all things work together for good to those who love God and are called by Him. Even in a tragic event like this, God can bring good. Let us pray for our dear brother and his family. The Scriptures also tell us that the effectual fervent prayer of a righteous man availeth much. Shawn is under the watch care of God. There isn't a terrorist, or dictator in the world, there isn't a demon in hell who can harm a child of God unless He allows it. I will remind you that when life seems the darkest, that is when the Lord does some of his greatest miracles. Let us commit our ways to the Lord. It is our responsibility as a church to pray and to care for those in need. With that in mind, I would ask each of you to commit before the Lord silently right now, every day to pray for all the hostages, their families, and let us also remember our President and other leaders who must make some very difficult decisions. We stand in need of prayer."

Pastor Jim went on and preached his sermon which also dealt with prayer.

CHAPTER THIRTY-ONE

Shawn woke up and actually felt refreshed. It had been five days since he had been taken hostage. He got dressed, brushed his teeth, washed his face and combed his hair. He had already read two chapters of "Last of the Breed," so he just sat quietly and thought about his family, Heather, and especially Angela. He figured by now the news had spread around the world. He wondered how his family was taking it, and if anyone had told Heather or not.

Shawn heard the rattling of keys and then the door opened. Do these people ever knock? He wondered. He walked to the dining room and was met in line by Jack Warren.

"Good morning, Shawn."

"Good morning, Jack." They walked through the line together. There were eggs, rice and sausage. The food was not bad so far, but it was not good either. Shawn had made up his mind that he would be as positive as he could and he would try to cheer other people up. He went and sat next to Harry Corman who was, of course, alone. Jack did not follow. Most of the people stayed away from Harry. They had enough to be depressed about, and they did not need any help from him.

"Mind if I sit here?" Shawn asked.

"Seat's empty isn't it?" snapped Harry. Once again Shawn bowed his head and prayed silently.

"Are you religious or something?" Harry asked coldly.

"I always pray before I eat."

"I was brought up Methodist, but I don't believe in God anymore. Organized religion is the reason we are here. Muslims, Christians, Jews, it makes no difference."

This was not how Shawn wanted to start his meal, but he was not one to back down, especially when it was something he strongly believed in.

"You don't believe in God."

"No, I don't, and if you had any sense, you wouldn't either. Look at the mess the world is in today, not to mention the one we are in. There's fighting, killing, disease, do you really think a God who loves us would do this to us?"

"Harry, God did not bring all that into the world, we brought it on ourselves. Besides if I were you, I would be very careful what I say about God."

"Why's that?"

"Because He may be the only friend we have left."

"I suppose you think God will get us out of all this?"

"I know He can, but I don't know if He will. Consider this, if He doesn't get us out, then we're all going to be seeing Him very soon. You may want to keep that in mind."

"I'm sorry. I know you are just trying to be nice but I have had a rotten life and God, if there is one, has never done one thing for me and now for it to end like this, well, it stinks. I don't know what these people are up to, but you know as well as I do that our country will never give in to their demands, and when they don't we are all going to be killed."

"Tell me something, what would it take for you to change your opinion about God?"

"A miracle."

"Suppose God did rescue you in spite of your attitude toward Him. Would you change then?"

"I have not been to church once since I was an adult and that's thirty years now. If there is a God and He 'delivers us' as you call it from this mess, I will go back to church."

"Harry, I'm going to pray that we get rescued just so you have to keep your promise."

"You're going to pray for me. Do you really think it will do any good?"

"Will it do any harm, Harry?" Shawn was finished with his breakfast and turned to leave.

"By the way Harry, you are wrong about God not having ever done anything for you."

"All right smart guy, what did God ever do for me?"

"He sent his son Jesus Christ to die for you. Whether or not you want to admit it, God loves you."

"Oh great, it's bad enough to be taken hostage by terrorists, I get to listen to a religious nut." Shawn went over and sat next to Jack who had also finished his breakfast.

"So how was breakfast?" asked Shawn.

"Lousy. I overheard some of your conversation. Sounds like we have an atheist in the crowd. That's too bad. We need all the help we can get," Jack said as he nodded upward.

"You know, Jack, I've met only a few atheists in my life and they are the most miserable people I know."

"Well, who knows? Maybe the Lord will free us all just to prove you right."

After breakfast they were all escorted back to their cells. Shawn walked back to his cell and brushed his teeth. He had four hours until lunch. He knew that sitting in his cell for twenty hours a day would get old very quickly. He had to find something to do. He decided to do exercises. Since he only showered twice a week, he would do his heavy exercises right before he showered and do light exercises the other days. Today he would start with some push ups and sit ups. Shawn had exercised regularly in the past. Amanda had also been into exercising. At one point she was training for a marathon. Shawn could never keep up with her.

Shawn decided to sit with some new people at lunch. He had counted twenty-six men and twenty-two women, so there were plenty of people to talk to. Shawn had judged that out of forty-eight hostages, only nine were probably younger than him. Two of the younger people that he struck up a conversation with were Brian and Renee. Renee was a beautiful girl from Oklahoma who could not have been older than eighteen or nineteen. Brian was a college student in his early twenties. How odd that love should blossom in the least romantic place on earth. Brian and Renee had met on the plane before the hijacking and enjoyed each others company. Since they only had three hours a day to even talk to each other, they were making every minute count. Brain and Renee liked having Shawn around because he was closer in age than most of the other hostages.

CHAPTER THIRTY-TWO

It had been one agonizing week since that horrible moment when Becky woke up with the awful realization once again that a man she loved was in great danger. She hadn't had a good night's sleep since. It was starting to wear on her. She finally decided she needed to be busy doing something. Not working this summer had its advantages and disadvantages. On the one hand it gave her time with Heather, her daughters, and their families at a time when they all needed each other. On the other hand, she had too much time to think. She needed a project. Something that would take awhile for her to do. An idea came to Becky. It was something she had wanted to do for some time now and never really got around to doing it. She wanted to go through all the old photos of her parents and grandparents, her husband's family, her children, her grandchildren, and make several scrap books. She would mount the pictures, put nice labels underneath and even try to put them in some order. To do it the way she wanted would take weeks. She had two trunks in her attic full of pictures.

She decided to get organized that Monday. Shannon, Sara, Jeff, and Ashley were over at her house that afternoon. Todd was coming later. Becky asked Shannon, who like her brother loved family history, to go through the trunks in the attic and start dividing up the pictures into groups. Becky needed to go to the store and get several things to begin the project. She needed photo albums, mounting paper, exacto knives, and labels. She was also going to the store to get some things for dinner. She wanted to have everybody over that night so that they could at least help her get started on her project.

Sara and Jeff were out in the yard watching Heather and Ashley play on the swings. Shannon was up in the attic going through photo after photo. She really enjoyed this. She was an amateur photographer herself. She had made ten piles of pictures. She found photos that went all the way back to the early 1900's. She found several photos of her great-grandfather who fought in World War I. It amazed her that she had never seen some of these photos before.

There were hundreds, maybe even thousands of photos to go through. This really would take a long time. Shannon took her time. She found herself spending time just looking at the pictures. Many of them were people she didn't recognize.

The pictures she spent the longest looking at were the ones of her father. Shannon and Sara had turned six a few months before the fatal crash that took their father's life. She only had a few childhood memories of her dad, but they were good memories. He had been a kind and loving man. Shannon more than the other two children absolutely worshipped her dad. He was a loss that had never been replaced. It had been hard growing up without a dad. Many times as a teenager and even as an adult she would have given anything to have a loving father to talk to and share her heart. Unlike Shawn, both Shannon and Sara were never very close to Uncle Henry. They loved him, but he wasn't Daddy. Fortunately, the Lord had blessed both girls with wonderful, caring husbands.

There was one photo in particular that caught Shannon's eye. She had never seen it before. It was a picture of her dad in Vietnam. He was standing on the flight deck of an aircraft carrier next to a tall, handsome black man. Behind them was a fighter plane, presumably the one they flew. Both men were in their flight suits and smiling at the camera. It looked like they had just finished a mission and were happy to be back. It wasn't her dad though that had her attention, it was the man standing next to him. She looked at the name on the flight suit. Connors. Shannon looked at the face. She looked back at the name. Her eyes grew wide. She spoke out loud to no one.

"Oh my gosh! It can't be him."

Sara would never forget Shannon's reaction that day, not in a hundred years. She was pushing Ashley while Jeff was pushing Heather on the swings. They could hear Shannon yelling before she ever left the attic. She came tearing out of the house waving a picture and screaming like a banshee.

"SARA! SARA!" She came running over to them. "LOOK WHAT I FOUND!" Shannon was so excited, she could hardly breathe.

"Shannon, settle down. Take deep breaths and . . ."

"Don't 'deep breaths' me. Look at this picture!" Sara had always been of the opinion that her sister was at times a little too animated for her own good.

"All right. Settle down and I'll look at it." Sara took the picture and looked at it.

"It's a picture of Daddy in Vietnam. He was a Navy pilot and a hero. We've known that our whole lives." Shannon slapped her sister lightly on the arm.

"No silly! I know Daddy was a pilot, look at the man standing next to him." Both Sara and Jeff looked at the photo.

"That's interesting. I didn't know dad's partner was black. Not that his race matters of course. Come to think of it, I've never seen a picture of his partner until now. That's what all the excitement was about. Dad's partner was black. I hate to break this to you, Shannon, but the military was integrated in 1947. This probably was not that uncommon." Shannon rolled her eyes.

"Sara, look at the name on his flight suit." Sara read the name out loud.

"Connors." Shannon continued.

"Don't you remember when Shawn was in college and we were trying to find out who dad's partner in Vietnam was? The man whose life he saved. Shawn told me he once heard Dad talking to this man and he called him 'Dave'."

Sara spoke again. "Dave Connors." Both Sara and Jeff gasped.

"How many black Navy pilots named David Connors could there have been in Vietnam?" said Shannon. Jeff spoke this time.

"And who were shot down in 1972." They all looked at the picture once again.

"It's him. Thirty some years younger, but it's him. Same eyes, same smile." said Sara.

"We need to have a chat with Mom when she comes home."

Becky arrived an hour later. The house was unusually quiet. She came into the living room with two bags of groceries. She noticed Sara, Shannon, and Jeff all sitting quietly on the couch looking at her. Sara spoke with a slight chill in her voice.

"Ashley, you and Heather go in the back and play."

"Okay Mommy." They were getting used to it. It took Becky two seconds to realize something was wrong. She put the groceries on the counter.

"Something's happened to Shawn."

"We haven't heard anything about Shawn."

"We need to talk to you about this." Shannon handed her the picture. Becky looked at it.

"It's an old picture of your dad from Vietnam."

"The man standing next to Dad, the man named Connors. Is his first name David?" Becky looked down at the photo and then at her daughters.

"Yes, his first name is David and yes, he's who you think he is."

"Is he the one who was shot down with dad?" asked Sara.

"Yes."

"So this is the man whose life dad saved?"

"Yes, he's the one." There was silence for a moment.

"Mom, why didn't you call him?" said Shannon. If Daddy saved his life surely he could do something now to help Shawn. It's the least he owes us."

"I didn't have to call him. He called me."

"He called here?"

"That's right. Last Monday. He told me they were doing everything they could. He told me the most difficult day of his life was when he found out the son of his best friend and the man who had saved his life was now in the middle of the hostage crisis. He told me if he thought he could get away with it, he would offer to exchange himself for Shawn. And do you know I believe him? I really do believe him."

"Why didn't you tell us?" asked Sara.

"Because he told me not to. He told me not to talk to the media or say anything at all. If the hostages found out Shawn's connection to him, it would put his life in danger. He told me not to tell even you at least not for a while. Since he's one of the few people who might be able to help Shawn, I decided to do what he asked."

"You did the right thing, Mom," said Shannon.

"Mom, can I ask another question?" asked Sara.

"Go ahead."

"You've known him for many years right?"

"Ever since your father saved his life."

"Why didn't you tell us about him? Why didn't you tell us he was the one whose life dad saved?" They all looked at Becky. She was slow and deliberate in her response.

"Girls, I can't tell you why. Call it mothers' intuition, but I really felt it was best that you not know of his relationship with your dad."

"You don't trust us, is that it? You thought we might shoot our mouth off and expect him to repay us for what dad did." Said Shannon.

"No, that's not it at all. I had my own reasons which I don't think I could explain even if I tried. I'm sorry girls. Maybe I should have told you. I hope you're not upset." Shannon and Sara looked at each other.

"Mom, we're not upset. You probably did the right thing. It was probably best that we did not know."

"I will ask one thing. You cannot tell anyone. Shannon, I know you're going to tell Todd, but you must not tell anyone else."

"Okay," both girls said at once.

"Sara, Shannon, I'm very serious. Remember Shawn needs all the help he can get."

CHAPTER THIRTY-THREE

The President rubbed his eyes wearily. He was tired. The last month and a half had probably taken ten years off his life. Losing the space shuttle, then the hijacking of a plane load of Americans, not to mention that the stock market had fallen over a thousand points in that time took its toll. The country was terrified and looked to him for answers. It was the worst crisis the country had seen since the Cuban Missile Crisis. As if that wasn't bad enough, he had an election coming up and the latest polls showed him in a dead heat with his Democratic opponent Senator Michael Graham of North Carolina. Senator Graham had been very critical of everything the President had done as if he could do any better. The President was a career military officer, Senator Graham had been in junior high during the Vietnam War and had never served in the military a day in his life. He was, however, a formidable candidate and the President knew he'd better take him seriously because the American people sure were. Just last week he had been named one of the fifty most beautiful people by 'People' Magazine. The media loved to show him riding horses, hiking, running, and doing all the manly things. If the election were a beauty contest, he would win hands down.

The President had a fund raiser to go to tonight, but he had no desire to go. He would never tell anyone this, but after the last two months, he would almost be glad to hand over the country and all its problems to Senator Graham. With his Presidential pension and his military pension, not to mention all the speaking engagements he would get, he could live quite well. He and his wife could buy another home in Winter Haven, Florida and he could live out his days playing golf, fishing, and fine dining. He would welcome quiet evenings with his wife. Win, lose, or draw though, he was not going to let Libyans or al Jihad disgrace his country and threaten his people. He would finish the job. It was his duty, and he could do nothing less.

Right now, he was meeting with his national security advisors in the White House. At the meeting was the Secretary of State, Secretary of Defense, the Joint Chiefs of Staff, the CIA director and the Vice President. Addressing the group was National Security Advisor Dr. Elizabeth Rhodes. She was unquestionably the smartest person in the room and the President's closest advisor. She had earned a Ph. D. in political science from Harvard at the age of twenty-six and had earned another one from Stanford in International Business. She was also the first African-American woman to hold the position of National Security Advisor. Her news today was not good. They were looking at a satellite picture taken only four hours before.

"Mr. President, this is where the hostages are being held, at this base. General Siad is in command and has personally overseen their imprisonment."

"Remind me again, what is his relationship to Qaddafi?" said the President.

"He's his nephew. How else would a thirty-five-year-old become one of the highest ranking officers in the country?" Dr. Rhodes continued.

"Mr. President, we know that General Siad met with Mohammad Azeim one week before the plane was hijacked. We assume their meeting was to iron out the details of the hijacking."

"Where is Azeim now?" This time the head of the CIA spoke.

"To be truthful, we don't know. The man is like a ghost. We have interrogated two members of al Jihad. They were handed over to us by Morocco. They don't know. Very few even in al Jihad know where he is. He moves around so much, even if we captured one of his operatives, and he told us where Azeim was, by the time we got our soldiers there, he would be gone. He probably left Libya before the plane landed. He has probably moved to Sudan or Algeria, or even Egypt."

"As much as I would like to get him, we have to focus on Libya right now. What have we got on them?" Dr. Rhodes clicked the slide. Another satellite picture came up.

"This is where they are building the bomb. It's disguised as a power plant, but we have proof positive it's where they are building their bomb."

"What is the earliest they could possibly have the bomb complete?"

"Assuming everything goes as planned for them, and they work around the clock, the earliest they could be finished would be the middle of August," said the CIA director.

"We can't let them finish building that bomb. We must stop them," said the Vice President.

"That bomb will not be completed. We will stop them. That's not even a question anymore." There was a determination in the President's voice. "Is there any way we can destroy the weapons plant and save the hostages?"

"That's the bad news." Said Dr. Rhodes. "We can go in there and bomb their weapon's plant, but they will most certainly kill the hostages." The President turned to the Secretary of Defense.

"Can we send in a special forces team to rescue them?"

"That's almost impossible," said the Secretary. "The base where they are being held is six hundred miles from the coast. If we sent in helicopters with a special forces team, they would probably be shot down before they even cleared the coast. Even if they weren't, security on that base is very tight. The Libyans could easily kill the hostages before we got to them, plus we might lose most, if not all, of the Special Forces."

"Mr. President," said the Secretary of State. "We know the Libyans are stalling for time. They want to drag this out as much as possible."

"What are you suggesting?"

"We want to make sure the hostages are okay. Let's make them think they are getting what they want. We can negotiate with them. Tell them we need an independent group to go in there and check on the hostages, like the UN." The President rolled his eyes.

"The UN and I are not exactly on speaking terms at the moment."

"Well, we could try the International Red Cross. We'll tell the Libyans we want the Red Cross to have access to the hostages. They must be able to visit the hostages and make sure they are being treated humanely. In fact, we could even insist that the Red Cross be allowed access to the hostages once a week until this crisis is over."

"Do you think the Libyans will go for it?"

"They'll have too."said Dr. Rhodes. "In fact, they'll probably want to. They'll make sure the hostages are taken care of and they'll also think they're getting what they want, more time."

"And how long do we allow this charade to go on?" asked the President.

"We, or rather you, give them an ultimatum. The middle of July at the latest. Go on national television and speak directly to Qaddafi. Tell him he must release the hostages, dismantle his weapon's plant, and turn over all members of al Jihad or we go to war." The President nodded.

"And do you think he will?" Dr. Rhodes had a sad look in her eye.

"It's highly unlikely, and when we send bombers in to destroy the plant, he will kill the hostages." The President again looked at the Secretary of Defense.

"What do we have in the area right now?"

"We have the U.S.S. John F. Kennedy fifty miles off the coast, and the U.S.S. Abraham Lincoln is also in the Mediterranean."

"Why don't we send in planes right now?"

"We're hoping Qaddafi will come to his senses which is unlikely, plus we want to let the world at least think we tried diplomacy," said the Secretary of State.

"What date would you recommend I give as an ultimatum?"

"July 15. There's not a chance they could have that bomb functional by then. If they don't do everything we ask, we bomb Tripoli and the weapon's factory." The President thought a moment.

"All right. Tomorrow night I'll address the nation. The Libyans have until midnight their time on July 15. If they don't hand over al Jihad, free the hostages, and dismantle the weapons program, we will use any means necessary to stop them. Whatever we do, I want it quick and decisive. I've already fought one Vietnam. I don't want another." Then as an afterthought, he said, "May God help the hostages."

CHAPTER THIRTY-FOUR

Shawn had been keeping track of the days on his watch and knew to the minute how long he had been there. On June 18, at 3:00 in the afternoon the guard came to his door. Shawn knew something was up because the guards had developed a routine almost to the minute of when they would come and get him for his showers and meals. The very fact that this was out of the ordinary scared him. His first thought was that they were going to take him out and shoot him, but something in the way the guard said "Follow me" suggested that maybe it was something else. Still, the prospects were frightening. The hostages were taken to the eating area and told to sit down. Shawn sat with the Smythes, Crystal, Jack, Brian, and Renee. They all received a shock. The guards escorted twenty-five people in who looked like American tourists. "Oh great, more hostages." thought Shawn. The man who had 'greeted' them when they first came, General Siad, explained that these visitors were from the International Red Cross. They had come to inspect the facilities and see that the hostages were well-taken care of.

This was courtesy of the President of the United States. He had insisted that before any discussion or negotiation of hostages take place, he had to be certain that the hostages were being treated humanely. They would not take the Libyans word for it. The Red Cross had to go in and see for themselves. Qaddafi was only too happy to oblige. He needed less than three months, and the longer he could keep the President at bay the better. He'd put them up in luxury hotels if he had to. He only had one stipulation. None of the Red Cross workers could be American.

As Shawn listened, he couldn't help but notice that everyone was listening to General Siad except one man. One of the Red Cross workers was slowly looking around the room. He seemed particularly focused on the guards. He was an older man, mid fifties. When Shawn looked at him, he looked away. The man was tall, lean, and muscularly built. He had gray hair and a neatly trimmed beard. After General Siad finished speaking, the hostages were all escorted back to their cells. A few minutes later a guard escorted a man in and shut the door. It was the same man Shawn had noticed earlier.

"Have a seat, please," Shawn said pointing to his only chair. Shawn sat on the bed across from him.

"Hello, young man, " he said as he stuck out his hand, "I'm Dr. George Taylor. I'm with the International Red Cross. You must be Shawn Miller."

"How did you know my name?"

"Your personal profile. All of us reviewed the files of each of the hostages before we came. We have quite a bit of information about you."

"What kind of doctor are you?"

"Actually, I'm not a medical doctor. She'll be in here in half an hour and give you a complete physical. My job is to see how you are holding up emotionally. The Libyans have told us we can ask any questions, so you can speak freely."

As he was saying that, Dr. Taylor was writing a message on a piece of paper. He handed it to Shawn. It read, "Be careful what you say, this cell is probably bugged." After Shawn finished reading it, Dr. Taylor ripped it up and put it in the toilet.

"You sound American?"

"Actually, I'm Canadian. I was born in Toronto, but I live in Vancouver. I did go to school in America though."

"So why are they letting you in to see us?"

"They want to appear humane and show that you are being treated well. They let us in so that we can tell the world how nice they are. It's a twisted logic they have."

"I'll say. I saw them kill two hostages and beat several others including me."

"I knew they killed some hostages. I was unaware that they had beaten any. When was this?"

"On the plane when they hijacked it." Dr. Taylor was writing some things down on a pad.

"Have they beaten any others?"

"Not that I'm aware of. Dr. Taylor, have you by chance been in contact with my family? I have heard nothing at all from anybody. I have a daughter that . . . "

"That would be Heather."

Shawn was stunned. "You know my daughter's name?"

"I reviewed your file before I came."

"Along with everybody else's I suppose."

"Well, not everybody's. We were each assigned a certain number and you were one of mine. You will be allowed to write letters to your immediate family. We will be here for several hours. We have to interview all the hostages, give them a physical, and interview some of the Libyans."

Dr. Taylor went on and asked many questions. He wrote as Shawn talked. Some of the questions were one's he expected: what emotions was he feeling, was he being threatened or intimidated, how often did the guards check on him, did they carry weapons.

The more Shawn talked to Dr. Taylor, the more Shawn liked him. Their conversation seemed to go from an interview to an informal chat though his pen never stopped moving. He was genuinely concerned about Shawn. He ended up staying longer than half an hour. After nearly an hour together, the guard opened the door. The doctor and nurse were standing outside the cell with a large medical bag.

"Well, that's my cue to go. I do have a little something that may cheer you up." He handed Shawn three envelopes. Shawn's heart leaped for joy. They were from home. "You can read these after the doctor finishes with you. Shawn wanted to rip them open and read them right then, but he let the doctor do her job. She and the nurse were both German. They proceeded to check Shawn out. The gave him a complete physical. They took samples of his bodily fluids.

They checked his temperature and blood pressure, listened to his heart and lungs, and asked a number of questions about everything from what he ate, to how much sleep he got, how many times he went to the bathroom, and a number of other embarrassing questions. He answered them all honestly. They stayed a half an hour and then left. Before the door shut behind them, Shawn was ripping open his first letter. It was from Angela.

Dear Shawn,

I hope everything is going well for you. These past few weeks have been the worst of my life. When I heard your plane had been hijacked, I felt as if my world was coming apart. Every time I pray for food, or pray before I go to bed, I pray that God will keep you safe and bring you back home to me. You are very special to me, Shawn. I miss you very much. I have talked to your family a few times. They seem to be taking this well, but they miss you also. Please take care of yourself and come back to us soon.

Love,
Angela

Shawn was moved almost to tears as he read Angela's letter. Just hearing from her had made his life almost bearable. Then he read his mother's letter.

Dear Son,

Hello. I am so glad to be able to write you. I want you to know that we pray for you day and night. We miss you so much and pray that God will keep you safe. Pastor Jim called a special prayer meeting on Friday night and many members of the church were there. Uncle Henry and Aunt Bonnie even came. Heather prays for you every night before she goes to bed. Last night she prayed, "Dear Jesus, please help Daddy not to be afraid and help him to come home soon." This morning she was eating her cereal and she started crying. I asked her what was wrong and she said, "I miss daddy." Please take care of yourself, son. I love you very much. Remember, you are still my little boy.

Love,
Mom

Shawn felt a big lump in his throat and more than anything else in the world he wanted to go home. He would have given all he had in the world for one minute at home with his family. He immediately got out a pen and paper supplied to him by Dr. Taylor and started writing.

Dear Angela,

Thank you so much for your letter. I hope one day to tell you just how much it meant to me. I am being treated okay so far. The worst part is the fear that I will never see you or my family again, but I know it is in God's hands, and when I hear of so many people praying for me I am encouraged. I want you to know how much your friendship has meant to me. The thought of seeing my family again, and spending more time getting to know you are what keeps me going. Thanks again for your prayers and support. Take care and God bless you.

Love,
Shawn

The next letter was to his mom.

Dear Mom,

Thank you so much for your letter. I have been locked up for two weeks and hearing from you was like water to a man dying of thirst. It means a lot to me to know that you and the church are praying for me. I have turned this matter over to God, and I know he will see me through whatever that may be. I don't know how many more times I will be able to write a letter, but I want you to know how much I love you. I have not always been good at saying thank you but I want you to know that you're the most wonderful mother in the world. I remember as a child watching you go to work, and then coming home and cooking supper, cleaning, helping us with our school work, and in twenty-four years I have never once heard you complain because I knew you loved us. So for all those times I never said thank you, let me say thank you now. You were my inspiration. You are the reason I became a teacher. Please give Heather a great big hug from me and tell her I love her very much. Mom, I don't know what's going to happen, so there's one matter I would like to take care of. If I do not make it home, I hope you can find it in your heart to take Heather and raise her. She loves you very much, and I know she will be raised right. I think it's what Amanda would have wanted also. Just make sure she knows how much her parents loved her. Please give my love to Sara, Jeff, Ashley, Todd, and Shannon. Take care and God bless you.

Love,
Shawn

After he wrote a letter to each of his sisters and Heather, Shawn sealed the envelopes and placed them on the bed. He was glad that he had an opportunity to write them, but he felt an overwhelming sadness at the thought of never seeing them again.

At supper that night Shawn sat with the Smythes, Jack, Mrs. McGregor, and Harry whom he had asked to sit with them. Brian and Renee wanted to be alone. Their spirits had been lifted since they had heard from their families. The only one who seemed to be more depressed than before was Jack. Shawn gathered that he and his daughter did not get along well, so he decided not to pry. Crystal had gotten a letter from her children and tried to tell Shawn about it, but could not stop crying to tell him. The Smythes had heard from their children, and even Harry seemed a little more cheerful as he told of hearing from his sister and her family. After supper, the hostages were given half an hour to walk around the courtyard and talk. Shawn always took this opportunity to talk to some of the people he did not know as well. He did manage to strike up a conversation with a doctor named Forrest Kemper. He was very polite and friendly and took an immediate liking to Shawn.

At 7:30 they were taken back to their cells and Shawn got out his book "Last of the Breed." What he would give to be able to do what the character in that story did.

CHAPTER THIRTY-FIVE

The President sat in the Oval Office looking dazed and tired. He hadn't been getting much sleep the last few nights. His eyes were bloodshot and he had dark circles under his eyes. With him were Dr. Rhodes, Defense Secretary Robert Kirkland, Secretary of State Paul Meijer, the Joint Chiefs of Staff and CIA director George Yates. Things seemed to be going from bad to worse for the President. One Congressman from Massachusetts was even calling for his impeachment. Even his own Cabinet couldn't agree what to do. The Secretary of Defense and the Secretary of State were arguing during his Cabinet meeting. The latest intelligence reports indicated that the Libyans were farther along on their weapons' program than previously thought. At the rate they were going, they could have a working bomb by the middle of August if not sooner. The space program was shut down until further notice because of the loss of the space shuttle, nobody had a clue even what country Mohammad Azeim was in, the stock market had dropped another five hundred points this week, and the latest polls showed Senator Michael Graham (who had just made the cover of GQ) two points ahead of the President. According to Senator Graham, everything was the President's fault.

"Mr. President, we need a decision," said Dr. Rhodes. The question before them was whether or not to bomb the weapons plant now or wait until July 15. The President rubbed his temple.

"And what happens to the hostages if we attack?"

CIA director Yates spoke up.

"They will very likely be killed. In fact, I can almost guarantee it. The only reason they're alive now is the threat of an attack. Once we attack and kill some of their people, they'll have no reason to keep them alive."

"Mr. President, if we don't attack now, they'll be holding the whole country hostage. What message are we sending to the rest of the world? The very fact we are waiting may send a message to other countries to take hostages if you want to bargain with the United States. We must act now, swiftly and decisively or we risk the appearance of being weak."

"I agree, Mr. President," said Dr. Rhodes. "If that bomb becomes operational, they'll blackmail us back to the Stone Age. We've done everything we can to save the hostages. Now we have to think of the rest of the country." The President looked thoughtful for a moment.

"We haven't done quite everything. We have one more thing we haven't tried. We must try. If it fails, I give the order to attack." The President walked over to his desk and picked up the phone.

"Betty, would you please send in Mr. Tiseman?"

Everyone else in the room just looked at each other blankly.

"Mr. President, who is Mr. Tiseman?"

A tall, dark-haired man walked into the room, a stranger to all but the President. He handed a manila folder to the President.

"Thank you. Everyone, I'd like you to meet Richard Tiseman. He's about to share a secret with you. A secret that until now only he and I and one other person knew. It's our best, last, and only option for getting the hostages out alive."

CHAPTER THIRTY-SIX

Shawn waited anxiously for the next visit. It came on June 28. At 3:00 that afternoon, the guard opened the door and in walked Dr. Taylor.

"Good to see you again!" he said. He smiled and shook Shawn's hand warmly. "I have something that will make your day a little brighter." He handed Shawn four letters and two books. One was a devotional and the other a Bible.

"So how are you doing today?" asked Dr. Taylor.

"I miss my family, and I want to go home."

Dr. Taylor was writing some things down on a clip board.

"Why don't you tell me about your family? Sometimes talking about them makes you feel better."

Shawn spent the next thirty minutes talking. Dr. Taylor listened carefully. Shawn found it odd that he wasn't writing anything down. Shawn told of his father's death, his high school days with Amanda, college, marriage, Heather, Amanda's death, and finally, of course, Angela.

"Wow," Dr. Taylor said. "You're thirty-four and you've experienced more than most people twice your age." There was silence for a moment. "And how do you feel about Angela?" Shawn turned and looked at him.

"Are you a hostage counselor or a love doctor?"

"I double as both. Which do you need now?"

"I guess both." Said Shawn. "I like Angela very much. If this hadn't happened, I could see our relationship going places."

"Do you have a picture of her in your wallet?" asked Dr. Taylor.

"No, I only have pictures of my family," said Shawn.

"Do you mind if I have a look?"

"Sure." Shawn opened his wallet and handed it to Dr. Taylor. The first photo was of Heather. Dr. Taylor smiled as he looked at it.

"Your daughter is very cute."

"I know. Everyone says that about her." The next photo was of Shawn, Heather, and Amanda.

"Now that's a nice looking family." He looked at the pictures of his sisters and their families. The last photo was of Becky. Dr. Taylor stared at it for a moment.

"Well, I can see where your family gets it good looks."

"Thank you." Just then a man and a woman in white lab coats came in.

"Shawn, this is Dr. Phil Thomas and Miss Cheryl Lapeer. They will give you another physical. If you'll excuse me, I must check on the others."

"Thank you for your help Dr. Taylor. I feel better after talking to you." Dr. Taylor turned to leave.

"By the way, Happy Birthday, George." Dr. Taylor stopped and gave a very annoyed look.

"Thank you, Cheryl."

Shawn spoke up. "Today's your birthday. Why didn't you say something?"

"Because he didn't want anyone to know," said Dr. Thomas. "I, on the other hand, glanced at his personnel file."

"Well, Happy Birthday, George. By the way, how old are you?" George didn't answer.

"He's fifty-eight today." Now George didn't look annoyed. He looked angry.

"Don't be so embarrassed George, you don't look a day over 50." George quickly left the room. Dr. Thomas got out the thermometer and blood pressure kit.

"Rather an unusual man, if I do say so myself," he muttered.

"How so?" asked Shawn.

"Well, he joined our team at the last minute. Everybody on the team has known each other for years and two days before we leave to come here, we're told we're going to have another psychologist. We've already got two and we really didn't need one more, but orders came straight from the top. The head of the Red Cross personally saw to it he was on the team."

"So you've never met him before?"

"Not until twelve days ago. I actually didn't meet him until we were at the airport on our way here. In fact, some days I wonder if he really is a psychologist." He took the blood pressure cuff off. "130/88. Your blood pressure is a little high, but you are under stress so I guess that's understandable. Temperature is 98.8." Dr. Thomas continued the exam.

"I'm sorry. You really have my curiosity up. Why do you say you wonder if he's really a psychologist?"

"Oh, I'm sure he is, it's just . . . well, I've had some course work in psychology, and sometimes when I ask him a question, he looks at me like he doesn't know what I'm talking about, and yet he supposedly graduated with honors from the most prestigious university in Canada. I don't know. Don't quote me on any of this. He's a good man. I probably shouldn't be saying anything."

"That's okay, doctor. Your secret's safe with me."

CHAPTER THIRTY-SEVEN

Friday morning, Pastor Jim usually spent making the final preparations for his sermons for Sunday. He followed a regular routine. He would get to his office at 8:00 and study for his sermons until 11:00. At 11:00, he would pick up his wife, go eat lunch, and then spend the afternoon making either home visits or hospital visits. You could almost set your watch by Pastor Jim's schedule. Today his schedule would be interrupted. At 9:00 his secretary buzzed him on the intercom.

"Pastor Jim, I'm sorry to bother you but there is someone here to see you." Pastor Jim looked at his day planner. He didn't have anyone scheduled for an appointment.

"Who is it?"

"It's Henry Evans."

"Please send him in." Uncle Henry walked into Pastor Jim's study. He could tell Henry had been crying.

"Pastor Jim, I need to talk to you."

"I'm glad you came, Henry. Have a seat."

On Sunday when Pastor Jim got up to speak, he did not read the scriptures first as he usually did. That, however, did not strike anyone as odd. What had caught their attention was Henry and Bonnie Evans sitting on the front row.

"Beloved, the Lord moves in strange and mysterious ways. On Friday of this week, a man that many of you know and love came to see me and has asked to speak to this congregation. I hope you will listen as he shares what is on his heart. Brother Henry."

Once again tears were in Henry's eyes but he spoke clearly.

"As Pastor Jim said, on Friday I came to see him in his office. I came there to ask his forgiveness for something I did a number of years ago. Eighteen years ago, when he was a candidate for this church, I opposed his becoming pastor. I said some things that were not true. I slandered this good man's name, and some of you believed me. I said that he was too young and inexperienced to be our pastor. That was a lie. The truth is, I didn't want him here because he's black. I couldn't handle a black man being our pastor. I got angry at this church and at God, and for eighteen years I have been a bitter man who was too proud to admit he was wrong. As you know, my nephew Shawn is one of the hostages. During this crisis, Pastor Jim has gone out of his way to show love and support to my sister, her family and even me. When a man can do that after what I have done to him, he's a better man than I. Yesterday, when I went to his study, I asked for his forgiveness, I knelt down and I asked God to forgive me, and now I ask you to forgive me." Henry finished and went and sat next to his wife on the front row. Pastor Jim got up once again to speak.

"Beloved, our God is a God of forgiveness. He commands us to forgive. In the Lord's Prayer, we are instructed to pray, 'Forgive us our debts as we forgive our debtors.' Each of us who know the Lord has been forgiven a great debt, and we now have an opportunity to show that Christ-like forgiveness to another. Jesus tells us to forgive seventy times seven. With his dying breath, Christ said, 'Father, forgive them, for they know not what they do.' Brother Henry has asked for my forgiveness and he has received it. He has asked God's forgiveness and now he asks yours. He and Bonnie have also asked to rejoin the church. They met with the deacons yesterday and we all agree that they should become members once again. If you are willing to forgive Brother Henry and to restore him to membership with this church, please signify by raising your right hand."

The vote was unanimous. Throughout the hostage situation, the congregation had prayed for a miracle, but they had just witnessed one that no one would ever forget. From that day on, North Hill Baptist Church was never the same. Few people could remember months later what Pastor Jim preached that morning, but they never forgot the day an angry, bitter racist became a forgiven happy Christian once again. At the end of the service the congregation sang, "Ring the Bells of Heaven." Pastor Jim and Henry stood next to each other as they sang.

> Ring the bells of Heaven,
> There is joy today,
> For a soul returning from the wild.
> See the father greet him out along the way,
> And is born a new and ransomed child.
> Glory, glory how the angels sing,
> Glory, glory how the loud harps ring,
> T'is the ransomed army like the mighty sea,
> Pealing forth the anthem of the free.

CHAPTER THIRTY-EIGHT

At 9:00 on the morning of July 10, the President gave the order. Operation Freedom Raid was approved. This was the last hope of getting the hostages out alive. The operation was so secret that when the plane took off from Germany, the flight crew did not know until they were airborne where they were going. The men on board this flight had all volunteered for this mission. They were American Special Forces, the most highly trained soldiers in the entire world, all of them that is, except one. Their commander was not a trained commando, but the entire fate of the mission rested on his shoulders. He would lead them into the valley of death and back out again.

The plan to most would seem foolhardy and yet the beauty of it was that the Libyans would never expect it. The plan was to fool them into thinking that the Special Forces team was actually Red Cross workers. The plane they were flying was identical to the one the Red Cross team flew. The team dressed as Red Cross workers and even had forged documents. They would ride the buses the Red Cross team usually rode in and when they arrived at the base, they would simply take out the guards quietly, release the hostages, drive back to the plane, and take off. They estimated that they could land, rescue the hostages, and take off within one hour. Everything depended on their commander, known to Shawn as Dr. George Taylor.

The plane landed in Libya at 8:00 that night. The guards patrolling the runway were a little surprised that a plane was landing. They had not been told of this. However, they did recognize the

Red Cross on the side of the plane, and they had seen this plane take off and land twice before. The plane taxied to the end of the runway and stopped. As the team disembarked, six guards wearing green uniforms, with machine guns slung over their shoulders greeted Dr. Taylor. Fortunately, they recognized him from his previous visits. The one in charge, a young captain named Ibrahim Rajah spoke.

"Dr. Taylor, we were not informed your team was making another visit. This is highly unusual."

"I know. They only decided at the last minute. We have word that two of the hostages are gravely ill, and in need of medical attention right away. We have asked to see that they are properly cared for. Your government is aware of the situation. We must go quickly." Captain Rajah stared at Dr. Taylor for a moment. Another guard spoke to him in Arabic. Dr. Taylor could tell he was hesitating.

"Captain. We must get to them quickly. If one of them dies because you delayed us, General Siad will not be pleased."

"Let me see your documents." Dr. Taylor handed him several pieces of paper. They carefully checked the papers and looked to see that the pictures on the documents matched the ones carrying them. They also checked the equipment they were carrying. It was clearly medical equipment. Satisfied that everything was in order, they directed them to the buses, parked in a hangar on the far end of the runway. The team boarded two buses and each had a soldier as a driver. No sooner were the lights of the airport out of view when a soldier slipped up behind the driver and quietly killed him. They dumped his body along the way but not before taking his uniform and putting it on one of their own.

Shawn was sitting in his cell reading when suddenly the door flung open. There was Dr. Taylor, only he didn't look anything like the quiet, caring psychologist Shawn had seen on his previous visits. He looked more like an older version of Rambo. He was wearing a green coat and hat that he had obviously 'borrowed' from a Libyan soldier, he had a machine gun in one hand and a pistol holster fastened to his waist.

"Come on, Shawn! Hurry!" Shawn scrambled to get his shoes on.

"HURRY!" George said in a very loud whisper.

"What's going on?" Shawn asked.

"We're trying to get you out of here!" Shawn ran out of his cell and nearly tripped over two Libyan guards lying dead near his cell. Dr. Taylor was gone, directing other hostages out of their cells. Another American soldier was directing them to the bus parked just outside their building. Shawn quickly boarded the bus. As soon as he was on the bus, another soldier instructed them to all lie down and not utter a sound. Shawn was one of the first ones on, so he made his way to the very back of the bus to make room for the others. In less than ten minutes all the hostages were on board the bus and, to all appearances, the Libyans were not yet aware of what was actually going on.

Shawn could over the whispers. He recognized Dr. Taylor's voice.

"Are all the hostages accounted for?"

"Yes, sir."

"Do we have all the team members back?"

"Yes sir."

"Then let's get out of here!"

Back at the airport Captain Rajah had the strange feeling that something just wasn't quite right. General Siad had always given him very specific instructions regarding the Red Cross team. Surely he would have told him of this, even if it was unexpected. He hesitated. General Siad did not like to be bothered at night. The Captain decided to risk it. He picked up the phone and dialed the number. Someone answered on the third ring.

"This had better be important!" came an angry voice on the other end. Rajah could hear a female voice laughing in the background. General Siad was a notorious womanizer.

"General, I'm sorry to bother you. This is Captain Rajah."

"Yes, what is it?"

"Sir, the Red Cross team left a half hour ago to the base to check on the hostages and I was wondering if . . ." General Siad sat straight up in bed. The female voice stopped laughing.

"Red Cross team. What Red Cross team?"

"They came here to check on some of the hostages who were ill. They landed about thirty minutes ago and left for the base as usual."

"You fool! There are no more Red Cross visits scheduled!"

Amazingly, within fifteen minutes, the two buses pulled out of the base and headed back to the airport. The confused guards let them pass, thinking it odd that they had just come in a few minutes before. No sooner had they pulled out of the base than sirens went off, and the entire base lit up like the fourth of July. Shawn's heart sank to the pit of his stomach. There were six army vehicles behind them and each had a machine gun mounted on top.

"Everyone, stay on the floor!" came the voice of Dr. Taylor. They did not have to be told twice. Machine gun fire roared across the sky as bullets sprayed the bus. Dr. Taylor made his way to the back of the bus. He was standing over Shawn.

"Put your face to the floor. I'm going to break this glass." Shawn did as he was told. With the butt of the rifle, George broke the glass of the window on the emergency exit. He and another of the special force's team began firing back. The Libyans were not prepared for return fire and so they widened the gap between them and the buses. Shawn knew it was only a matter of time before they caught up with them again. The Libyans opened fired on the bus but amazingly, they didn't hit anyone. Apparently they didn't realize they were all on the floor. George spoke to the man next to him.

"Keep shooting! I need to tell the driver something." George made his way to the front of the bus. "Take a very sharp turn in about one minute."

"Whatever you say," said the driver. George went to the back.

"What was that all about?" asked Shawn.

"Ever play pool, my boy?" George asked. Suddenly the bus took a hard right turn into the sand causing the jeeps to take a sharp turn. George opened fired on the first jeep blowing out two of its tires and hitting the engine. The jeep flipped end over end and knocked out two other jeeps behind it.

"Eight ball in the side pocket!" yelled George. The bus cheered and everyone applauded the good Dr. Taylor.

"There's still three to go." George said. This time the Libyans began firing and didn't stop. Hundreds of bullets hit the bus, but most were over their heads. The man next to George was shot in the shoulder and could no longer continue to shoot. George looked down at Shawn.

"Do you know how to shoot?"

"I do hunt."

"Close enough. You're taking his place." Shawn jumped up, grabbed the rifle from the wounded man and began to shoot. Nothing happened.

"You're out of ammunition." Said George. "Hold on." He grabbed another clip from the wounded man's pack. He took out the old clip, inserted the new, and cocked it. "There you go. Fire at will." Both Shawn and George began firing at the jeeps. Shawn heard fighter planes overhead. They were obviously very close and Shawn knew that they did not have a chance against fighter planes. Shawn waited for the explosion of the bus and his immediate death afterwards, but it didn't come. In fact they fired a missile at the jeeps and took out two of them, then continued in the direction of the base. The explosions that followed were so loud that it literally hurt Shawn's ears. The night sky lit up as bright as day.

"They're ours!" Yelled one of the soldiers in the bus. The Libyans behind them quickly abandoned the chase. Another explosion shook the ground so hard the bus nearly turned over. Again another cheer went out from the bus.

"Where did you learn to shoot like that?" asked Shawn.

"I was in the military for a while. I spent some time in Vietnam." Shawn looked at him.

"All right 'Dr.' Taylor. Who are you really? You're not a psychologist and you're not Canadian."

"What makes you say that?"

"There were no Canadian troops in combat in Vietnam. You're American. We both know it." The bus slowed down. They arrived at the airstrip where the plane awaited. The airstrip seemed to be in the middle of nowhere. The bus stopped at one of the hangars and the hostages got out. The pilot had already started the engine and prepared for take off. As they were about to board the plane gunfire echoed across the night.

"Run quickly!" yelled George and the hostages broke into a dead run for the plane. Shawn was the last one out of the bus. The gunfire was coming from near one of the hangars and Shawn saw several dark figures in the distance heading toward them.

"HURRY!" Someone yelled as more gunfire rang out. Shawn still had the rifle in his hand. He began to fire in the direction of the dark objects. He thought if he could keep them pinned down for a few seconds, they would be safe. As the hostages boarded the plane, Shawn stood his ground.

"Shawn, get out of here!" Shawn turned and ran toward the plane that was at least twenty yards away. Suddenly a grenade exploded behind him and knocked him down as if a large hand had smacked him. The explosion nearly knocked him out. As he lay on the ground, he could not move. He tried, but his head was spinning and he was completely disoriented. "So this is it." He thought. "I made it this far, only to be caught like this." There was an exchange of gunfire between the Libyans and one of the Americans standing at the door of the plane. Shawn knew he could not make it to the plane. He could not even stand up. They would have to leave him or they would all die. Mustering all the strength he could, Shawn yelled,

"Go on! Leave me! Get out of here!" Then a strong arm grabbed him, threw his arm around him and headed toward the plane, half carrying him, half dragging him. Shawn did not have to look at the face to know who it was.

"Thanks, George," he said. As they made it to the plane, the soldier at the door fired off the remaining bullets, grabbed Shawn and dragged him inside. Shawn collapsed into the seat beside the door. The plane was already moving. George was right behind him. The plane was taxing down the runway. Shawn turned to George who was leaning against the wall of the plane.

"Dr. Taylor," he said trying to look at him. "I want to thank you for saving . . ." That's when Shawn noticed it. A large red spot in the middle of Dr. Taylor's stomach. Some of the other hostages were helping him lie down. That was the last thing Shawn remembered before he passed out.

CHAPTER THIRTY-NINE

Shawn woke up an hour later with Mrs. Smythe gently rubbing his head with a wet cloth. He sat up but his head was still spinning. As the plane hit an air pocket, Shawn realized they were flying. "We made it." He thought, then he remembered Dr. Taylor.

"How's George?" he asked. Mrs. Smythe had a very concerned look on her face.

"He's alive." She said but that was all. Shawn stood up and looked toward the back of the plane and saw Dr. Kemper and several others leaning over George who was lying on the floor. As Shawn walked down the aisle toward them he nearly stumbled and felt as if he were going to throw up.

"How is he?" Shawn asked. The others just looked away.

"You had better sit down. You took quite a blow," said Dr. Kemper.

"I'm fine. Is he going to be all right?" George was lying on the floor struggling for breath. His shirt was off and there were bandages over his wound. Shawn couldn't help but notice the ugly scar on George's left shoulder. Shawn sat down. Dr. Kemper sat next to him.

"Shawn, it's very serious. I think his lungs are filling with blood and he's bleeding internally."

"Well, you're a doctor, can't you do something?" asked Shawn. Dr. Kemper looked down.

"I haven't been totally honest with you. I'm a chiropractor. I haven't dealt with internal medicine in twenty years. This is way out of my league."

"Well, you have had some medical training. Is there anything you can do?"

"If he were at Johns Hopkins and had a team of the finest doctors in the world, there's a slight chance they might save his life. All I have is this." He held up the medical kit. "There's nothing I can do. Besides we have other problems at the moment."

"What's wrong?"

"We're running out of fuel. One of the bullets put a hole in the fuel tank. We are going to have to make an emergency landing in about thirty minutes."

"How long have we been flying?" asked Shawn.

"Almost an hour."

"Oh, no. That means we're still in Libya."

"No, we aren't." Said Dr. Kemper.

"We aren't flying north?"

"If we flew north, the Libyans would track us and shoot us down long before we were out of their airspace. So we flew south. You were only seventy miles from the border of Chad. We were going to fly to the capital and then go to one of the embassies, but we will not make it."

"You mean we're going to crash?"

"I prefer to think of it as an emergency landing. We will land somewhere in the grasslands and hope to God we are near civilization."

"How long ago did we cross the border?"

"We crossed over into Chad about thirty minutes ago. For whatever it's worth, we did make it out of Libya alive. That was a miracle in itself." Over the intercom they heard the captain's voice.

"Prepare for emergency landing." Shawn and Dr. Kemper went back to where George lay. They carefully buckled him into a seat and then sat on either side of him to hold him. For five minutes it was quiet. Shawn looked out the window and then at his watch. It was nearly midnight. Suddenly the plane jerked as if it were choking. Shawn knew they would be coming down soon.

"Everybody brace yourself," came a voice. The plane jerked again and lost altitude. Shawn could tell because his ears hurt. For several minutes his heart seemed to quiver at the bottom of his stomach. He grabbed George tight so he would not be bounced around so much. The plane continued to jerk and drop. Two of the engines went out. Shawn looked at George. He was still gasping for breath.

The plane came down with a hard thud and bounced, then came another hard thud. Shawn was knocked around as the plane slid through the grass. Shawn waited, half expecting the plane to blow up, but it did not. The plane slid for a few seconds as it turned sideways and came to a halt. He waited for a second and then stood up. Other than being jerked around and sick to their stomachs, no one was seriously hurt. Shawn looked at Dr. Kemper.

"That pilot should get a raise," he said. Everyone quickly exited the plane except Shawn and a few others who were carrying George very carefully. His breathing was becoming more difficult. They carried him from the plane into the darkness. Other than the emergency lights on the plane, there was no light whatsoever. Shawn's eyes adjusted to the darkness. The fact that they had not hit a tree on their way down was a testament to their pilot's skills.

"You did a fine job landing the plane, sir. You are to be commended," Jack said to the pilot, Juan Hernandez.

"Thank you," said the pilot. Shawn and the others carried George to a tree about thirty feet from the plane. They laid him down and used several blankets balled up as pillows to make him more comfortable.

"Do you have any idea where we are?" asked Mr. Smythe to Trevor Hines, one of the special forces officers. Trevor was holding an object that looked like a miniature electronic game. He punched a few buttons before he spoke.

"We are 187.6 miles from the capital."

"What is that thing?" asked Jack.

"It's a GPS. That's short for Global Positioning System. You could put me anywhere on this planet with one of these and I couldn't get lost if I tried."

"So you know exactly where we are?" asked Jack.

"Absolutely," said Trevor.

"It's not going to do us any good if nobody else knows where we are," said Harry in his usual pessimistic voice.

"Oh, they know where we are. The plane has a tracking device on it. I dare say by tomorrow morning. Satellites will be photographing us from space."

"That's wonderful," said Mrs. Smythe.

"Well, that's the good news."

"And what's the bad news?" asked Jack.

"The bad news is they're going to have a devil of a time trying to get us. The nearest American military base is in Italy, 3000 miles away. Chad, if you have been reading the papers, is in the middle of a civil war, and the guy the Americans were supporting was shot last week. Their current leader is the one who had him shot. We're not exactly on his Christmas card list."

"Do you think our lives are still in danger?" asked Jack.

"Oh, he won't do anything to hurt us, not unless he wants a very short Presidency. In fact, he'll let us go, and even allow an American plane to come pick us up, but not before he milks it for all it's worth. The earliest we'll get out of here is three days, but it may be as long as a week. That's where we have a problem. We have a limited amount of food and water. If we divide it evenly amongst everybody, it'll last two days. If we conserve, maybe three, but our biggest problem is them." He said pointing toward Dr. Taylor. "I have six wounded men, three critically. If we don't get help soon, they're going to die."

"What are we going to do?" asked Mrs. Smythe.

"I don't know yet. Give me a few minutes to put a plan together. I know what I'm not going to do. I'm not going to sit here and watch my men die without doing something."

Shawn and Dr. Kemper were not part of the conversation. They were doing their best to try to make George and the other wounded soldiers comfortable. Dr. Kemper called him aside. He had a sad look in his eye.

"I'm afraid he doesn't have long. His lungs are filling with blood. There's nothing I can do." Shawn looked at George lying ten feet away.

"How long does he have?" Dr. Kemper thought for a moment.

"He may have fifteen minutes, no more than thirty." Shawn shook his head.

"Shawn, I don't mean to sound callous. This man saved our lives, but I've got two more that are severely wounded. There's a chance I might be able to save them."

"I'll stay with him." He made his way over to George who was fighting for breath. Shawn knelt down and took George's hand in his. Shawn looked into his eyes. There was a sadness in those eyes that came from years of loneliness and heartache. A sadness that Shawn was familiar with. It came from having someone very dear and precious to you being taken away. This was a man whom many years ago had a wife and children and a little boy he loved very much. Then one day they were separated through no fault of his own. Tears filled his eyes as Shawn gently squeezed the feeble hand.

"We've missed you. We've missed you so very much. Mom's missed you, the girls have missed you, and I've missed you."

"How did you know?"

"Your 58th birthday on June 28th. You aren't Canadian. You sure aren't a psychologist, and the clincher, that scar." Shawn put a hand on his shoulder. "I remember your scar from when I was a child. You got it when you were shot down in Vietnam."

"You always were too smart for your own good." He said with a slight chuckle.

"But why? Why did you leave us?" George was growing weaker by the minute.

"I don't have time to explain everything. I have a friend who works in the government. He will answer your questions. Just know this. I never wanted to leave you. I had to do it to protect you."

"How will I find your friend?"

"If I know my friend, he'll find you. Listen, I have a few things to tell you before I die. Tell your mother I love her. She was and is the great love of my life. I've never loved another. Tell the girls I love them and I'm sorry I couldn't be there to watch them grow up, and you, there isn't a father in the world more proud of his son than I. I've kept track of all of you. There hasn't been one day that went by that I didn't think of you."

"Dad, I love you."

"I love you, son." And with that Shawn Miller lost his father for the second time in his life.

CHAPTER FORTY

Dawn comes quickly close to the equator. The golden rays of the sun were peeking just over the horizon. Shawn decided to keep George's true identity a secret for the time being. No one would have believed him anyway. Dr. Kemper put a blanket over George's body.

Trevor Hines was talking with Jack, Mr. Smythe, Dr. Kemper and several of the men on his team. Curious to find out what they were discussing, Shawn made his way over to them.

"We'll have to send some people out to scout around. There's no other way around it," said Trevor. "We've got to find a town or village with a doctor and we must find them soon. We've already lost one man."

"Okay, who do you want to go?"

"I was thinking we need to send at least four. Each goes in a different direction. If they find something, they get help or come back and help us. We do have one problem, though. I will need at least one other person to go. Several of my men are wounded, and I would like to keep a few here in case we have trouble."

"I'll go!" said Jack.

"No offence, Jack, but I need someone young and in good physical shape." Jack was hurt by this.

"What do you mean good physical shape? I'm in great condition."

"How old are you, Jack?"

"I'm 48." Trevor laughed. Jack was clearly older than that.

"I meant this year."

"Actually I'm 58 but . . ."

"I'll go," said Shawn. Trevor took one look at him.

"This won't be easy. You sure you're up to it?"

"I'm sure."

"All right. I'll brief you on what you do." He handed Shawn a pistol. "No thanks."

"You'll need this."

"It'll weigh me down. Besides, I might blow my toe off. I really don't want it." Trevor put the gun back in his holster.

"All right, I won't force you to take it, but you are taking this or you don't go." He handed Shawn his GPS.

"You want me to take a play station?" Trevor looked disgusted.

"If one more person calls this a game, I'll shoot them. This, for your information, is a Global Positioning System, otherwise called a GPS." Shawn looked at it curiously. Trevor spent a few minutes explaining what it was.

"You mean this will tell me exactly where I am anywhere in the world?"

"Walk about thirty feet in that direction." Said Trevor pointing toward the vast open grassland. "And look at your GPS as you walk." Shawn obeyed. After he walked the required distance, he noticed that the last digit on his GPS had changed. He walked back to Trevor and noticed the digit change back again.

"See what I mean? It will tell you within fifty feet where you are anywhere in the world."

"That's amazing. Which way do I go?"

"You're going south." Trevor took the GPS and punched a button. "This little arrow will always point south. Follow it for a day. See if you see a village of any kind. If you do, mark its location by hitting this button," he said as he pointed, "once you've done that, press this button," once again pointing, "and the arrow will point in this direction until you get here."

"That's all there is to it?"

"That's it. A smart guy like you should have no problem. If you don't find anything by tomorrow morning, come back. Don't make us come looking you."

"All right. When do you want us to leave?"

"I'll send you and my other men out in an hour. We have some unfinished business before you leave." He pointed in the direction of George's body and for the first time Shawn noticed that some of the special forces team were digging a grave with a small shovel they found on board the plane. Using two sticks cut from a tree, they made a crude cross.

A few minutes later, everyone gathered around. Using rope, they lowered his body into the shallow grave. The men of the special forces unit saluted as he was lowered into the grave. Major Hines spoke in a clear and distinct voice.

"Almighty God, we commit to your care the soul of our beloved friend and comrade George Taylor, a good and brave man who willingly sacrificed his life to save others. We lay his body in the earth with the sure and certain knowledge that he will rise again in the resurrection day when the trumpet sounds and the dead shall be raised. We ask that you receive him into your presence. Ashes to ashes, dust to dust. From dust thou art, and to dust thou shalt return." There was a moment of silence, then one of the men began to sing. The others soon joined in.

Amazing grace, how sweet the sound,

That saved a wretch like me.

I once was lost but now am found,

Was blind but now I see.

Tears flowed freely from many of the nearly sixty people gathered together under the tree. Strangely, Shawn didn't feel a great deal of emotion at that moment. His mind was still clouded from the blow to his head, and with the rescue, the plane crash, being reunited with his father, and now suddenly losing him again, not to mention the lack of sleep; he was still in a state of shock. His mind had not grasped the reality of who this man they were about to bury really was. All was quiet and everyone was looking at Shawn. He realized they were waiting for him to pray. Trevor had asked him to close with a short prayer. He started to open his mouth, but for the life of him he couldn't think of what to say. Then he remembered the prayer Pastor Jim would close the service with sometimes when he dismissed the service at North Hill. It was found in the Bible, but at the moment he could not remember the passage. He cleared his throat and spoke.

"Now Lord, let thy servants depart in peace according to thy Word. Amen." Many others also said 'Amen' also.

CHAPTER FORTY-ONE

Ten minutes later Shawn and the three men from the special forces team began their quest to find help. They were each given a quart of their precious water, some food in a plastic container and a GPS. They were warned to use their water sparingly.

Shawn left at a jog. He decided to jog until he was tired but not exhausted. For one solid hour he jogged south. Finally, he slowed to a fast walk. He figured he had gone about six miles. All he had seen were trees, grass, and a few wild animals. He looked at his watch. It was 11:00. The sun was high overhead and it was very hot. Shawn guessed it had to be over a hundred degrees. He was getting very thirsty, but he decided he would go as long as he could without taking a sip in the hopes his water would last him. He began alternating between jogging and walking. After two more hours of jogging or running over uneven ground and grass up to his knees, his legs became like Jell-O. Every few minutes he would look at his GPS to make sure he was headed in the right direction. He was getting very dizzy and he knew he needed to stop and rest. He found a tree with a little shade and he sat down under it. He took a big gulp of water. He knew he needed to conserve, but it felt so good to his parched throat that he took another big gulp. He resisted the urged to take a third drink. He opened his pouch of food and began to eat. With half his rations gone, he decided to continue his journey, praying he would find help soon.

Jogging was too tiresome, so he decided to walk as fast as he could. After a few hours the sky turned a beautiful orange color and Shawn looked off to the west and saw the sun setting over a tree. He saw some giraffes wander by about half a mile away. The scene reminded him of the National Geographic Specials he had seen on television.

Darkness came, but Shawn did not stop. He kept going as fast as he could. Fortunately, his GPS was equipped with a little light so he could see what direction he was supposed to go. Soon it was very dark and the only light was from the stars. Shawn kept going. It started to get a little chilly. His throat was dry and his legs ached horribly, but he kept going. All through the night he went. He refused to stop. He heard strange noises all around him. He thought of the people whose lives depended on him. He began to feel extremely fatigued, but he kept going. He would not even stop and rest for a minute for fear he might not get back up. The first light of dawn broke across the sky. A sickening feeling came over him. As far as the eye could see, there was absolutely nothing except grass and trees. He looked at his GPS. He had traveled twenty-five miles. The trip back would be more difficult because he had fewer supplies, and he was already near the point of exhaustion as it was. He had to make a decision. He could go on and hope to find help, or he could turn back now.

He decided to go on. He would go until noon. If he found nothing by then, he would turn back. He continued to look at his GPS. He had traveled twenty-eight miles. His watch read 8:00. He had been away from the group for nearly twenty-four hours. His whole body began to ache and his legs were in great pain. He stopped, but he didn't dare sit down. He took a long gulp of his water. When he finished there was only a tiny bit left. He decided to finish it off. That little bit would probably not make any difference anyway. The container was no good to him any more, so he threw it aside and continued his journey.

Finally, his legs gave out completely. He collapsed on the ground too exhausted even to stand up. He had to literally crawl to a tree a hundred yards away. He lay down underneath its shade. He started to look at his GPS but decided against it. At the moment, he really didn't want to know how far he had to go to get back to the group. Sitting up slightly, he looked around. There was nothing but grassland as far as the eye could see.

Shawn never remembered going to sleep. The last thing he remembered was putting his head down. He had planned to take a ten minute rest. When he awoke, he looked at his watch. It was 3:00. He had slept more than five hours. The sun was blazing overhead and he was covered in sweat. He had planned to head back three hours ago, but he knew he would never make it back. He had well over thirty miles to go and no water whatsoever. Furthermore, his legs were so weak, he wasn't sure he could even stand up. Shawn did the only thing he could do. He prayed.

Suddenly, Shawn felt something on his chest. He looked down and saw a black hand. Startled, he looked up and saw the face of a young African man. His first feeling was fear.

"Please, don't eat me," he said out loud. The young man was alone and had no weapons. His only clothing was a garment wrapped around his waist. He did have two leather containers around him. Shawn judged him to be about twenty years old. His white teeth contrasted sharply with his dark skin. Slowly the fear went away. This man had a kind face. He was not going to hurt him. He looked at Shawn and tilted his head to one side.

"White man need help?" he asked.

Relieved he spoke English, Shawn replied quickly.

"Yes, white man need help very much." His throat was so dry he wasn't even sure the man heard him. The man took off one container which appeared to hold water. It looked to be made of animal skin. The man opened the top, knelt down and put it to Shawn's mouth. It was water. As ice cold as the water from his refrigerator back home. Never in his life had it tasted so good. Shawn chuckled a little at the thought of this man filling up his leather animal skin container from a Whirlpool refrigerator in his hut.

"Thank you." Shawn wiped his mouth and handed the container to him. There was still some water left in it. He didn't want to leave the man an empty container. The man gestured at him with the bottle.

"You drink." He didn't have to be told twice. Shawn took another long refreshing gulp and then another. He drank the container empty and handed it back to the man.

"Sorry, I drank all your water. I hope you can get some more." The man opened his other leather pouch and handed Shawn several pieces of bread. Each one was the size of one of his mother's homemade biscuits. The bread was absolutely wonderful. It must have been made that day. It was soft and fluffy. As he ate, the man spoke again.

"What your name?"

"Shawn, Shawn Miller." His voice was muffled by the bread. "What your name?"

"Jeunda."

"Jeunda. That's a good name."

"You seek village?"

"Village?" It took Shawn a second to register what he was asking. "Yes!" he said with great excitement. "I seek village! You know where village is?"

Jeunda smiled.

"Village there." He said pointing toward the east. Shawn started to stand up, but his legs gave out on him and he collapsed. Jeunda grabbed one arm and helped him to his feet. He was stronger than he looked. Shawn was finally able to stand and walk, though his legs ached.

"Follow smoke." Shawn looked east in the direction Jeunda had pointed. He strained his eyes and just over the top of some trees he saw it. He could just make out a very faint puff of smoke. He would never have seen it had Jeunda not pointed it out to him. He had been heading south and would have missed it completely. This man saved his life.

"My friend, I want to thank . . ." Shawn turned around. There was no one there.

Shawn walked in the direction of the smoke. The bread and water and the knowledge that help was close by had given him a new surge of strength. He walked quickly. As he got closer, he could make out huts. He was sure he had seen this village in a National Geographic Special.

As he approached the village, he noticed something strange. There were no people anywhere. The village looked completely deserted, then he heard it. Singing, beautiful singing. He recognized the song though the words were not in English. "What a Friend We Have in Jesus." He followed the singing and through an opening he saw that the whole village was in a large building with a cross on top. An elderly white man was leading them in the singing. Shawn entered the back door. The singing stopped and all eyes turned to him.

"Good day," he said out of breath. "My name is Shawn Miller and I need your help." With that he collapsed on the floor.

CHAPTER FORTY-TWO

Something cool and wet was pressing on his forehead as Shawn regained consciousness. An elderly white lady was patting a wet cloth on his head. He was in one of the huts and several people were standing over him. All of them were black except the elderly lady attending him and the gentleman he had seen leading music earlier.

"Hello," the older gentleman said. "Are you feeling better young man?"

"May I please have something to drink?"

The gentleman turned to a teenage African boy.

"Peter, go get some water please." The boy quickly left the hut.

"You gave us all quite a shock. We don't have many American tourists come our way. Do you mind if I ask how you got here?" Peter returned with a pitcher of water and a sandwich. "Here, have some food." Shawn took the plate and drink and put it aside.

"Sir, I need your help. I was on a plane that crashed about thirty miles north of here. There's a group of people who are stranded. Some of them are wounded and they have very little food or water. We must help them quickly."

"Eat up, young man."

"Sir, I don't think you understand. They'll die if we don't help them soon. I won't eat or drink until I know they're safe."

"Don't worry Shawn Miller, while you're eating, I'll arrange a rescue party. We'll be on our way within the hour."

"You know my name. What's yours?"

"My name is Dr. Carl Layman and this is my wife Mary. We are with the British Foreign Mission Board."

"Wow, a doctor, way out here. How fortunate."

"The need in this area is great. Besides fortune had nothing to do with it. God brought you to us. He directed you to this village."

"You may be more right than even you realize," said Shawn.

"We only have two trucks in the entire village. How many would you say is in your group?"

"Between fifty and sixty."

Dr. Layman frowned.

"Well, we'll have to make more than one trip. The most critical can go first. The rest will have to wait a couple of hours. I'll pack some pillows, blankets, food and water. You finish eating. I'll be back in thirty minutes."

"I'm coming with you."

"No, you're not. You're going to stay her and rest a few minutes. Doctors' orders. I can get everything ready. We need you with us when we leave." The elderly missionary turned to leave.

"Dr. Layman, you'll save many lives today. Thank you."

"It's the least I can do for my Lord." Dr. Layman left as Shawn finished off his sandwich.

"Would you like another?" asked Mrs. Layman speaking for the first time.

"As long as you're asking, yes." Mrs. Layman spoke something in African to Peter. He nodded and left.

"I appreciate your kindness," said Shawn.

"You're more than welcome young man."

"How long have you been missionaries?" Mrs. Layman thought for a moment.

"Let's see. Carl first came to Africa in 1952. He had just graduated from college. He wasn't even a doctor then. He was here for two years and then left and went to medical school. That's where we met. I was studying to be a nurse and he a doctor."

"What school did you attend?"

"The University of Edinburgh. He graduated third in his class. We were married in 1957 and left the next day for Africa."

"Have you been in Chad all this time?"

"No, we've been all over this continent. We started out in South Africa, then we went to Nigeria, Kenya, and now Chad. Carl has been in Africa a total of forty years. I've been here thirty-eight."

"Do you think you'll ever retire?"

"Retire? I doubt it. This is our home. I would be as out of place back in England as a penguin in the desert, though I wouldn't mind seeing my children again."

"How many children do you have?" She had a far away look in her eye.

"We had six. Two of them are in heaven."

"How did they die, if you don't mind my asking?"

"Our youngest child, his name was Michael died of the African fever when we were in Nigeria. In fact, he would be, let's see . . ." Just then Dr. Layman walked in.

"They're packing the truck with provisions now. We have to dig up some gasoline to put in them, and then we'll be ready to roll. How are you feeling young man?"

"Much better. Thank you. I really appreciate your kindness."

"You're more than welcome." Dr. Layman started to leave. His wife spoke to him.

"Carl, how old would Michael be this year?" He thought a moment.

"Thirty-five next month."

"That's about your age, isn't it?" asked Mrs. Layman.

"Pretty close. I'm thirty-four."

"He even had blond hair and blue eyes like you. Our daughter Elizabeth died eighteen months later. She was in college in England. She and some of her friends went for a canoe ride and she drowned."

"I'm sorry," was all Shawn could say.

"They're in heaven." Dr. Layman said. "We'll see them again. The Bible says to be absent from the body is to be present with the Lord. We miss them, of course. We always will, but God has blessed us with four other children and eleven grandchildren. Losing my children has given me a better understanding of the love of God. When we lost Michael, I got a tiny glimpse of what is must have been like for God to give His Son to die." Shawn couldn't help but smile.

"You're so right. You know you remind me a lot of my pastor back home and believe me, that's a very big compliment. That's just the kind of thing he would say."

"Are you a believer?" asked Dr. Layman.

"Yes, I am. I accepted the Lord when I was eleven years old during my Sunday school class." Peter came back in and spoke to Dr. Layman.

"I've got to run and grab my medical kit. They're filling the trucks up with gas now." He left. Shawn leaned over and tied his shoes and tried to brush some dirt off him.

"You sound like someone who's experienced the loss of a loved one."

"I have. My wife died a year ago and just recently I lost my father." He didn't elaborate.

"Were they also believers?"

"Yes ma'am, they were."

Dr. Layman reappeared.

"Time to go," he said.

CHAPTER FORTY-THREE

S hawn got in the truck next to Dr. Layman. Another truck with two Africans was right behind them.

"You'll have to lead the way, my friend." Shawn pulled out his GPS, punched a few buttons.

"You need to head that way," he said pointing north.

"What is that thing?" asked Dr. Layman.

"It's a Global Positioning System. It tells us exactly where we are. The plane wreck is 36.2 miles that way." He again pointed north. "Tell me about Peter. He seems like a really nice kid."

"Yes, he is. His mother was one of our first converts when we came to this village. Her husband died right before Peter was born. She asked us to take him under our wing and help her raise him. She even asked us to give him a Christian name. I've always enjoyed reading about the apostle Peter so I suggested Peter. My wife has taught him to read and we're corresponding with some people now who we hope will sponsor him to go to college in England in a few years."

"Wow, that would be great. So your wife taught him to read."

"Yes, Mary has a small school where she teaches some of the children. Not very big, she only has about twelve students. They're all bright, but Peter is the star of the class."

"He seems very sharp."

"Yeah, he's the pride of the village. He lives with his mother, but we consider him our adopted son."

It took them more than two hours to reach the hostages. Everyone cheered Shawn as if he were a hometown hero returning from a big football win. The other men who had gone out in search of help had returned empty handed. Shawn was the man of the hour. People were slapping him on the back and hugging him. They even sang, "For He's a Jolly Good Fellow."

"We had just about given you up for dead. I had already picked out a couple of men to go looking you. Thank God you found help."

Fortunately, the trucks were quite large. The six wounded were laid in the back of one truck. Dr. Kemper and eighteen of the others were able to fit in the other. Shawn, Major Hines, and several others unloaded the food, water, and blankets that they had brought with them. Within ten minutes, the two trucks were on their way. Shawn stayed behind with the others.

CHAPTER FORTY-FOUR

It was 3:00 in the morning as the President and First Lady rushed down the hall in their pajamas to the elevator. When the elevator door opened, Dr. Rhodes, two Secret Service agents, and two military officers met them. They skipped all the pleasantries.

"Mr. President, we just received a call from the British embassy in Chad. They are alive!" Dr. Rhodes said excitedly. The President's countenance changed to one of a giddy schoolboy being let out for the summer.

"Thank God. What happened to them?" he asked.

"Their plane was supposed to land at the capital, but apparently it was having some trouble and they had to do an emergency landing. They managed to make it to a small village with the help of a missionary doctor."

"How long before we can get them out?"

"We're working on that now, sir. As you know, we aren't very popular over there."

"You tell President . . . by the way, who is the President of Chad this week?"

"Mosharif."

"You tell President Mosharif to let our hostages go in a timely manner or, never mind, I'll tell him myself. Tell the Secretary of State I want a meeting in my office at 9:00."

"Uh, Mr. President, that's going to be rather difficult," said Dr. Rhodes.

"And why's that?"

"Because he's in Beijing." The President chuckled.

"That's right, and I sent him there. I want a National Security meeting then at 9:00. I want those hostages on their way home today."

"Mr. President." Dr. Rhodes said. "I think you should know there have been some casualties."

"Who?"

"Well, our information is sketchy at best. We heard from the missionary doctor's wife. She called the British embassy and informed them that one of the hostages made it to their village. Her husband and a few others left to bring them back, but there was one killed and several wounded."

"Any names?"

"No, she wasn't able to give them that information."

"So how do we get them out?"

"The British have offered to send vehicles to pick up the hostages. In fact they may have already left. They will pick them up and take them straight to the airport. We have a military transport plane already in flight on its way to the capital. From there they will be taken to the base at Heidelberg, Germany."

"Keep me informed."

"Yes sir."

It was nearly 10:00 at night when Shawn and the last of the hostages finally arrived back in the village. Dr. Layman was nowhere in sight. Hopping down from the truck, he looked around. Numbers of villagers crowded around them. He saw Jack, who had left with the first group. Shawn ran toward him.

"Hey Jack, have you seen Dr. Layman?"

"I think he's still in surgery."

"Surgery."

"Yeah, a couple of those wounded were in bad shape. I just heard a few minutes ago though that it looks like they're going to pull through."

"That's wonderful," said Shawn. Just then Dr. Kemper came walking toward them. He looked extremely tired. He stopped and spoke to Shawn.

"That man is truly a God send."

"Who?" asked Jack.

"Dr. Layman. I assisted him in surgery. The man is incredible. He saved their lives, no doubt about it. If they had been left to me, they'd have died for sure."

"Don't be so hard on yourself. You're the reason they lived long enough to get here," said Shawn.

"No, I'm not knocking myself. I'm just saying the surgery he performed on both men was not easy. Only an extremely skilled surgeon would even try." Peter came up to them.

"Mr. Miller, Dr. Layman has asked you to come with me."

"They've made arrangements for all of us tonight. I think he's going to show you where you're to sleep."

"Well then, gentlemen, until tomorrow."

"Hopefully, we'll be on our way home," said Dr. Kemper. Shawn followed Peter. He took him to a house made out of mud bricks. Shawn could hear a generator running behind the house.

He guessed this was Dr. Layman's home. Peter led him inside. It was a simple and yet tastefully decorated home. Most of the furniture was wicker. There was a nice dining room set in the kitchen and on the walls were several pieces of African art. The stove and refrigerator were gas.

"Dr. Layman said you can sleep here." Peter pointed to the bedroom. Shawn walked in. A large queen size bed sat in the middle of the room. It looked to be right out of a Sears catalog. On the bed were some clothes, soap, shampoo, towels, and a note. 'Dear Shawn, these clothes should fit you. They belonged to Carl but he's 'outgrown' them as it were. Peter will show you how to work the shower. I've also left some bread and meat for a sandwich in the refrigerator. Help yourself. We're staying with a friend tonight. We'll see you in the morning. Mary.'

"I'll show you how to work the shower," said Peter.

"Thank you. These are very kind people. Dr. Layman told me a little about you. He said you plan to go to college in England. What do you want to study?"

"I want to be a doctor and come back here and help my people."

He could see the sincerity in the boy's face.

"Well, my friend, I wish you the very best. I know you'll make an excellent doctor. You're very lucky to have someone like Dr. Layman around."

"Not lucky. We are blessed to have him."

"You're absolutely right. Forgive me. You are blessed, indeed."

CHAPTER FORTY-FIVE

Shawn was asleep as soon as his head hit the pillow. He was so out of it that he did not even hear the buses come into the village at 4:00 in the morning. They were courtesy of the British embassy. There were three buses in all. One had been made into a makeshift ambulance to carry the wounded. Two doctors and three nurses had also accompanied the entourage.

Peter woke him up at 6:00 that morning. He could smell something cooking in the kitchen and it smelled delicious. He walked into the kitchen to find Mrs. Layman cooking eggs and sausage.

"Good morning," she said cheerfully. "I trust you slept well."

"Yes I did. Thank you for your kindness. I felt guilty sleeping in your bed while you stayed somewhere else."

"Oh don't be. In fact," she said pointing to Peter, "we stayed with Peter and his mom. We don't mind a bit. By the way, are you ready to go home?" she said smiling.

"Home? Am I ever. Any idea when we'll be able to leave?"

"In about an hour. Your taxi came in two hours ago." Shawn rushed to the door and opened it. Sure enough, sitting in the middle of the village were three large buses. Many of the villagers as well as the hostages were standing around staring at them.

"I don't believe it. I'm finally going home. I never thought I'd see home again."

Shawn ate so fast he nearly choked on his food. As soon as he was done, he gave Mrs. Layman a sincere thanks and went outside.

He could overhear Major Hines talking to Dr. Layman.

"I want to thank you, doctor, for saving my men's lives. They would have died if it had not been for you."

"I was only too happy to help. Besides, it was God who brought you to us. I was merely his instrument."

"Well, I'll be sure to thank Him, too, but if there's anything we can do, please don't hesitate to ask."

"I only ask one thing in return. Tell people in your country that the need in this place is great. These people need medicine, food, clothes, and school supplies. We do what we can, but there is so much more we could do if people in my country and yours would open their eyes and their hearts to these people."

"Dr. Layman, not only will I tell people what I have seen, I will personally see to it that a large quantity of food, medicine, and supplies are sent to this village courtesy of the United States' government. It is the least we can do for you."

"I would be most grateful."

"Dr. Layman," said Shawn. "I, too, will be telling people what I have seen and I might be able to talk my church into making a one time donation along with my own."

"Like I said, it was God who brought you to us. He moves in mysterious ways."

"Dr. Layman, would you mind, before we all left, praying with us?"

"Why, I would be honored."

At 7:00 that morning all the hostages and most of the villagers gathered around in one huge circle. Dr. Layman was in the middle. All bowed their heads and closed their eyes as he prayed.

"Dear Lord, we thank you for your guidance and deliverance. We thank you for these people you have sent our way. We pray that you would guide them on their final journey home. Go before them, may they fear no evil because you are with them and may we be reunited again at thy throne. In the name of our Lord Jesus Christ we pray, Amen."

Shawn listened closely to his prayer. It sounded as if Dr. Layman were talking to an old friend. Then Shawn realized he was. As he finished one of the Africans began to sing, "God be with you 'til we meet again." Soon they all joined in. Even Harry was singing.

By 2:00 that afternoon all the hostages were on the plane bound for Germany. Shawn had huge butterflies in his stomach. His last two experiences on a plane had been horrible. As the plane taxied down the runway, he looked out the window and watched the ground disappear beneath him. Everyone on the plane cheered. They were finally leaving and going home. Theirs had been a long and difficult journey and yet it had brought them closer together. They had been through a terrible ordeal with each other. They were now friends for life. They would each leave and go their separate ways, but there would always be a bond between them.

For the first time in two days his thoughts turned to his father. Shawn had tried to avoid thinking about it because it was such an emotional thing, and until now he needed to keep his wits about him. Now as he began to reflect what had happened in the last two days, he was still troubled. He had more questions than answers. What was his dad involved in that would cause him to fake his own death and leave a family he loved? How was he able to get onto the Red Cross team and pass himself off as a psychologist? Who was the mysterious friend of his father's, who seemed to know all the answers, and yet his dad would not even tell Shawn his name? How would his family take this? Would they even believe him when he told them? When would be the right time to tell them? Shawn took out a notebook and pen. On it he wrote; Who is Dave? And below that: Why?

The flight to Germany took several hours. The whole way there, those questions were on Shawn's mind. He wrote down every conceivable possibility no matter how preposterous. As the plane descended, his mind still went over those two questions. About the only thing he was sure of, was that he had to find this man Dave. If he could talk to him, he would probably be able to answer the other question; Why? Why would a man leave his family and disappear for twenty-four years?

With his mind so deep in thought, Shawn almost forgot to be excited at the fact they were finally on American soil. They had landed on an American Air Force Base. His mind quickly came back to where he was when he heard someone say, "Look, there's the American flag!" Shawn looked out his window and sure enough, there she was; the star-spangled banner. A lump formed in his throat. Never in his entire life had seeing that flag brought more joy and pride than at that moment. It was the visible symbol of the nation he loved so much.

All the hostages were taken immediately to the base hospital. Most of them would be leaving the next day for the United States. A few of the more seriously wounded would be held over a few more days.

Shawn had never liked doctors. As an adult he positively hated going to the doctor. Part of it was the long hours he had spent at the doctors office and hospital when Amanda was so sick. He admired the profession, but they were, in his mind, a necessary evil. He had physicals before, but he had never had one so complete as this one. They examined every part of his body. They took samples of bodily fluids and poked and prodded him until he felt like a pin cushion. The doctor examining him was an Air Force major named Bill Ward. He looked to be about Shawn's age and actually bore a slight physical resemblance to Shawn, something several of the nurses pointed out. He was friendly enough.

Having to spend the night in a hospital bed was not how Shawn thought he would spend his first night of freedom. He felt fine. Dr. Ward though had told him that he did have a sight concussion and he wanted to wait for the test results before he would allow him to leave.

The highlight of the evening however was when a nurse came in and told him he had a telephone call. He picked up the phone in his room and in between sobs recognized his mother's voice on the other line.

They didn't talk very long. She was crying so hard about all he could make out was that she loved him, missed him, and was very happy he was safe. She then gave the phone to Heather who had no idea who was on the other line. A more excited little girl in the entire world would have been hard to find at that moment (or for that matter a more excited father). It was then that it truly hit him. He was going home. Shawn did not want her to go, but his sisters were there and he felt he needed to speak to them, also.

The next morning, all of the American hostages left for the United States. Shawn said a tearful goodbye to Mr. and Mrs. Smythe.

They promised to write and visit each other if ever they could.

As he boarded the plane, the thought occurred to him that the next time he left that door, he would be in the United States. The flight would take approximately nine hours. To him, they would seem like nine years. Shawn noticed that all the window seats were taken. He found an empty seat next to Jack.

Spirits on that plane were very high. They were going home and that was the most important thing, but they had also found out that they and their families would be eating dinner at the White House with the President. Having never met a President before, the prospects for Shawn were exciting. Shawn couldn't help but compare in his mind the differences between this same group of people now, and when they were first taken hostage. Shawn overheard Crystal telling someone she was going to take her boys to McDonald's and get a quarter pounder with cheese and a McFlurry.

"What are you going to do when you get home?" she asked Shawn. He had to think a minute.

"I'm going to take my daughter and my girlfriend on a picnic to the park and we're going to fly a kite." Crystal just laughed.

"Sounds like fun. What about you Jack?" Jack had been staring out the window oblivious to the conversation around him. "Jack?" he turned to Crystal. "I said, what are you going to do when you get home?"

"Not much, I have a car I've been working on. I'll probably finish fixing it."

Crystal and the others continued their conversation. Shawn nudged him.

"Hey, friend, haven't you heard? We're free. We're going home." There was silence. "That's supposed to be good news. We'll see our families again. You're supposed to be happy." Not only was Jack not happy, he looked downright miserable. "Look Jack, I'm not trying to be nosy at all, but you don't look too excited about going home. Mind if I ask what's wrong?"

"Well," he said slowly, "You're going home to your family. I don't have a family. All I have is a house to go to. A very lonely house. There isn't one person in this world who cares a hoot about me."

"Jack, I know that's not true. I care, and I thought you told me you had children."

"I do. I have one daughter." He paused. "I guess I can tell you. Shawn, I was the worst father in the entire world. I used to come home drunk every night. I would scream and curse at my family. He paused. "And I beat them. I beat my daughter so badly once she had to have stitches and I nearly killed my wife. In fact, I probably did kill her." Shawn just listened in total disbelief. He wasn't sure what to say. Jack continued, his voice cracking slightly. "They finally left me. They had left many times before, but they always came back. I made promises I never intended to keep. I'd stop the drinking and the beatings. They believed me and they'd always come back. Then one day I beat my wife so badly, she ended up in the hospital. Jennifer, my daughter, moved in with my wife's sister. After Ruth got out of the hospital, my daughter begged her to leave me for her own good. She finally did. She wrote me a letter and told me she loved me. She said she would always love me but she could no longer live with me. She had to protect her daughter and herself before I killed them both." Tears rolled down Jack's face but he continued. "Six months later, Ruth died of a heart attack. I don't care what the doctors say. She died of a broken heart. The man she loved had beaten her and crushed her spirit until there was nothing left. I killed her. I'm as guilty of murder as any inmate on death row. The ironic part is, I really believed until the day she died she still loved me." Shawn put a hand on Jack's shoulder and gently patted him. He didn't say anything. He just listened.

"A few days later they had her funeral. As I looked into her coffin, I would have gladly switched places with her if I could. I would have given everything in the world I owned to be able to tell her just one more time I loved her and I was sorry for all the pain I caused. It was too late. My own family wouldn't even speak to me at the funeral. A few days later I went to my sister-in-law's house to speak to Jennifer. She was a freshman in college at the time. I wanted to tell her how sorry I was. She wouldn't even let me get the words out of my mouth. She got angry and started screaming 'You killed her! You killed her!' She told me she never wanted to see me or hear from me again. As far as she was concerned, I didn't even exist." There was another pause as Jack took out a handkerchief and wiped his eyes. "That was fifteen years ago, and we have not spoken since. She's gone on and made something of her life. She's a nurse. She's married a fine young man and now has two children whom I've never even seen. She'll never forgive me for the hell I put her and her mother through. I just wish I could tell her how sorry I am and that I love her. If I could just tell her that, I'd never bother her again."

"Do you know where she lives?"

"Yes, she lives in Alexandria, Virginia. I've memorized her address in the hopes that one day she would forgive me. I know God has forgiven me. I made my peace with Him several years ago in a little country church. But Jennifer? She never will."

"Have you ever asked for God's help?"

"Well, I asked Him to forgive me."

"I know you asked for His forgiveness, but have you ever asked Him to bring you and your daughter back together again?" Jack thought for moment and then said,

"No, I guess I never did. I guess after what I did to her I never thought He would."

"Maybe the reason He hasn't is because you never asked Him."

"It'd take a miracle to bring us back together."

"Jack, don't tell me you don't believe in miracles after all we've been through."

"Oh, of course I believe in miracles but wouldn't it be too presumptuous for me to ask God for one more. I mean, isn't there a limit to how many miracles He gives one person?"

"The Bible says, 'Ye have not because ye ask not.' God limits His miracles because of our lack of faith. Let me ask you something. Do you believe that God can bring you and your daughter back together again?"

"Yes, I know He can. I guess I just thought I didn't deserve her back again."

"Aren't you glad God doesn't always give us what we deserve?"

Jack smiled. "You'll never know how much." There was a slight twinkle in his eye. "You think I could ask Him now?"

"Why not? The sooner you ask, the sooner he'll answer."

"Will you pray with me?"

"I'd be honored." Together they bowed their heads and Shawn prayed first.

"Dear Lord, I thank you that soon we will be home and with the ones we love. Lord, I pray for Jack. He's asked your forgiveness, and we pray that he will be reunited with his daughter and her family soon. We know you can change the hearts of people. Thank you. Amen." Then Jack prayed.

"Lord, you know I've been the worst kind of sinner and I don't deserve what I'm asking, but you've proven that you love me in spite of myself. If it's not asking too much," Jack was trying to choke back the tears, "Please let me see my little girl again." Jack could not finish his prayer. Shawn put his hand on Jack's shoulder.

"Well, now that you've asked, all we have to do is wait for the answer. You said your daughter lives in Alexandria?"

"Yes, she's a nurse."

"We're landing at Andrews Air Force Base. That's not too far away. Who knows, maybe she'll be there waiting for you."

CHAPTER FORTY-SIX

It was a beautiful, clear day as the plane began its descent to home and family. There was barely a cloud in the sky. Shawn could see for miles around. There was something comforting about finally being over the United States again. The plane circled a few times and made its approach to the runway at Andrews. Shawn saw a large number of military aircraft parked there. He remembered reading that Air Force One was kept at Andrews when it was not in use. His ears were popping, but he didn't care. When the wheels finally touched down the entire plane erupted into cheering and clapping. Even Jack was smiling. They had made it home.

It seemed like an eternity before they finally were able to disembark the plane. In reality it was only a few minutes. As Shawn walked out the door of the plane, a crowd of hundreds of people began to cheer. A huge banner read, "Welcome Home."

He was three steps from the bottom when he spotted a little blond headed girl running toward him with all her might. When he reached the ground, he bent down just as Heather rushed into his arms.

"Daddy!" Shawn squeezed her so hard he had to make sure her didn't hurt her. "Daddy, we missed you!" His mother, his sisters, and their families also came running to him. He picked Heather up and carried her in one arm and gave a rather awkward hug to each of them.

"And what about me?" came a voice. Shawn turned and looked. "Angela!"

His family was quick to notice that her hug was longer than theirs. They were directed to a small reception area inside where they were able to sit and talk for a while. After a few minutes of laughing, crying, and a few more hugs, Shawn looked over and saw Jack standing off to the side drinking a glass of tea. When he caught Jack's eye, Jack slowly shook his head 'no.' Shawn never felt so sorry for anyone in the world as he did for Jack at that moment. No one had come to see him. His thoughts were interrupted as a well-dressed man came up and spoke.

"Excuse me, Mr. Miller?" Shawn looked up, instantly recognizing him as the President's Chief of Staff, Andrew Perry. Shawn stood up and shook his hand.

"Mr. Perry, this is an honor, sir."

"The honor is mine. Welcome home. As I'm sure you and your family are aware, the President has invited all of you along with the other hostages and their families for dinner at the White House tonight. He sends his apologies. He had planned to be here now, but something came up. He's most anxious to meet all of you tonight."

"Well, we're pretty excited about meeting him."

"Mr. Miller, I know you've just arrived and are anxious to spend time with your family, but the President was wondering if it would be possible for him to meet with you privately for a few minutes." Shawn's reaction was a mixture of surprise and puzzlement.

"The President wants to meet me?"

"Yes, sir. If that's okay. Unfortunately he's leaving tonight right after dinner for the G-8 Summit in Madrid. He'll then be visiting Eastern Europe. He won't be back for two weeks and the only time he can meet with you is this afternoon. I realize this is short notice, and I do apologize but . . ."

"Mr. Perry, I will be more than happy to meet the President now or whenever is convenient for him." A smile came across his face and he winked, "Of course, I'll have to cancel my meetings with the Pope and the Queen of England."

An hour later Shawn was in a limousine on his way to the White House. His family was getting settled in their hotel rooms courtesy of the U. S. government. They, along with all the other hostages and families would be coming later.

Pulling into the gate of the White House was an impressive site. Shawn had only seen it once. As a teenager he came to Washington and saw the White House from the street. He had never been in. He felt a little out of place.

Shawn followed the military aide to the West Wing. He had seen the TV show. Now he was in the real thing. They stopped in front of one of the secretary's desks. She was talking on the phone. She pointed to a chair and whispered, "Please, have a seat." After a minute she hung up.

"Hello, Mr. Miller. The President will see you in just a few minutes." After a couple of minutes, she answered the intercom. "Yes sir." She looked at Shawn. "The President will see you now. Just go right through there." The butterflies in his stomach were now the size of elephants. Shawn stepped into the most famous office in the world. The President was on the phone and had his back to him. He turned when Shawn entered and motioned for him to sit on the couch.

"I'll be with you in just a minute."

Shawn did as he was asked. He couldn't help but stare at the President. Many times he had seen him on TV making speeches or giving his State of the Union address. He felt uncomfortable with the fact that he was alone in the Oval Office with the most powerful man in the entire world. It was nothing against the President. Shawn liked this man. He was a natural born leader. This man would be in the history books hundreds of years from now. He was a man you couldn't help but admire, whether or not you agreed with his politics. Born to humble origins, he had served as a Navy officer for thirty years before becoming the youngest Chairman of the Joint Chiefs in history. After his retirement from the Navy he served for two years as the Secretary of State for his predecessor, a Democrat, before running for President himself as a moderate Republican. The history books would long remember his service in the military and state department, but he would always be remembered as the first President of the United States to be of African-American descent. Yes, there was much about President David Connors to admire.

The President hung up the phone and walked over to Shawn. Shawn stood and shook his hand.

"Mr. President, this is truly and honor. I'm . . ."

"Shawn Allan Miller. Born January 9, 1970. Graduated from Wilson High School in 1988. Earned a degree in Elementary Education from UNC. Recent widower and father of one. It's good to see you again." "Again?" thought Shawn. He was feeling very uncomfortable right now.

"Wow. I'm impressed. Did the CIA tell you all that?"

The President laughed. "The CIA, now that's funny. Actually they're not too happy with me right now. They told me they needed 30 billion more dollars to fight the terrorists and I told them . . . well, never mind."

The President studied him for a moment.

"You look like him."

"Look like who, sir?"

"Your dad. Duke Miller." Shawn felt the room spinning. He had not heard his dad called that in twenty-five years. No one but his closest friends knew his nickname. He was totally unprepared for this.

"You? You're my dad's friend who works for the government? So you're 'Dave.'" The President turned misty eyed for a moment.

"Let me level with you for a minute. This job," he said pointing to his desk. "This job may be the loneliest job in the world. When you take away the cheering crowds and the state dinners, and the weight of an entire nation under attack falls on your shoulders, it really is lonely. One reason for that, is you're never quite sure who your friends are. When the going is good, the country's at peace, and the economy is growing, friends come out of the woodwork. A crisis hits, and you couldn't buy a friend. Besides my own family, the one person in this whole world whom I knew would stick with me through thick and thin was your dad. Losing him was painful beyond words. He was the finest, most honorable man I ever knew and without question, the bravest."

"Mr. President, I'm at a loss for words. I never knew you even met my father, let alone were his closest friend. I have so many questions I want to ask you."

"I tell you what. Why don't I just start from the beginning? I'll tell you all I can and maybe more than I should, but I think you have the right to know."

Shawn nodded silently.

"Your father and I served in Vietnam together. You've probably guessed that by now. We flew missions together and became the best of friends. One day in December of 1972, we were flying over North Vietnam when our plane was shot down by a surface to air missile. Both of us were wounded, but I was severely wounded. We landed in enemy territory. We were fifteen miles from safety, and enemy soldiers were all around us. I was losing blood and unable to even walk. I knew I was slowing him down, and if I didn't get help soon, I would die. No sense in both of us getting captured, so I told him to leave me behind. He could come back later for me. He flatly refused to leave me. He said either we were both going to make it out alive or neither of us would. Several times I told him to leave me, but he wouldn't do it. Through the grace of God and your father's determination, he was able to drag me bleeding and dying to safety. I owed him my life. There was absolutely no question in my mind whatsoever that I would have died out there in the jungles of Vietnam if it hadn't been for your father. That's when I knew I had a friend I could trust, and I'm very grateful to say that I believed your father shared that trust with me."

Shawn cut right to the chase. "But why did he disappear for so many years?"

"I still can't tell you everything, but I'll tell you all I can. Have you ever heard of the Bowman Affair?"

"I have."

"Tell me what you know about it."

"Well, only what I've read in the history books. Apparently there was a network of spies within the military who were giving some very sensitive secrets to the Russians."

"The history books are too kind. There was a network of spies, but unfortunately they were also involved in assassination, sabotage, espionage, and a whole list of other atrocities. Do you recall how we discovered them?"

"Well, a man code named the Informant turned them in. He was a CIA agent, if my memory serves me correctly. His identity has been one of the most closely guarded secrets ever next to the identity of Deep Throat. Some even suggested it was the same person."

"The history books say he was a CIA agent. In reality, he was a Navy officer. We chose to keep his identity to protect him." He paused. "And his family."

"You mean, my dad was the Informant?" The President didn't answer.

"We knew for years there was a secret spy ring working inside the government, particularly the Navy, but also the CIA and the FBI. We set up a team to investigate it. The operation was run largely by Naval Intelligence. The only problem was, the man supervising the investigation, a highly decorated officer, was one of the spies. When two of the investigators died under mysterious circumstances, the third member became suspicious of his supervisor and passed the information along to your father's commanding officer Captain Russell Anderson. The problem was, the spies had been following the movements of all the investigators and knew he had passed the information to Captain Anderson. You were old enough to remember what happened to Anderson and his family, so I won't rehash it, but before he died, he gave copies of everything to your dad, and then Anderson and his whole family were brutally murdered. The message was clear. They would kill anyone who tried to turn this information over to the proper authorities. When your house burned down, Duke thought they might be on to him. That's when he called me and I heard something in his voice I never heard before."

"What was that?" asked Shawn.

"Fear. More than fear. Sheer terror. Duke wasn't afraid of dying. He proved that in Vietnam. But he was mortally afraid of what they would do to you. What he saw in the Anderson home that morning was the most horrible thing he'd ever seen. All he could think about was what would they do to you and your mom and sisters."

"I remember that. He sent us to my uncle's house."

"That's right, and he drove through the night to get to Washington. I was working in the Pentagon at the time. We talked for many hours. Duke knew he had to turn over what he had, but what would they do to him and more importantly, you." The President got up and walked over to his intercom.

"Betty, would you please send in Mr. Tiseman? Thank you." A

few seconds later a tall dark haired man walked into the room. Shawn immediately recognized him. Here was the mysterious stranger he had seen so many times in his life. The man who showed up at important events throughout his life and then disappeared into thin air.

"Shawn, I'd like you to meet Mr. Richard Tiseman." They shook hands. The President continued. "God works in mysterious ways. The day before Duke came to see me, I overheard someone talking about Mr. Tiseman here. He works with the Federal Witness Protection Program. Now normally the witness protection program hides people who testify about criminals, usually drug lords or mafia families. Mr. Tiseman, however, works with a special division of the Federal Witness Protection Program. He handles individuals whose identities must be concealed for National Security reasons. His clients, if you want to call them that, are among our country's most closely guarded secrets. He alone knows their true identities. In fact, he's not even supposed to tell me who they really are, though I would never ask." The President continued.

"When Duke came to see me, he told me everything. He knew he had to turn over the information he had, but he also knew he was in great danger. You see, Shawn, we didn't have all of them."

"You mean the spies?"

"I mean the spies, assassins, predators, all rolled into one. The information Anderson gave your dad pinpointed most of them, but there were two of these monsters unaccounted for."

"So my dad was worried the ones you didn't catch would figure out who turned them in and have that person killed."

"And his family." Said the President soberly.

"Whatever happened to the ones you didn't catch?"

"Oh, we caught them, and I think Duke knew we would, the question was, would we get them before they got you. Duke didn't want to take that chance. He gave me the information and I gave it directly to the Secretary of Defense, but even he didn't know where it had come from. He then set me up with Mr. Tiseman here. We tried to talk Duke into allowing your whole family to enter the Federal Witness Protection Program, but he refused. We even offered to send you to another country like Canada, or New

Zealand, but again he refused. You must remember. We were dealing with the KGB. He felt there was no where in the world he could go that they wouldn't find him. The thought of seeing what happened to the Anderson family happen to you . . . " the President's voice trailed off.

"So whose idea was it for him to fake his death?" asked Shawn.

"Actually, it was Duke's. He said the only way to get the KGB off his back was if they thought he was dead and someone else turned over the information. We waited a month after his supposed death before we arrested them but of course we kept them under observation all the time. We made it look like Anderson had turned over the information before he died. Fortunately, they never made the connection. The night after I gave the information to the Secretary, Mr. Tiseman arranged for your father to have an accident. The plan was simple yet brilliant. He was able to take the body of a homeless man from the morgue. He was about the same size and age as Duke. He put your dad's uniform on him, then put him in the driver's seat of his car and pushed the car over the cliff. He then went to a gas station and called the police."

"So that explains it." Said Shawn quietly. "And he hadn't been drinking then?"

Mr. Tiseman spoke up. "No, he hadn't."

"So who was the Navy officer who went into the bar that night and left drunk?"

Mr. Tiseman smiled. "I never was a very good actor."

"We had an understanding that Mr. Tiseman would look in on your family occasionally."

"Mr. Tiseman," Shawn said. "I owe you a 'thank you' for helping my dad out."

"I was honored to know him."

With that, Mr. Tiseman left. The President and Shawn were quiet for a moment. Shawn broke the silence.

"Did you ever catch the other two?"

"You mean the other two spies? Yes, we did. We caught one in Stockholm trying to give the secrets of SDI to the Russians. He worked for a Defense Contractor. The other one, well, we just caught him last year. He was by the far the most difficult one to catch."

"Who was he?" asked Shawn.

"I probably shouldn't tell you this, but I will. Have you heard of Philip Hanford?"

"The FBI agent they arrested for . . ."

"He's the one. He was giving vital secrets to the Russians."

"Wow, everyone in the country's heard of him. That was all over the news. So why didn't my dad come home after that?"

"He thought about it, I know. But he finally decided it was in everybody's best interest to stay where he was. I don't think he ever got over what he saw that night at the Anderson home. People in the intelligence community have long memories. He still didn't want to take a chance that someone out there might want to seek revenge."

"So, did you see him a lot?"

"Actually, I haven't seen him since the night of the accident. We would write to each other a few times a year, but our mail always went through Mr. Tiseman. I had no idea where Duke was."

"So where was he all this time?"

"He moved up to Vancouver and started a small but successful computer company. He was pretty much a loner that whole time. Really his only outlet was a home for boys he worked with as a volunteer. He would work there ten to fifteen hours a week. They loved him there. He donated thousands of dollars worth of food, clothes, and sports equipment. He spent very little on himself."

"How did he ever get on the Red Cross team?"

"Well, that's a whole different story. He heard about the hijacking, but he had no idea who was on that plane until he picked up a copy of USATODAY. They had a list of all the hostages, their ages, and where they lived. When he saw Miller, Shawn A., age 34, Wilson, North Carolina, he was livid. He absolutely demanded to speak to me. Richard told me Duke wanted to talk to me and I gave in."

"What did he say?"

"He asked me if we were going to do anything about it. I told him we were. He asked me what and I told him what I could. I mentioned that a Red Cross team would be going in to check on you. He demanded that he be on that team. I, of course, told him no, and then, well, let's just say Duke could be very persistent when he wanted to be."

"What did he say?" Shawn said smiling.

"He told me that after everything he had done for this country, after all he had given up, the very least we could do, was let him into Libya to see his son. We owed it to him." Once again the President turned misty eyed. "He never could bring himself to say that I owed it to him. I tried my darnedest to talk him out of it. I told him it was dangerous, as if that might have actually made him reconsider. I told him if he went and were captured, we would deny all knowledge of his existence. Of course that made no difference to him. He finally told me, "I'm going in and I'll do it with or without your help." The President laughed. "You know, I wouldn't have been at all surprised if he had walked right into that prison all by himself and walked right out again with all of you. I know he would have died trying." He paused. "I guess he did die trying."

"So you fixed it so that he could be on the team?"

"I won't bore you with all the details of how I did that. Let's just say I had to call in a lot of favors. I had to do it. I owed it to him. I knew I had to do it. Fortunately, the head of the International Red Cross is a close personal friend. I was able to arrange it." The President thought for a moment. "Here's something I didn't know until today. The day before your dad left, he willed everything he owned to that boy's home. His house, car, all the money in his bank account, even his clothes. He wasn't a wealthy man, but he had managed to save some money. I think he knew he was not coming back." The President spoke almost philosophically. "One way or the other, he wasn't coming back."

"So the escape was his idea?"

"Mostly, I say that because we did have a couple of ideas floating around, but Duke filled us in with all the necessary details. I'm not sure you realize how smart your dad was. I'm sure he was a genius or near genius. His mind was like a camcorder. From the second he walked into the place, he memorized the dimensions of the base, how many guards there were, how far apart they were, how often they changed, what kind of weapons they used, where all the prison cells were, how far apart they were, and how often the guards patrolled. The man was a walking encyclopedia. We never could have pulled off what we did without him." The buzzer on the intercom went off.

"Excuse me a second." The President answered the phone. Shawn overheard him say, "Just give me about five more minutes, then send him in." He hung up.

"I have a meeting with the French ambassador, but he can wait a few minutes. After the way they acted during this hostage situation, I don't mind making him wait a while." The President smiled. Shawn stood to his feet. It was clear the President had other things he needed to do and his time was precious.

"Mr. President, this has been such an honor. I feel so over-whelmed now, I don't know what to say."

"Duke was my closest friend. I will miss him very much. I'm glad to have met you again."

"If I may say so sir, you were a very good friend to him too. He obviously trusted you, and with good reason. My family and I thank you from the bottom of our hearts."

"I appreciate that. By the way, there's one more thing I need to tell you. I haven't told your family about this situation. I thought I would leave that in your capable hands. You tell them whenever you're ready."

"Thank you." Shawn turned and walked to the door. As he opened it, he looked back at the President.

"Mr. President, may I ask you one more question?"

"Sure."

"Did we ever meet before?"

Again he smiled. "We did. A long time ago. You were three or four at the time. Your dad and I took you and my nephew David fishing. You walked into the lake and . . ."

"And I slipped on a rock. You helped me up and carried me back to shore." Again the President smiled and nodded. "I remember that. For a long time I was deathly afraid of water, but I remember a man helping me out of the lake. All these years I thought it was just a childhood dream or something."

CHAPTER FORTY-SEVEN

Dinner at the White House that night was marvelous. Shawn had never experienced anything like it. To have dinner with the President was something he never dreamed of. He actually didn't discuss much of his meeting with President Connors and his family. They didn't seem too willing to bring it up and he didn't want to get into the whole story right there.

During the meal, Shawn spotted Jack sitting at another table. He made his way over there and bent down so no one could hear their conversation.

"How's it going, Jack?"

"Good." He said unconvincingly. "I just wish . . . " his voice trailed off.

"I know. Have you heard from any of your family?"

"If by family you mean my daughter, then no, I haven't heard from her. I fly back to Seattle tomorrow and I just can't help but wonder if I'll ever see her again."

"You say she lives not too far away from here?"

"Less than ten miles."

"Well, why don't you go see her tonight?" Jack looked at him like he had lost his mind.

"You gotta be kidding me." Jack said a little too loudly. People were now looking at the two. Shawn just smiled and waved. Jack lowered his voice.

"I appreciate what you are trying to do, but to just show up on her front doorstep after fifteen years and say, 'Hi honey, it's me, your miserable excuse for a father.' She'd throw me out on my ear."

"Jack, where's your faith?"

"After what I did, it's hard to have faith that anyone would forgive me."

"Jack excuse me for just a minute." Shawn left and went and spoke to his mother. Jack had no idea what they were saying but Mrs. Miller was nodding her head in agreement. Shawn came back.

"Jack, I've got it all worked out. Let's go to your daughter's house together. My mom will let me use her car. As soon as this is over, I'll drive you over there. I'm putting feet to my prayers."

"Shawn, I really don't think this is such a good idea. I'm grateful for all you've done, but this really isn't your concern."

"Jack, for fifteen years you've been miserable. You clearly still love your daughter. If you don't go now, you may never get another chance. At least if you go to her house and talk to her, you'll know one way or the other and you won't have to wonder for the rest of your life. Jack, do you believe God can bring you two back together?"

"I don't know. I suppose He can, but I don't know if He will."

"Jack. You can at least try. The Bible says if we have faith the size of a mustard seed we can move mountains. Give God a chance to work. Who knows, maybe this is exactly what He wants to show you your faith is not in vain." Jack just stared at his plate for a moment. "Jack, you see that pretty little girl over there." Shawn pointed to Heather who was discussing her hero, 'Barney the purple dinosaur' with the First Lady and Becky. "I love her so much it hurts. If anything ever came between us, I would do everything I could to make things right again. I know you want to do the same. Stop thinking with your head and start thinking with your heart."

"I don't even know if she's home."

"We won't know until we try."

It was 9:30 before all the former hostages and their families left the White House. Jack and Shawn got in Becky's Park Avenue and headed toward Arlington.

Jennifer Saunders was sitting on the couch watching her favorite TV show, "Survivor." She had taped it earlier in the week and had not had a chance to finish it. Her husband Tim, who was an English teacher at the local high school was busily grading papers. He taught at a community college during the summer. The two of them had been happily married for nine years and had two children, two boys aged seven and five, named Tyler and Camden.

When she heard a knock at the door, she paused the video and looked at her watch. It was 9:45. Who in the world would be visiting at this hour. She opened the door and saw a tall, blond man with blue eyes and a nice smile standing on her doorstep.

"Good evening, is this the home of Jennifer Saunders?" he asked.

"Yes, I'm Mrs. Saunders, may I help you?"

"My name is Shawn Miller, would it be possible for me to speak with you for a few minutes?"

"Who is it honey?" A tall slender man with brown hair came up behind her.

"There's a man here who wants to talk to us."

"It's kind of late. Do you mind if I ask what this is about?" asked Tim.

"Actually, it's about Jennifer's dad." It was quiet for a moment.

"I recognize you." Tim said. "You're one of the hostages they just freed. I saw you on CNN this afternoon. That was quite an ordeal you went through. Please come in."

"Thank you." Tim motioned for them to sit on the couch.

"So how can we help you?" He asked.

"I came to talk to you about your dad, Jennifer. He was one of the hostages in Libya." A deadening silence came over the room. The tone in Jennifer's voice changed.

"I heard he was one of the hostages." She said with a definite coldness in her voice. "This is not going well." Thought Shawn.

"Your father is a very brave man. He was willing to risk his life to save others." This time there was anger in Jennifer's voice.

"My dad is the meanest, cruelest man in the world. You must be talking about a different man. He's one I never want to see again. Is that all you came to say?" Shawn felt the need for diplomacy here. Odd, he thought, he was more nervous talking to an angry woman than he was the prison guards in Libya.

"Jennifer, I am talking about a different man. Your father told me about his drinking, and abusing you and your mother. Believe me, if he could do anything in the world to go back and change that he would, but he can't. He can only ask for forgiveness. He's changed. He's made his peace with God and now he wants to make his peace with you." Jennifer began to cry. Tim sat quietly patting her hand.

"You don't know what that man did to me. My life will never be normal because of him. You just don't know." She sobbed.

"Jennifer," Shawn said gently, "you're right. I don't know what you've been through, but God does and He's willing to forgive him, why don't you do the same also."

"It won't be easy," she said still weeping.

"No, it won't. It takes courage."

"I guess you know something about courage."

"Courage is shown in many ways. To forgive someone for a lifetime of wrongdoing takes more courage than I've ever had." Jennifer looked at Tim. They were silent for a moment.

"Honey, it's your decision, but I think he's right. We talked about this very thing yesterday." Jennifer thought for a minute. It was clear that she was struggling with it in her mind. Silently she nodded.

"I don't even know where he is," she said wiping her eyes.

"I do. Would you excuse me for a minute?" Shawn walked outside and came back in. "I'd like to introduce you to a friend of mine." Shawn stepped aside to reveal Jack standing behind him.

"Daddy?"

"Jenny." The two hugged each other and cried like children. Shawn felt a happiness inside him he had never known. It was worth everything he had been through just to see a family reunited.

"Can you ever forgive me?"

"Oh, Daddy, forgive me." There was more crying. Finally Jennifer said, "Daddy, I'd like you to meet some very special people. This is my husband Tim." The two men shook hands. Jenny went and woke up the boys. "And these are your grandsons, Tyler and Camden."

"Jenny, they're such fine looking boys." He gave them each a hug.

"You were right, my friend," Jack said to Shawn. "You were absolutely right."

"And I want to thank you also, Shawn. Tonight a great burden has been lifted off my shoulders," said Jenny.

"It's what God did. I'm merely his servant."

"I see you've met my guardian angel here." Said Jack as he put a hand on Shawn's shoulder.

Shawn and Jack left an hour later. Jenny invited her father over for breakfast the next day before he left for Seattle. Few times in his life had Shawn ever felt so good.

CHAPTER FORTY-EIGHT

The long awaited family meeting would finally take place
Sunday afternoon. Sunday morning at 10:00, the whole Miller
family and Angela were at church on time. Many people came up to
him and shook his hand or hugged him and let him know that they
had been praying for him. In the service that morning, Pastor Jim
took a moment and gave a prayer of thanks for bringing the
hostages and especially Shawn safely home. What Shawn could not
get over was seeing Uncle Henry and Aunt Bonnie on the second
row of the church. Uncle Henry was smiling and happy, and not just
because Shawn was home. He was a totally different man. After the
service, he saw Henry and Pastor Jim talking and laughing like old
friends. Pastor Jim was asking Uncle Henry to sing in the choir. He
had heard that Henry had a beautiful tenor voice.

Shawn had asked Angela to be with him during the family
meeting, but she refused. She came for Sunday lunch but not the
meeting. This would be a very personal and private meeting
between the family. She did not belong there. She did, however,
agree to watch Heather and Ashley. She would take them to her
house and let them play and bring them to church that night.

After lunch was over, the dishes cleared, and Angela and the
girls were gone, Shawn, Becky, Sara, Shannon, Jeff, and Todd all
gathered around a circle in the living room. They all sat and listened
in rapt attention as Shawn spoke.

"I have something I need to tell you, all of you, about what happened." He paused. "Everything I've told you so far about what took place in Africa was true, but there were some things I didn't tell you. I did that intentionally because I wanted to wait until we were all together and could talk about it." Shawn choked on his words. He wasn't crying. He just wasn't quite sure how to say it and make sense. His mother sensed his hesitation.

"Son, whatever it is, you can tell us. We're here for you. Take your time if you need to." Shawn decided to get right to the point. He spoke quietly but firmly.

"Dad didn't die in that car accident twenty-four years ago. He died in Africa saving our lives." You could have heard a pin drop. For the next two hours Shawn slowly and carefully told the entire story. He left nothing out. He told of the Dirty Dozen, the house fire, the Andersons, the rescue, and his father's death. No one interrupted, moved, or even asked a question. When he was done, his audience was silent again. His sisters and brothers-in-law sat wide eyed with a look of shock and surprise and yet acceptance, but what really threw them all for a loop was the look on his mother's face. There was no look of shock or horror in her eyes, just a smile and a nod of acceptance. The shock of finding out his father was still alive was nothing compared to the stunning realization that came to him now. Like a bolt of lightening from heaven, he suddenly realized why; why his mother refused to discuss his father's death, why she never discussed their relationship with President Connors, and most of all, the real reason she never married Dr. Seth Greene. Mother and son's eyes met. Shawn's voice trembled a little.

"You knew. All this time you knew he was still alive and you never told us? Why?" Becky studied her hand for a moment.

"Shawn, sometimes the truth is best left unsaid. I didn't know for sure, in fact at first I believed he was dead, but then some strange things started happening."

"Like what?"

"Like the Navy giving us $200,000 worth of life insurance I wasn't aware we had. Like mysterious people checking on us. I made an appointment to speak to someone in the Department of the Navy and they strongly recommended I leave the situation alone. Do you remember the fall of 1985 when we went to Washington,

D.C. and saw the Vietnam Memorial?"

"Yes, I remember it well."

"I wouldn't swear to it in court, but I saw a man standing under a tree about fifty feet away from us, that bore a striking resemblance to your father. He was wearing sunglasses and seemed to be watching us. If it wasn't him, then it was someone who sure looked like him." Shawn spoke up.

"I remember that. You were very upset and we had a hard time calming you down."

"Why didn't you tell us what you suspected?" Sara asked.

"Because I had no proof and because if I had you'd have gone investigating on your own. You did anyway. Like the time you drove up to Richmond and interviewed the policeman who arrived on the scene of the accident first."

"You knew about that?" said a very surprised Shawn.

"Of course I did. He called the next day wanting to talk to you. He told me the whole story. If I had told you I thought your father was still alive, you'd have bugged very FBI agent and Naval officer from here to California. If your father was still alive and hiding somewhere, he probably had a very good reason. I didn't want you or him in danger."

"You know, mom, I think it's time we all stopped keeping secrets from each other." They all gave each other a group hug and just held each other for a few moments.

"Well," Becky said. "Since we're not keeping secrets anymore, I should tell you, I'm going to be a grandmother once again."

"Mom!" Sara said playfully. "You weren't supposed to tell."

"Well, you know how bad I am at keeping secrets like that."

"Actually," Shannon spoke up. "Mom, you're going to be a grandmother twice again."

CHAPTER FORTY-NINE

In the two months since his return home, three major events happened that would change Shawn's life. The first one happened a week after he got home. He found out that his friend Mrs. Jones, the principal of Mountain View Elementary School would be moving to Raleigh to take a job with the State Department of Education. The current assistant principal of Mountain View, Mrs. Pullman, would become the new principal beginning in the fall of 2004. This created an opening for assistant principal. Even before the hostage situation, Shawn's name had come up, unbeknownst to him, as a possible candidate for the job by Mrs. Jones and Mrs. Pullman. This time Colin Daniels agreed. Shawn was called into Mr. Daniels office and asked to consider the position. It would be an increase in both pay and responsibility. Shawn eagerly accepted. There was one draw back though, he would now be Angela's boss.

The second event happened in early August. In a quiet cere-mony in the White House, the President posthumously awarded the Congressional Medal of Honor to John Miller. Shawn accepted the award on behalf of his family. He looked down at the medal. The golden star, the blue ribbon with fourteen white stars on it. It wasn't very big but it spoke volumes about the courage of its recipient. Shawn was surprised they had awarded it to his dad, not because he didn't think his father deserved it but because they only awarded it to people in the armed forces. The President explained that his father had never been discharged from the Navy, so technically he was still active duty, and he died in combat.

The third event happened two weeks before the funeral at Arlington National Cemetery. He and Angela had been special friends for many months. Since his return home, they had spent quite a lot of time in each others company. There was a little coffee and yogurt place they liked to go. They went at least twice a week. They were creatures of habit. They got the same thing every time. She got an iced mocha, and Shawn got a vanilla yogurt with Oreos on top. Friday, August 30, seemed like any other Friday to Angela. She met Shawn at 6:00. They had dinner at her house, and then they went to the yogurt shop. This time however, Shawn had something important to say. They sat quietly for a minute enjoying each other's company. Angela was looking off into the distance and Shawn was looking at her. She had an innocent, almost childlike look in her eye. She seemed deep in thought. To Shawn, she had never looked more beautiful.

"I love you," he said in a quiet and sincere voice.

"I love you, too." She paused for a moment and then added, "very much."

"So what do we do about it?" asked Shawn.

"I don't know. I'm new at this." She continued. "I want you to know. I'm not trying to replace Amanda."

"I know that."

"I don't want you to be afraid to talk about her around me. I know that she was your first love and Heather's mother. I don't want you to think that I expect you to give any of that up for me."

"I never thought that."

"I just wanted to make sure you knew my intentions."

"And now I want you to know mine. What happens when two people fall in love?" Angela didn't say anything. "We're both old enough that I think we don't have to play the teenage games of dating. We know what we want, and there's no beating around the bush."

"You mean we're not going to swap class rings?" she said jokingly.

"Oh, I intend to give you a ring, but I'm afraid it won't be my class ring. I lost it a couple of years ago. The ring I had in mind has a diamond on it."

"I have my old high school ring at my parent's house. I could give them a call and have them mail it."

"No thanks, just a plain gold band will do."

"My cousin's a jeweler. I'm sure I can get a discount." She said.

"Tell your family not to make any plans this winter. Nothing that can't be changed."

"I'm sure they'll understand."

Shawn held her left hand and looked at it.

"When I officially ask you . . . "

"I'd rather you not tell me anything about that. I'd rather be surprised."

"I was just going to tell you that I'm a little shy. So I thought I'd write you a note with a yes, no, check one box, and pass it to you."

A week later, Shawn drove to Nags Head, North Carolina to stay in a condo owned by his aunt. Angela was also going with her father and mother. They rented a condo for the weekend one mile away from the condo Shawn's aunt owned. They all drove down Thursday night.

Friday morning Shawn played golf with Mr. Bierman. It was just the two of them. Shawn had something he wanted to ask him. Angela warned him not to beat her dad too badly in golf. They finished nine holes and had lunch at the clubhouse. Shawn finally got around to asking.

"Mr. Bierman, there's something I need to ask you."

"Please, call me Ken. I was wondering when you would get to that," he said smiling.

"You know by now that I'm in love with your daughter, and she's given the indication that she may be in love with me." Ken laughed a big hearty laugh.

"Given the indication, you've got to be kidding. My boy, you are all she's talked about for months. Every time we talk to her we hear about you. Her mother and I, no offense, are a little tired of hearing about you all the time."

"Well, that's good to hear," said Shawn. "I would like your permission to marry her. I promise you that I will love her and take good care of her. We may never be rich, but I really believe we will be happy together and more important, I believe God has brought us together and we can serve him best by being together."

"You have a daughter. I know you love her very much."

"Yes sir, I do."

"I told God the night Angela was born I would do my best to bring her up right. She's been my pride and joy for twenty-eight years. I want what's best for her, and you're right, she will be happy with you. You have my permission to marry her, but I'm going to hold you to your promise to love her and take care of her, and if you ever don't, you'll have to answer to me."

"Agreed." The two men then went and played the back nine.

That night, Shawn and Angela went to the Olive Garden for dinner. The time at the restaurant passed uneventfully. They had dessert and coffee and talked about some of the sights they were going to see. Shawn had purchased the ring a week before. A lady in their church who was good friends with Becky owned a jewelry store. Shawn saw the ring he wanted within thirty seconds after he walked in the store. Not wanting to rush into buying it though, he looked at some other rings, but none were as pretty as the first one he saw. It was half a carat, in the middle with little diamond chips surrounding it. The quality was good and Shawn's mind was made up. The price tag was $3,000 but the lady marked it down to $1,400.

Shawn asked Angela is she would like to take a walk on one of the popular beaches. She, of course, agreed and so hand in hand they walked down the beach. There were a few other people but they were far enough away that they would not hear Angela and Shawn's conversation. The ring in his pocket felt like a millstone. They stopped and looked at the full moon which was reflecting on the water. It was a beautiful sight.

"Angela."

"Yes, Shawn." She had a starry look in her eyes.

"When I was a hostage, I promised myself that if I made it out of there alive, I'd never be afraid to love again. Life is too short and too hard to go through it alone. I believe God brings people together so that we can be stronger as a couple than we could ever be separate. I love you very much. Will you marry me?" She looked up at him and smiled a huge smile.

"Yes, I will marry you."

Shawn pulled the ring out of his pocket and placed it on her finger. Of the three events, this one was the most life changing.

Arlington National Cemetery, September 2004

The day could not have been more beautiful if they had planned it. The sky was blue, very few clouds, the weather was not too warm, and the faint smell of autumn was in the air. On one side of Shawn stood his entire family, along with Angela. On the other side was President Connors, along with Dr. Rhodes, the Secretary of Defense, and several high-ranking officers. Nearly all of the former hostages, as well as the special forces team were there. Directly behind Shawn, sat Jack, his daughter Jennifer and her husband. It was the ultimate poetic justice that the very morning of John Robert Miller's funeral, news spread around the world that American forces had captured Mohammad Azeim in a small village in the Sudan. He had been captured, not as a brave warrior leading an army against the infidels, but rather as a coward, living in disguise in a tiny hut. The man who was responsible for shooting down the space shuttle and hijacking American citizens would now face justice. His capture had dealt a crippling, though not fatal, blow to the dreaded al Jihad organization. Its founder and CEO would be brought to trial and most certainly face the death penalty. He would die like a common criminal.

An honor guard carried the flag-draped coffin as bagpipes played "Amazing Grace." President Connors gave the eulogy, not as President of the United States, but as a man who had lost his closest and most trusted friend. His final words were particularly moving.

". . . No man ever loved his country more or sacrificed more to protect her. In the history of our nation, few will ever equal, and none will ever exceed the courage of John Robert Miller. His was truly a sacrifice of honor. Those of us who knew him and loved him have suffered a loss beyond words, and yet we can take comfort in knowing that the Lord the righteous judge, has promised a reward in heaven for those who have fought the good fight, who've finished their course, who've kept the faith. I can see our friend now, standing at the gates of paradise, saluting St. Peter and saying 'Lt. Commander John Miller, reporting for duty, sir.'"

A soldier took the flag off the coffin, folded it and gave it to

Becky. The coffin was then lowered into the ground as taps were played. The President saluted and Shawn him say in a quiet voice, "Goodbye, old friend, I'll see you in heaven."

The crowd slowly walked away. Shawn stayed for just a moment longer, Angela by his side. Neither said a word, they just held each other, then they too, slowly turned and walked away arm in arm. Their wedding would take place on December 16th at North Hill. Pastor Jim had already cleared his calender for that day. They would leave right after the wedding for a ten-day trip to Italy with stops in Florence, Venice, and Rome. Theirs would be an unusual wedding in one way. There would be four bridesmaids, and four groomsmen, and a maid of honor, but there would be no best man. The place where the best man would have stood would be empty. The best man Shawn knew, was now in heaven.

Printed in the United States
23472LVS00005B/1-48

9 781594 679124